THE CURIOUS CONSPIRACY

AND OTHER CRIMES

MICHAEL GILBERT

MICHAEL GILBERT

THE CURIOUS CONSPIRACY
AND OTHER CRIMES

Crippen & Landru Publishers
Norfolk, Virginia
2002

ISBN (limited edition): 1-885941-72-2

ISBN (trade edition): 1-885941-73-0

FIRST EDITION

10 9 8 7 6 5 4 3 2 1

Printed in the United States of America on acid-free, recycled paper

Crippen & Landru, Publishers
P. O. Box 9315
Norfolk, VA 23505
USA

E-Mail: CrippenL@Pilot.Infi.Net
Web: www.crippenlandru.com

CONTENTS

INTRODUCTION

When one considers the stories that make up this collection, one is immediately struck by the impossibility of categorising them. Normally in such cases the lynchpin will be the character responsible for solving — or, at least, for attempting to solve — the problems that the author has dreamed up for him. *The Adventures of Sherlock Holmes, Dr. Thorndyke's Famous Cases, The Father Brown Stories.* There are many examples.

In most cases such a title is neat and satisfactory. The reader knows what to expect. A tangle of difficulties deftly unravelled for him by the selected expert. The stories which are collected here differ from any such pattern. In many of them no indictable crime is committed, and the leading characters are rarely policemen; ranging, as they do, from Grandmother Clatterwick and her faithful attendant McGuffog, via the implacable Miss Bell, to such an unlikely performer as Mr. Prosper, the head cashier of Messrs. Maybury and Goodnight, whom the younger members of the firm suppose to be unhappy — "Adding up and subtracting all day long, poor old chap."

In a time scale the stories range from the Peninsular War to the present day. In location they cover London from the streets and alleys of Southwark to Hampstead Heath, dropping in for a pint at the Wapping Giant, visiting a Prep School at Broadstairs and a Public School at Windsor, and spending a lot of time in the Middle East, particularly in and around the Independent Principality of the Island of Ibbelin whose Ruler made a series of such remarkable purchases.

Were one compelled to find an adjective to cover the whole compilation one might, falling back on the true meaning of the word, describe it as "catholic" — with the predictable result that uninstructed readers would expect the stories to deal with clerical and ecclesiastical topics; not having at hand that great bible of the English tongue, twelve volumes of *Oxford English Dictionary*, which offers us, as the meaning of catholic, "of universal human interest; touching the needs, interests or sympathies of all men."

That seems to me to cover the ground adequately.

Michael Gilbert
Gravesend, Kent

AUDITED AND FOUND CORRECT

At the offices of Messrs. Maybury and Goodnight, Solicitors, the order of departure was an established ritual. It varied only when Mr. Goodnight left early, as he usually did: in the summer for a game of golf or in the winter for a meeting of one of the many societies in which he was interested.

When he was not there, Sal and Beth started at five o'clock packing up their typewriters and tidying their desks. They would be away by a quarter past five, closely followed, and occasionally preceded by young Mr. Manifold, the articled clerk. At five thirty the litigation clerk, Mr. Prince, and the conveyancing clerk, Mr. Dallow, left, though not together since they had not been on speaking terms for two years.

There remained only Sergeant Pike, late of the Royal Marine Corps, who had the job of locking up; and Mr. Prosper, the cashier.

As the girls hurried past on the pavement they could look down into the lighted semi-basement room where Mr. Prosper sat at his work. They used to make jokes about him. He was a bachelor who lived by himself, so people said, in a small North London flat.

"Not much to go home to," said Sal. "No wonder he stays late."

"When does he go home, anyway?" said Beth. She was the warmer-hearted of the two. "What a life, eh? Adding up and subtracting and that sort of thing all day long."

"He chose it," said Sal. "If he's bloody miserable, it's his own fault, isn't it?" Sal was the cynic.

Mr. Prosper was not miserable. He was happy. He had a job which suited him precisely and he would have asked for none other.

Since childhood he had been fascinated by figures. He could add and subtract before he could spell. He liked arranging figures, setting them out in orderly columns, correcting and adjusting them, comparing the totals he arrived at. He compared primes and cube roots as another boy might have compared birds' eggs or stamps.

If his mind had been of a more theoretical bent he might have become a qualified accountant. It was a step he had considered more than once, but rejected. It was the figures themselves which interested him, not the intricacies of taxation and company law which he would have had to master to become an accountant. He was happy to be a bookkeeper and a cashier. That was his metier.

He had joined Messrs. Maybury and Goodnight thirty-five years before, when Alfred Maybury was alive and Richard Goodnight was quite a young man. He had watched over its fortunes from the earliest days, when no-one knew where the next week's wages were coming from, until the happy moment when they had acquired Jim Collard as a client. At that time Jim, who was now boss of the Collard Empire of shops and offices, had been at the beginning of *his* career. Richard Goodnight had done a job for him, and done it well. Their company work went, of course, to a large City firm, but all the conveyancing and much of the day-to-day contract work and debt collecting, inseparable from Collard enterprises, came to them.

Mr. Prosper worried about it sometimes. He said to Sergeant Pike, who was his only confidant in such matters, "We're a one-man firm with a one-man client."

"Should last out our time," said Pike. "And old Goodnight's."

"He'll take in young Manifold, as soon as he's qualified."

"Don't care for him," said Pike. "Too much grease on his hair."

They neither of them cared for Manifold, who had been to a famous public school, and wore the knowledge of it like a badge in the button hole of his well-cut suit.

"Ought to be in some large outfit," said Pike. "Doesn't fit here."

The smallness of the firm was an added attraction to Mr. Prosper. In a larger organisation he would have had assistants. He would have been forced to delegate. Here, he could keep his eye on everything. Once a year a qualified accountant was called in to audit his books, for the satisfaction of the watchdogs at the Law Society. He had an easy task. "I wish they were all like yours," he used to say. "Never a record mislaid or a penny missing."

The early evening was Mr. Prosper's favourite time. His papers, like good children, were all in bed, tucked up in their folders. Perhaps he might have, on the desk in front of him, a single sheet of foolscap ruled in double columns on which he would be making some last-minute calculations, or he might be reconciling the client balances or adjusting the PAYE records. An adjustment and reconciliation which was entirely superfluous. But only part of his mind would be on the job. His real thoughts were running down other tracks.

It was his habit, during such moments of agreeable relaxation, to weigh up his colleagues and acquaintances, their achievements and failures, their gains and losses, just as though they were business enterprises, each with his own personal balance sheet, which he himself was charged with the job of inspecting.

How would Richard Goodnight come out of such an audit?

There were undeniable items on the debit side. He did a minimum of work to justify the profits of the firm which, since Mr. Maybury's death, came into his hands alone. Mr. Prosper knew little about his private life, but was aware that he had a flat near Sloane Square, a house in the country, shares in a shooting syndicate in Kent, and fishing in Scotland. He seemed to change his car every year.

Nor was his day an onerous one. His average time of arrival over the past six months had been 10.27. His average time of departure 4.59. Subtract from this an average lunch hour of one hour and fifty-two minutes, and this left a working day of four hours and forty minutes, during which he saw a few old clients and dictated a few letters.

The real work of the firm was done by Mr. Prince and Mr. Dallow.

On the credit side, Mr. Prosper conceded, there were two balancing items. First, the fact that if anything did go really wrong — and the number of things which could go wrong with a one-man solicitor's firm were legion — the disaster would fall on Mr. Goodnight alone. The rest of them would lose their jobs. He would lose all that he possessed. Again, credit had to be given for his share in setting up the firm, his part in the early struggles, and the fact that Jim Collard's work, on which the firm depended, had come through him. Yes, his account was roughly in balance.

At the other end of the scale, take Sergeant Pike. There were substantial, if imponderable assets on the credit side of *his* balance sheet.

Twenty years of service in the Marines. The confidence which his record inspired. (Three firms had competed for him when he left the Service.) Excellent health. The financial security of his pension. Yes. A lot of pluses there and very few minuses.

In contrast, what could be said for young Manifold? Too much grease in his hair, Pike had said. Too much grease all round, thought Mr. Prosper. He had been given his articles in the firm, in preference to a number of abler young men, simply because he was Jim Collard's nephew. He did the simplest work, and made mistakes which even the girls laughed at. All he seemed interested in was playing games. Indeed, thought Mr. Prosper, he spent a great deal more time in squash and racquets courts than he did in the law courts; and for these inconsiderable services he was paid rather more than Sergeant Pike and almost as much as Mr. Prosper himself. Moreover it was clear from his conduct and his manner that he already saw himself as future head of the firm.

It was at this point that the well-sharpened pencil in Mr. Prosper's hand checked for a moment, moved on, checked again, and then went back.

The task to which he had been devoting himself that evening was his periodical check of disbursement books. These were records, kept by everyone in the firm, of the petty cash which they expended in the course of their duties: fares, searches, commissioners' fees, and the like. They were operated on a simple in-and-out system. You paid the money out of your own pocket, noted it in your book, and recovered what was owing to you at the end of the week.

The disbursement book in front of him belonged to young Manifold, and the item at which his pencil had checked was dated September 20th. It said "Collard's. Purchase of shop 220 Holloway Road. Taxis £3.80."

Mr. Prosper climbed stiffly to his feet, went out into the passage, and made his way along to Manifold's room. Papers on the table, papers on the window ledge, papers on the floor.

"No idea of system and order," said Mr. Prosper. It took him some minutes to locate the file he wanted in the bottom drawer of one of the cabinets. He sat down to study it. The solicitors acting for the owners of that particular shop had been Blumfeldts, and it was at their offices, at the far end of Holborn, that the purchase would have been completed.

"Ten minutes' walk, five minutes in a bus," said Mr. Prosper.

The memory which had stopped him was of something he had overheard Sal saying to Beth. "Guess what, I came back in the bus with Prince Andrew last Thursday, and he paid my fare."

Last Thursday had been September 20th and Prince Andrew was the name which the girls had bestowed on young Manifold. It was possible, of course, that the bus trip had been unconnected with the completion of 220 Holloway Road, but in any event £3.80 was an incredible amount for a taxi fare to and from the end of Holborn.

Collard's were always buying and selling small shop and office properties, and after the conveyancing work had been done by Mr. Dallow it would have been normal for the routine job of completing the purchase, paying over the money, and collecting the deeds to be entrusted to the articled clerk. There were a dozen files in the cabinet which related to such transactions.

Panting slightly with the exertion, Mr. Prosper gathered them up, and left the room.

In the passage he encountered Sergeant Pike, who said, "Let me carry those for you."

"Quite all right," said Mr. Prosper breathlessly. "I can manage."

It annoyed him that the slightest exertion made him puff and wheeze.

Back in his own room he spread the files on his desk and started to read them. From time to time he referred back from a file to the disbursement book. Now that his suspicions had been aroused it was only too easy to detect the signs of small but systematic cheating that had been going on.

In one case completion had been postponed at the last moment, from Friday in one week until Wednesday in the week following.

Manifold had claimed taxi expenses for *both* occasions. Then there were the local search fees. Search fees had to be paid, of course, but there seemed to be altogether too many of them. An analysis of the transactions that Manifold had been engaged in over the last six months showed thirteen purchases, eleven sales, and no fewer than *sixty* fees. Mr. Prosper's pencil scurried across a fresh sheet of paper, analysing, computing, comparing.

Sergeant Pike pushed his head in and said, "I'm off. I'll leave the front door on the latch. Bang it as you go out." He spotted the pile of files and peered at the notes Mr. Prosper was making.

"Has our golden boy been putting his foot in it again?"

"Yes," said Mr. Prosper. "I really think he has."

He was a man who liked to take his time and move slowly. He needed incontrovertible proof.

Next morning he had a word with Sal. He realised that one member of the staff would be unlikely to incriminate another, and he had to proceed with craft.

Fortunately he had found, in the girl's own disbursement book, an item for a single bus fare to the Bank of England dated September 20th, and described, in her school girl writing, as "Documents by hand."

He said to her, "I've been checking these books. Surely you've been undercharging. Why only a single bus fare? Did you walk back?"

Sal thought about it, and said, "No, that's quite right. Thursday afternoon, Mr. Manifold paid my fare. He got on at St. Paul's. We came back together."

"Ah, that accounts for it," said Mr. Prosper, handing her back the book. It did, in fact, account for it. The completion had been that afternoon. Blumfeldt's office was within a stone's throw of St. Paul's.

His next call was on Mr. Dallow, a precise and solemn man with the air of an undertaker. He said, "I've been looking through these disbursements books, and I've been puzzled by all these references to local search fees. Could you explain about that?"

"I usually get the articled clerk to do the local searches. Something wrong with them?"

"Nothing wrong, no. I wondered if you could explain. Just exactly what *are* local search fees? How many do you have to make?"

"That depends. Normally, one Borough Council and one County Council. If you're dealing with a County Borough, of course, you only have to make one search."

"I see," said Mr. Prosper. He had been wondering whether it would be safe to take Mr. Dallow fully into his confidence. He decided to do so. Mr. Dallow was the soul of discretion.

He pushed the disbursement book across. Mr. Dallow cast an eye down the entries and uttered a series of "tuts" and "tchks" like an electric kettle coming to the boil.

He said, "This is nonsense, absolute nonsense. Purchase of Malpas House. Three search fees! Why, that sale never went through at all. It was cancelled before it even started. And what's this? Six separate searches for 3, 5 and 7 Caxton House. They're all flats in the same block, and St. Alban's is a County Borough. One search would have covered the lot. What's the boy playing at?"

"I should hardly describe it as play," said Mr. Prosper coldly.

"And why wasn't it picked up in the bill?"

"It wasn't picked up," said Mr. Prosper, "because they were all Collard's transactions. Instead of sending them a separate bill for each one, as we should do, we debit them quarterly with all their costs for the last three months. I've often pointed out to Mr. Goodnight that this was a slack and dangerous way of doing business and likely to lead to errors."

"Which it has."

"Not errors, Dallow. Systematic fraud."

"We shall have to tell Mr. Goodnight."

"I'd rather you said nothing about it until I've had a word with Manifold. He might have some explanation."

But Mr. Prosper did not say this as though be believed it.

In the luncheon interval he left a note on Manifold's desk, *I would like to see you about your disbursements book. Please look in at 5.30 this evening.* J.P.

"Well," said Manifold. "So what's it all about? I hope it's not going to take too long. I've got a court booked for six o'clock."

He indicated the handle of the squash racquet sticking out of the top of his briefcase. He did not seem at all apprehensive.

"How long it takes depends entirely on you," said Mr. Prosper. He had the offending disbursement book on the desk in front of him, and had marked a dozen places in it with slips of paper. "I'd like an explanation, if there is an explanation, of some of these sums of money you've been claiming."

"What do you mean, explanation? They're my petty cash expenses. Fares and so on."

"Money you've actually spent?"

Manifold looked at him for a long moment, then burst into laughter.

It had quite a genuine ring about it. "You've been snooping," he said. He picked up the book and started to look at the entries which Mr. Prosper had marked. Occasionally he chuckled. "Quite a neat bit of detection." He said, "but you've missed one or two.   Those commissioners' fees — £4.20. That was a bit of a try on. And a couple of extra taxi fares there."

Mr. Prosper was almost speechless. At last he managed to say, "Do I understand that you admit it?"

"Fiddling the petty cash? Of course I admit it. Everyone does it."

"I beg your pardon," said Mr. Prosper. "Everyone does *not* do it. Not in a decent, honest, old-fashioned firm like this."

"Old-fashioned is right," said Manifold, looking round Mr. Prosper's basement room, with its wooden cabinets, black deed boxes, and solid furniture. "Dickensian is the word that occurs to me. I think it's time we caught up with the twentieth century."

Mr. Prosper said, picking his words carefully, "Nineteenth, twentieth, or twenty-first century, it makes no difference. Honesty is still honesty, and dishonesty is dishonesty."

"And realism is realism," said Manifold. He had perched himself on the corner of the desk and seemed to have forgotten the urgency of his appointment on the squash court. "Have you ever worked out exactly what the effect of a transaction like that is?" He tapped the disbursement book. "The effect on the client, I mean."

"The effect is, that if he knew about it, he'd realise he was being cheated."

"You're still not thinking about this realistically. Look. Suppose I help myself to £100 in this way. Everything I claim appears as an item in the Collard Company bill. Right?"

Mr. Prosper said nothing.

"It's an expense, and allowable for tax in the accounts of the company. Corporation tax at 52%. Then the profits of the company pay tax and surtax when they come into Uncle Jim's hands. Do you know, he once told me that for every hundred pounds that goes in at the bottom, he can only count on touching ten pounds when it comes out at the top?"

Mr. Prosper still said nothing.

"Work it out for yourself. If I asked Uncle Jim for a hundred pounds — which I'm sure he'd be very happy to give me — it would cost him a thousand quid to raise it. Right? If, on the other hand, I work it this way, it costs him ten pounds, and the Chancellor of the Exchequer provides the other ninety, and loses nine hundred into the bargain."

His face white, his mouth compressed to a thin line, Mr. Prosper said, "Fraud is fraud, however you wrap it up."

Manifold got up off the desk. As he did so, Mr. Prosper realised that he was a large and athletic young man, twice as big and twice as strong as he was himself. It also occurred to him that they might be alone in the building. Sergeant Pike sometimes got away early, leaving him to lock the street door. However, he had no intention of climbing down. He waited for Manifold's answer, which came in a very different way from the light and chaffing tone he had employed up to that point.

He said, "What are you going to do about it?"

"I shall report it."

"Who to?"

"Mr. Goodnight."

"And what do you suppose he'll do about it?"

"Inform the Law Society and have your articles cancelled."

"He won't."

"He'll have no option."

"He won't do it for two good reasons. The first is, that if he did so, he'd lose all the Collard work. I'd guarantee that."

Mr. Prosper looked at him with loathing.

"The second reason is, that if old Goodnight starts stirring up trouble he may find it bounces. Have you ever wondered why you don't look after his private tax? Why he handles it all himself?"

"What are you getting at?"

"How do you imagine he lives at the rate he does? Two houses, two cars, an expensive wife, shooting, fishing. He's been fiddling his tax for years. And the best of British luck to him."

By this time Mr. Prosper was profoundly shocked and almost speechless. If Manifold had cut short the interview at this point, the worst might not have occurred. Unfortunately, he changed gear, and said, with an unhappy assumption of bonhomie, "Come along, old chap, don't be an ass. Forget the whole thing."

Mr. Prosper took a deep breath, and said, "No."

"You're determined to make a fuss?" Manifold's mouth hardened. "You'd risk your job, and the jobs of everyone else here, for a few pounds that no-one cares about, least of all the man who's paying it?"

"I won't be blackmailed into being accessory to a fraud."

"I imagine," said Manifold with calculated brutality, "that other people here will be able to find themselves jobs. The typists and Sergeant Pike, and so on. But one thing I'm sure about, and that is that you won't."

"Insolence won't help you."

"You're not only stupid, you're old-fashioned. You're out of date. People like you aren't needed any more."

Anger was having its way with Mr. Prosper now — a red-hot, scalding anger that drove out fear.

"That job you're doing, counting on your fingers, it can be done by any school dropout with a pocket calculator. You're not just out of date. You're obsolete."

Mr. Prosper was on his feet now. His groping fingers touched the heavy round ruler on his desk and closed on it. He took two steps toward the astonished Manifold and swung a blow, downward, at his head.

Manifold had no difficulty at all in avoiding it. His reactions were twice as fast as Mr. Prosper's. He jumped back nimbly. The blow fell on thin air. Mr. Prosper overbalanced and collapsed, hitting his head on the corner of the desk as he went down. As he did so, the ruler shot out of his hand and hit Manifold on the shin.

Manifold laughed, picked up the ruler, and said, "Watch it, old boy. You'll be hurting someone."

He was struck by the way Mr. Prosper was lying and went down on to one knee beside him. He said, "Come along, get up off the floor."

The arm he was holding felt curiously limp.

A sound made him jerk his head round. Sergeant Pike was standing in the doorway. He said, "You'd better get hold of a doctor, Sergeant. Mr. Prosper's had a fall."

Sergeant Pike came over, pushed Manifold roughly out of the way, and knelt beside Mr. Prosper. After a long moment he got up, walked across the room, and locked the door, pocketing the key. Then he picked up the telephone and started to dial.

Manifold said, "What are you doing?"

"I'm calling the police," said Sergeant Pike.

✠   ✠   ✠

Cosmo Franks deployed the case for the Crown with the dispassionate care which is expected of Senior Treasury Counsel.

In answer to his questions, Mr. Dallow told the Court that the deceased had been on the point of exposing a systematic series of frauds by the accused. Sergeant Pike spoke of hearing a crash, coming into the room, and finding the accused bending over the body. He had been holding a heavy ruler in his hand and had put it down as the Sergeant came through the door. An officer from the Forensic Science Laboratory said that the fingerprints of the accused were on the ruler. The only surprise was the medical evidence.

Dr. Summerson, the Home Office Pathologist who had carried out the autopsy, gave it as his opinion that although a blow from such a weapon might have been a contributory cause of death, it would not have killed a man of normal health. Mr. Prosper, it appeared, was suffering from an advanced cardiac degeneration, a condition popularly known as fatty degeneration of the heart, probably the result of his life-long sedentary occupation.

"If it hadn't been for Summerson," said Junior Counsel, as he and Franks walked back from Court, "he'd have been booked for murder, that's for sure."

"It was illogical, whichever way you look at it," said Franks. "If he meant to kill him, the fact that he didn't hit him hard enough to kill a healthy man, and only happened to kill him because he was unhealthy, shouldn't have reduced the charge from murder to manslaughter."

"He was lucky," said Junior Counsel.

"It's not the sort of luck I'd care for myself," said Franks. "A hardened criminal might laugh off a five-year sentence. Not Manifold. It'll crucify him."

They walked on for some distance in silence. Franks said, "And he's not the only person in trouble."

This was true. When Jim Collard removed his work to another firm,

Mr. Goodnight decided that it was time he retired. He had overlooked the fact that this step invited an automatic inspection of his affairs by the Revenue. He was now faced with criminal charges of tax evasion, the certainty of a crippling fine, and the possibility of imprisonment.

"When you think it through," said Junior Counsel, "really the only person who came well out of it was old Prosper. A quick death instead of months of hospital and misery."

"I suppose that's right," said Franks absently. He was already thinking about his next case.

FRIENDS OF THE GROOM

Chief Inspector Hazlerigg hated weddings. This may have been due to certain early passages in his career when, as a junior constable, he had had the jobs of controlling the crowds and, on at least one occasion, keeping a fatherly eye on the presents, at these fashionable junketings.

On this occasion, of course, his role was a more privileged one. He had received an invitation, bought a present and hired his morning dress like the best of them.

✠ ✠ ✠

It still did not quite reconcile him to the occasion.

"If there's one thing more dreary than drinking champagne in the early afternoon, it's watching other people drink champagne in the early afternoon," he confided to Inspector Marsh who, by happy coincidence, was also a guest. "Which of 'em do you know?"

"I've known Blatcham ever since I picked him off Eros on Boat Race night, more years ago than I like to remember," said Marsh, clanking at the tow-headed, young-old bridegroom surrounded by guests at the far end of the room. "Keeps his figure, doesn't he? He must be nearly forty."

"He's a regular cavalry officer," said Hazlerigg. "Probably wears stays."

Blatcham's uninhibited laugh rang out at that moment almost as if he had heard the remark. Listening to the laugh left one in no doubt why his friends in the 16th-21st called him "Horse" Blatcham. They were round him now, a cluster of them, bow-legged, serious characters with the baffled look of men who have watched, in their own short lifetimes, an officer's charger turning into a Sherman tank.

"Which is yours?" asked Marsh.

"Oh, I know the bride," said Hazlerigg with a smirk. "Baby" Bunting, now Mrs. Blatcham, was a well-known character in the West End, and likeable in spite of it all. "I wonder," he added, "that you've got time to come to these functions. I always thought that DDIs were hard-working men. That's what they tell us at the Yard."

"I'm not entirely here on pleasure," said Marsh stiffly.

"Ah," said Hazlerigg. "Just as I thought. You've been told off to keep an eye on the presents."

He nodded at the long table against the wall, where an array of silver toast racks, mugs, inscribed salvers, letter trays and coffee pots mingled oddly with dozens of oven ware and canteens of cutlery.

"Certainly not," said Marsh. "We can't spare policemen for that lark nowadays. In any case," he added unkindly, "there's nothing there that a self-respecting burglar would consider worth the hire of a dress suit."

"Tell me all," said Hazlerigg. "It'll be half an hour before they cut the cake."

✠   ✠   ✠

"As a matter of fact," said Marsh, "I've been wanting to. It's a silly little thing, but it's been worrying me. You know I've got a lot of those types in my manor." He looked again at the cavalrymen. "Their clubs —" he mentioned the name of three of them "— and their banks as well."

"It started last year. A young man walked into the Porto Street branch of the Home and Overseas Bank and presented an open cheque for £60, signed by Muncer — Captain Bertie Muncer. He's the tall, dark one in the corner.

"The clerk cashed it without hesitation. When it was put to him afterwards he seemed rather surprised. He said, first of all, that he knew Muncer's signature very well — none of these chaps write fluently, and it makes 'em very difficult to copy, or so I should imagine.

"But it wasn't only that. He said he'd been dealing with army types for 30 years and he was certain this must be a friend of Muncer's. Right clothes, right voice, right manner. He'd never given it a second thought. Muncer had a healthy account and was fond of racing. He'd often borrow cash from friends on the course, and give them a cheque for it.

"Well, when the cheque was cleared Muncer queried it, and the fun began."

✠   ✠   ✠

"Even Muncer had to admit that the signature was perfect. It would have deceived him easily, he said. The rest of the writing on the cheque wasn't Muncer's. But, of course, the bank clerk hadn't looked particularly at that.

"The cheque, too, was out of a book which had been issued to Muncer. Not his current book, and not, in fact, a recent one. One he'd had almost a year before. The used cheques out of that book had been returned to him and, of course, he'd destroyed or lost them, so there was no way of following up further on that; but it was plain enough by the serial number that that was the particular book it had come from."

"You were thinking," said Hazlerigg, "that he might have issued the cheque for a smaller amount — or spoilt it, perhaps and thrown it away — and someone got hold of it, took out all the writing except the signature and filled it up again. It's not all that easy to erase writing on a cheque form — as I needn't tell you."

✠ ✠ ✠

"We thought it might be something like that," agreed Marsh. "As a matter of fact, our number-one theory was that Muncer had signed the cheque himself and forgotten all about it. He was quite capable of it. So we weren't, perhaps, taking it as seriously as we ought when the next one came along."

"The next one?"

"Different victim, different bank, but exactly the same trick. A young man walked into 'Crab' Rolloway's bank and took £75 out of his account. That one hadn't even been reported to us — it takes time to clear the cheques and Calloway only got his statement quarterly — when two more happened.

"Crabtree and Fitz-Tucker. Fifty-five pounds off one and £40 off another. The same system exactly. The man breezed in about five minutes before closing time — which showed a nice sense of psychology. In both cases he'd made certain that the supposed signer of the cheque was out of town or otherwise engaged."

"Two more members of Muncer's regiment?"

"Not the same regiment, but the same circle. Two or three regiments which had been brigaded together in the war. You know how they stick together."

"Very cliquey," agreed Hazlerigg. "And was it the same man who presented the cheques in each case?"

"We think so. Not much description except, again, that he looked just 'right,' and none of the bank clerks had any suspicion.

"One of them — the one who cashed Crabtree's cheque — went so far as to say that he recognised the man as one of Crabtree's friends, who'd been in the bank with him on some previous occasion. When we pressed him he weakened on it, and said, No, but he was just like lots of his friends.

"Well, all those three were reported more or less together, and you can imagine we sat up and began to take notice."

✠ ✠ ✠

"We did what we should have done sooner — sent the cheques to an expert. His report said first, that the body of the cheques hadn't been tampered with. Secondly, that they were none of them signed by hand. I can't go into the reasons, but he was quite definite. They'd all been done with very finely made, very accurate rubber stamps."

"Ah," said Hazlerigg. "I wondered about that. Couldn't anyone do that? You get a specimen of someone's signature, photograph it — I'm not an expert on it, but there's some process or other. You end up with the signature engraved on steel. Then you make a rubber stamp. Managing directors do it, when they have to sign off thousands of letters."

"Certainly", said Marsh. "It can be done. But it's not all that easy. There are firms who have the necessary equipment, but they're all above suspicion. Anyway, we checked round them all, without finding anyone in the least resembling our young bank-robber. It would take a professional to make a plate like that, and professionals are few and far between. Of course, once you had the plate anyone with a bit of care could manufacture a rubber stamp."

Chief Inspector Hazlerigg swears that at this point the room rotated completely around him.

"What's wrong with you?" said Marsh.

"No time to lose," croaked Hazlerigg. "Which of them are here?"

"Which of who?"

"Muncer, Rolloway, Crabtree, what's his name — Fitz-Tucker?"

Marsh looked round.

"Muncer and Crabtree. I think Rolloway's in Korea and ..."

"Never mind. They'll do. Can't you manoeuvre them over here?"

It says much for Hazlerigg's personality that within three minutes he was in friendly conversation with Captain Muncer on one side and Major Crabtree on the other. Marsh caught fragments of the conversation.

"No, the first time we did it was for Pongo's wedding — good idea, really, all club together, saves money — you and me and Fitz and Crab — who was the other? Oh yes, it was Horse."

After about five minutes of this they all wandered over to the sideboard to inspect the presents and Hazlerigg slipped out of the room.

A minute later the loungers in Pall Mall caught a glimpse of a large man in black tail-coat and striped trousers, flying down the street. The time was a quarter to three.

At seven minutes to three an air of drowsy solemnity hung over the Charles Street Branch of the Northern and Western Bank.

It was scarcely disturbed by the opening of the door and the unobtrusive entry of a young man. He was unremarkably, but somehow correctly, dressed and carried himself with the easy charm which was the mark of his caste.

He put down a cheque for £60 on the counter, smiled at the cashier, and said, "Half in ones and half in tens, please."

Then a surprising thing happened; not the least surprising of which was the flinging open of the door of the manager's room and the appearance from it of the manager, followed by a Chief Inspector in full formal morning dress.

✠   ✠   ✠

"Marvellous," said Marsh enviously. "But how did you know he was going to go for Blatcham's money at just that precise moment?"

"He'd always waited till his victims were otherwise engaged," said Hazlerigg. What better time than when one of them is cutting his own wedding cake?"

"Hmp," said Marsh. "Once you realised that it actually was one of his cavalry friends I suppose it made better sense. I'd always assumed it was an impostor. After all, in those sort of circles people don't look after their cheque books at all — I suppose it was easy for — what was his name — ?"

"Littleton," said Hazlerigg. "Pongo Littleton."

"For Littleton to collect stray cheques. What I still don't see is how he turned their signatures into stamps. Unless he's an expert. Which I gather he isn't."

"They were very cliquey," said Hazlerigg. "Six of them. When one of them got married the other five gave him a silver salver with their signatures reproduced on it. I'd seen the thing with my own eyes, five minutes before I talked to you."

THE BLACKMAILER

I have known Miss Prince for a good many years, and I have liked her as long as I have known her. I have also respected her and, occasionally, feared her; but I have never pretended to understand her.

The first thing about her was her early Victorian sense of justice. She seemed to possess, in the fullest degree, those clear, hard, unsentimental, unshifting ideas of the difference between right and wrong that belonged to the first years of the Young Queen.

Then she was a practical philanthropist. She chose her objects wisely and gave generously. She imposed only one condition on her gifts. If her name was so much as whispered in connection with them, she never gave to that cause again.

There was one other thing; I happened to know roughly what her income was. Most of it came from investments, and she was still enjoying some patent rights from her father's inventions. She lived in modest comfort in North London and she kept a maid. But on occasions her gifts seemed to exceed her means.

In the summer of last year, in particular, her donations reached a high point of generosity. It was entirely by accident that I discovered the source of this money. Packer — she's the maid I mentioned — is a good-hearted, garrulous creature and some of the details came from her. The other facts were there, for everybody to read, in the newspapers.

✠ ✠ ✠

One fine May morning Miss Titmus, who rented the top floor of a quiet house in a quiet crescent in North London, folded a blanket on the linoleum of the kitchen floor, sat down on it, laid her grey head back on to the pillow she had placed inside the gas oven, and turned on the tap. Her landlady, who lived in the basement, smelled the gas and hobbled up to see what it was about. She was too late by half an hour.

✠ ✠ ✠

Spring turned to summer and summer faded into the white mists of autumn and on one of those dark November days, when the second instalment of the taxes is overdue and the Christmas bonus is still in the distant and problematical future, Mr. Medlicott, who had a house not far from the North Circular Road, swallowed a glass of salts-of-lemon and died before the morning, in great agony, but stiff-lipped to the end.

Inquiry revealed that Mr. Medlicott was overdrawn at the bank and had been worried by debts.

✠   ✠   ✠

The next case, which came along with the first daffodils in the spring of the new year, was of a somewhat different type.

Miss Merrant was a small woman of about 60. At 6 in the evening, when light was fading, she climbed the protective barrier and walked out on to the parapet of one of London's roadway viaducts. It was a straight drop of nearly 100 feet to the concrete below. But she was evidently a woman who believed in taking no chances and therefore she waited until she saw a heavy truck, towing a heavy trailer, come swinging down the hill. She judged her moment had arrived and stepped off into space.

The driver caught a glimpse of her body flailing through the air and stamped on the brake, pulling his monster to a screaming standstill. He climbed out, white-faced. For a moment he thought his imagination had been playing tricks with him, and then he heard a moan from somewhere above his head. Looking up, he saw Miss Merrant, voiceless, winded, but otherwise intact, in the sagging canopy of his truck.

In due course the court missioner made a report. It concluded: "Miss Merrant, though not rich or even particularly well off, was financially quite solvent until the end of last year. She had an income from some investments left to her by her father, and a small 'nest egg' in the Post Office Savings Bank. In the last three months she appears to have sold these securities and drawn out the money in her savings account and spent it. She is very reticent about this and I cannot understand exactly where this money, amounting to £800 or £900, has gone. Miss Merrant herself either cannot or will not help me."

✠   ✠   ✠

"There is a man to see you, Miss Prince."

Miss Prince folded her fat, white, cornelian-ringed hands in pleasant anticipation. "A man. Well now. Isn't that nice. Should I, perhaps, be asking him to tea, Packer?"

"I rather fancy not, Miss Prince. He's not really — not quite ..."

"I see. I wonder what he can be coming to see me about. Are we ready to receive him?"

Packer made a few deft arrangements while Miss Prince looked on approvingly.

The man who made his appearance a few moments later was on the young side of middle-age, a little fat, a little bald, entirely nondescript. After an interval of hesitation, which was just long enough to be thunderingly rude, Miss Prince invited the stranger to be seated.

"Miss Prince?"

"You have the advantage of me, I am afraid."

"My name's Smith. I won't keep you long. Very good of you to see me."

"Not at all," said Miss Prince. "An old woman like me comes to be glad of any company."

"Ah — oh, yes, I see. Well, now Miss Prince, can I start the ball rolling by asking you a question? Do you know a Mrs. Preston?"

A sudden silence fell in that pleasant upstairs room. Miss Prince sat motionless. The stranger appeared to be in no hurry to break the silence. There was a little spurt of fire, a cinder fell tinkling from the grate, and with an apparent effort Miss Prince spoke. "Well. What an extraordinary question! Why do you ask it? Who are you?"

"Never mind for a moment who I am. Shall we stick to the question?"

"And if I refuse to answer your question?"

"Well," said the man reasonably, "either you do know Mrs. Preston or you don't. If you do, there's no harm in saying so." There was a plain edge to the voice now. "If you don't, perhaps you will explain how ..." a little notebook came into play... "at 11.15 precisely this morning you approached the assistant in the sub-post office on Millpath Road, produced a Post Office Savings book purporting to be made out in Mrs. Preston's name, and withdrew three pounds?"

"I — you — I ..." said Miss Prince. "Oh dear, oh dear, oh dear."

Out of his experience Smith gave her three minutes to get over it, and to cover the interval he went on talking, half to himself.

"Commonest form of crime," he said. "You ought to hear what the judges say. Very harsh about it. Always recommending the law to be tightened up. But it never does any good. So long as it's 'easy come, easy go,' 'Produce your book and we'll pay the money,' there's bound to be fraud. People," said Mr. Smith virtuously, "will always take advantage of any system based on public trust. Ingenious, too, some of them. Get hold of an old savings account book, like you did, and get to work on it. Ingenious," said Mr. Smith. "Very ingenious. But illegal."

"Do you …" said Miss Prince. "Are you a policeman?"

"Certainly not," said Mr. Smith. "I'm a member of the public. One of the people you've been defrauding. I'm your victim, see." He showed his yellow teeth in a quiet smile.

"How did you … ?"

"Lady," said Mr. Smith, "I just watch for it. I stand in post offices and places and watch for it. If that young lady behind the counter hadn't been so busy gossiping to her girl friend she'd have spotted it a mile away. Your face, your voice, your hands. It was written in letters a mile and a half high, really it was."

Miss Prince seemed to have recovered a little of her former composure. She drew herself up in her chair, dabbed at her eyes with a lace handkerchief, and said: "What are you going to do about it?"

"Well, now," said Mr. Smith. The interview seemed, in some way, to have reached a turning point. "You'll excuse me, I'm sure, but I'm too old a bird to be caught with chaff." He got up with surprising speed, glanced round the room, looked behind the old leather and brass-nailed screen, peered behind the curtains.

"There," he said. "You'd be surprised what people think of. However, now we know we're alone, anything we talk about can be just between the two of us. Now if I did no more than my plain duty you'd be in the dock. But there's worse places than the dock. There's Holloway Prison. Do you know the first thing they do to you at Holloway?"

Miss Prince made a very faint noise of inquiry.

"They cut all your hair off and wash you with yellow soap."

Miss Prince shuddered. "Don't talk like that. Please don't talk like that. It isn't — it's not only me. My family. My father would never have got over it. How lucky that he's dead! He was an inventor, you know."

They were always Army officers or inventors, thought Mr. Smith.

"He invented the first English phonograph," said Miss Prince. "But the big gramophone companies ..."

"Quite," said Mr. Smith. "But the important thing at the moment is that I need some capital. And capital is a thing which is hard to come by. Income, now — I'd laugh at income. What's £5 a week? Two pounds ten in the tax collector's pocket. But a nice round capital sum of £500."

"Five hundred! I couldn't possibly ..."

"It's going to save a lot of trouble if I tell you straight out that I've been devoting a little time lately to having a look at your affairs. I know exactly what you've got in that current account of yours and I know what securities your nice kind bank manager is holding for you. It may mean realising a little of that war stock."

"I don't think ..."

"The offer's open for two minutes. At the end of that time the price goes up — to £800."

Mr. Smith took out a watch.

Miss Prince's nerve held for exactly ten seconds, then she gave a little moan and said, "You must give me time."

"Three days," said Mr. Smith.

✠ ✠ ✠

I have no exact information about how Miss Prince spent the intervening three days. For the first 48 hours she does not seem to have done anything very much. Packer tells me that she doesn't think she was sleeping very well just then.

On the morning of the third day she saw her bank manager and drew £500 in pound notes.

And a few hours later she was saying, "Well, Mr. Smith, I'm glad you were able to get here."

"Like hell you are," said Mr. Smith shortly. "Have you got the money?"

"Yes, I've got the money." She took a sealed envelope out of her handbag and passed it over to Mr. Smith. "You'll find it's all there, just as you said. Five hundred pounds. I got it in one pound notes."

"Very kind of you," said Mr. Smith. "I think I'll count it." He was fumbling open the envelope with impatient fingers. "Not that I don't trust you, but mistakes will happen."

"There is just one thing I'd like to be sure about," said Miss Prince mildly. "How am I to know that once you have this money you won't soon be back asking for more?"

Mr. Smith looked up from his counting. "You'll have to trust me."

"Like Miss Merrant trusted you?" said Miss Prince softly.

Mr. Smith's fingers faltered, then stopped. There was silence in the room as he searched Miss Prince's face. Then he said, and for the first time there was a note of uncertainty in his voice, "What do you know about Miss Merrant?"

"Why, she is one of my dearest friends," said Miss Prince. "We're all a great big family up here in North London you know. I knew Miss Titmus, too, slightly. We had a nodding acquaintance, in the queues. Mr. Medlicott as well. I didn't know him personally. But I knew of him. He used to work in the same office — before he retired, of course — as my young cousin Alfred —"

"So what," said Mr. Smith shortly. "What's all this leading up to? Why are you telling me all this?"

"It must have been almost exactly three months ago —" Miss Prince over-rode the interruption "— when they let Miss Merrant out of the nursing home. She came to see me and sat in that very chair you are sitting in now and between the two of us —" Miss Prince pounced forward a little in her chair like a fat but well-muscled cat "— we hatched up a little *PLOT!*"

"What … ?" said Mr. Smith. "What … ?"

"The advantage we had," went on Miss Prince, "was that we knew what was wrong in each case. We knew about Miss Titmus and her — well, I suppose there's no object in false modesty now — about her so-called husband and the letters that used to come to her every week. And we knew about Mr. Medlicott and the silly, silly things he did with his Post Office Savings book. I expect it was really that which gave us our idea. And Miss Merrant — she told me everything. It didn't seem a very big thing for her to have paid £900 for, but I suppose that tastes differ. The thing about it all which struck us," Miss Prince rapped one hand delicately on the table —" the common factor in them all was that they were all *Post Office* matters — Miss Titmus's letters and Mr. Medlicott's savings account and Miss Merrant's silly telegrams. So we got the idea — I'm sure you'll tell me if we were wrong — that this person who was doing it all was obviously a person who hung around post offices a good deal to see if he could pick up information."

The shot went home.

"After that it was straightforward, but very, very tedious. We paid some money into an account in Packer's name —"

"That's a lie."

"Her name really is Mrs. Preston. Didn't you know? I call all my personal maids Packer. It's so much easier."

Mr. Smith found nothing to say to this.

"Then I drew out £3 at a time for her in the most *furtive* manner — I'm really quite an actress, Mr. Smith — from practically every sub-office in North London. It was quite fatiguing."

"How are you going to prove this?"

"Of course, we'd thought of that. I can assure you I took the very best legal advice — without mentioning any names. I was told that I ought to have witnesses to two things. A witness that you asked for the money, and a witness that I paid it to you. Well, I've done just that. I suppose because you looked behind the screen the *first* time you forgot to this time. You can come out now, Packer. The gentleman won't hurt you."

"Thank you, ma'am," said Packer.

"You take your money back," said Mr. Smith. He shovelled it urgently across the table.

"Certainly, if you insist. I don't think that will make any difference to the *legal* position. The great thing, so I'm told, is that you took it in the first place."

"You'll never prove it," said Mr. Smith. "I'm not admitting anything."

"If only," said Miss Prince severely, "you had listened properly to what I said the first time you came. I told you — it was indiscreet of me really, but I do boast sometimes — that my father was an inventor. He was a great hand with phonographs. You remember? He was almost the first man in London to see the possibilities of wax recording. Do sit down, Mr. Smith, and let's listen to our first conversation in comfort. Press that switch down, Packer. That's right."

A startlingly life-like voice rang out. "My name's Smith. I won't keep you long. Very good of you to see me …"

Smith seemed suddenly to deflate. The stuffing was out of him. He sat down slowly, and his face was yellow. "What are you going to do?"

It was almost an echo. How many people had said those very words *to him?*

"Seven years' penal servitude would seem to be the normal sort of sentence," said Miss Prince. "I don't think they actually shave your head in Dartmoor now. Just a very short crop, I should think."

"What do you want?" said Mr. Smith.

"Eight hundred pounds — just for a start," said Miss Prince. "And it's no good saying that you haven't got it, because what with Miss Titmus and Mr. Medlicott and poor Miss Merrant there must be quite a lot of money there. I've no doubt we'll have some more from time to time."

"Eight hundred pounds is a great deal …"

"If it was income," said Miss Prince gaily, "I wouldn't say 'thank you' for it. But a nice capital sum …"

For the first time Mr. Smith really looked at Miss Prince, at the prim lips, the shining jet eyes, the firm lines fencing the mouth. He saw nothing to comfort him.

SQUEEZE PLAY

M r. Rose was a big man in all senses of the word.

His body was huge. A lot of it was muscle run to fat but time could not deprive him of his powerful shoulders and the thick, strong wrists which had made him a sabre champion thirty years before.

His mind was capacious. It was a mind which had been able to embrace and master all the intricacies of the profession of a diamond dealer and yet find room as it were in some spare storage space, to tuck away such odd trifles as azalea-growing and contract bridge. He grew perfect azaleas in the large garden of his home in Hampstead. His contract bridge was feared in half the bridge clubs in Whitehall.

His business was enormous. He was a leader of the Diamond Ring. In his time he had made a great deal of money. He had also made a number of enemies. These had failed because they had made the mistake of attacking Mr. Rose directly. It is patently absurd to attack a man who is mentally big enough to out-manoeuvre you, financially big enough to buy you up, and physically big enough to throw you into the river.

This February night he was waiting in the drawing room of his Hampstead home, for the first opponent who threatened to defeat him simply because he had avoided the attack direct.

He had attacked Mr. Rose through his daughter.

Jessica was the child of Mr. Rose's old age. She was nearly eighteen; she was as beautiful as a tiny, jewelled humming bird, and about as witless. Nevertheless he loved her dearly and it was this love which was making it so difficult for him to deal adequately with Ronald.

Ronald was coming to see Mr. Rose that night, after dinner, and whilst he was waiting for him Mr. Rose reflected on the forthcoming interview, and on the character of Ronald. His studied conclusion was, that in a long and varied life, he had never met anybody who appealed to him less. He had met many criminals, but none who combined in that

35

particular degree a false front of bonhomie with a cold inner selfishness. Ronald was apparently prepared to torment a young girl to gain his own ends, but he was not prepared to suffer either pain or inconvenience himself. Unless Mr. Rose was much mistaken he was a coward as well as a liar.

After a career in the Air Force which was nine parts pure fiction to one part of debatable fact he had, so far as Mr. Rose had been able to discover, been living on susceptible girls ever since.

Jessica Rose had been easy meat to him. He was so well equipped for the conquest, with his Jaguar Sports Car (loaned to him by a trustful garage), his carefully dyed RAF overcoat, and his carefully cultivated RAF slang; his casual mentions of a DFC (though never when there was anyone present who might check it up); above all his endless leisure and seemingly endless money.

Mr. Rose had sized him up the first time he had met him and had been horrified to think that his daughter should have such a friend. He had not made the obvious mistake of warning her against him. Jessica might sometimes be witless, but she had a will of her own.

Then, a fortnight before — the bombshell.

They were going to get married.

Mr. Rose's first reaction to this news had been to put a reliable firm of private detectives on to the job of uncovering Ronald's past.

What they had discovered had confirmed Mr. Rose's worst suspicions, but unfortunately it was apparent that he was dealing with a discreet rogue. Ronald's actions had often been despicable but rarely criminal. Moreover, he had, unfortunately, not committed the crowning indiscretion of marrying before.

The private detective, when he reported these negative results, added that he supposed that Mr. Rose knew that he could withhold his consent to the match. Mr. Rose thanked him and said that he had realised this. He did not add that, in his view, the remedy usually caused more undesirable publicity than the ill it was designed to cure.

Then Ronald had made a proposition so barefaced that even Mr. Rose was startled.

He had suggested, in short, that Mr. Rose might care to purchase his daughter's immunity. It was not the proposition itself, but the price which had shaken him. Ronald had demanded the Collander matching diamonds.

When Mr. Rose realised that Ronald was serious and that there was no other way out of it, he had taken one of his quick decisions.

He had asked Ronald to come up to the house to discuss the matter with him.

As he reached this point in his meditations the bell rang; he went to the front door himself and let the young man in.

It was evident at once that Ronald had been fortifying himself for a difficult interview with drink. Nevertheless he was far from drunk.

He stood in the hall and demanded truculently "Where are we going to talk?"

"There's a fire in the drawing room," suggested Mr. Rose, "that is, if you've no objection."

"Well, I do object," said Ronald. "Let's go into some other room."

Mr. Rose thought for a moment.

"I see," he said, with the suggestion of a smile on his big, pale face. "You are thinking of microphones in the wainscoting and policemen behind screens."

"Never you mind what I'm thinking of," said Ronald. "We'll go in the dining-room, or we won't talk at all."

Mr. Rose nodded. He led the way into the heavy, old-fashioned dining-room, turned on the lights, and then switched on the electric log fire. Neither man sat down.

Mr. Rose came straight to the point.

"I suppose you realise what you are asking for?" he said.

"You can take that as read," said Ronald.

"You know that although the Collander diamonds are mine — mine to dispose of, I mean — I really hold them on trust?"

"Surely."

"You know the reason for the trust, and just what sort of heel I should look if I gave them away?"

"Jess told me something about it."

Mr. Rose winced as if he had been hit. Outside of her own family nobody called his daughter Jess. When he had recovered his voice he said, "What if I won't do it?"

Ronald took a careful pull at his cigarette, looked at the glowing tip, and then said, "Somehow, do you know, I don't think our marriage is going to be a very happy one."

"Suppose I tell my daughter what you have suggested?"

"She won't believe you. We both know you don't approve of me."

" 'Approve' is a wild understatement," said Mr. Rose. He seemed to have recovered some of his good humour. "Well, now, this is what you might call a squeeze, isn't it?"

"You don't get anywhere by insults," said Ronald.

"The remark was not intended as an insult," said Mr. Rose gently. "I was employing a metaphor from contract bridge. Possibly you don't play?"

"I don't mind a hand if the stakes are right. I prefer poker."

"A squeeze, in bridge," went on Mr. Rose, "is achieved when you make your opponent guard two suits and then force him into an impossible position, where he has to discard from one of them. Is it straining the expression too far to say that you are squeezing me in Hearts and Diamonds?"

"Very neat," said Ronald. "Very well put. Well, then, which are you going to throw away?"

"Neither," said Mr. Rose. He put his hands into his pockets and took out a short, weighted, deadly looking leather cosh. "I am afraid you have made the common mistake of not counting your cards. I still have a Club."

Ronald took a step towards the door. He seemed less happy than he had been. "Look here, don't try any of that sort of stuff," he said.

"Why not?" said Mr. Rose. "Why should I not break your neck with this little fellow," he swung the cosh affectionately, "and take your body out in the car and drop it in Epping Forest?"

"You can't do it," said Ronald. "I'm not such a mug as that. There's only one way out of this house, isn't there? On to the road in front. There's a callbox at the corner. I've got a friend there. If he sees your car come out he's going to ring the police. How do you like that?"

"Capital," said Mr. Rose. "Capital." He flicked the cosh up and down and it whiffled unpleasantly in the air. "So you've got the Club suit blocked as well?"

"I fancy so," said Ronald.

"The trouble with you inferior bridge players," said Mr. Rose "is that you fail to take *all* the necessary factors into account. There are at least two things you have omitted from your calculations. One, I admit, you could hardly have known about. Before I sent for you tonight —" Mr. Rose rocked his enormous bulk backwards and forwards on his feet and regarded Ronald dispassionately, "I had a talk with my doctor. He confirmed a previous diagnosis. Reluctantly, I think, but quite definitely I have only got two months more to live. I won't bother you with details, but my engine has outgrown its pumping system. This, as you will appreciate, radically alters my outlook towards certain matters. Where there is a necessary — removal operation, shall we say, to be conducted, and provided that there is no *immediate* risk of detection —"

"You can't do it," said Ronald hoarsely. "I tell you, my friend will —"

"Your friend will see nothing," said Mr. Rose. "That is your second mistake. I have no real intention of removing you by the front entrance. I mentioned that merely in order to discover what precautions you *had* taken. I spent a pleasant two hours this evening trenching a new azalea bed. I shall shortly —" Mr. Rose moved lazily but so that he stood between Ronald and the door — "I shall very shortly be filling that trench in again."

His arm went up; and came down again, once. Five minutes later he was unbolting the tool shed in the garden breathing rather heavily; under the burden he carried.

As he did so a thought struck him, and his face creased into a smile of genuine, unmalicious, mirth.

"Poor old Ronald," he said. "Not a good player, really. It never even occurred to him that I might have a Spade left as well."

UNDER THE LAST SCUTTLEFUL

"And don't forget the boiler," said Mrs. Cotton. "I opened it up so that we can have a nice bath. It'll need two scuttles of coke."

Sam Cotton groaned.

When they had moved into the Old Rectory at Marlhammer he had felt, in his bones, that he was making his last move. He was only 49. But the time comes in every man's life when he will settle down to enjoy the fruits of his toil.

Starting as an unskilled, untrained, almost unpaid assistant to an assistant in a shaky firm of chartered accountants, he had worked. How he had worked! Twelve, fourteen, sixteen hours a day. In his spare time, at night, during weekends. Now he was a qualified accountant, a partner, a director of four companies, and a very rich man indeed.

Too fat, not healthy, seldom happy — but rich.

The Old Rectory had cost money. It was a plain, Georgian house, of dark red brick and darker red tile with more solid wood in its window frames and box shutters than a builder would put into a whole row of houses these days. It stood back from the road, a little isolated by beech trees. It had its private path to the little church, but it was nearly a quarter of a mile from its nearest human neighbour.

"It's pretty," agreed Mrs. Cotton, "but it's got too many rooms."

This, like most of Bertha Cotton's deceptively simple remarks, was true. The house had been designed for and occupied by old-fashioned country parsons. It had many bedrooms and vast boxrooms. It had a pantry, which the Cottons used as a kitchen; a kitchen, which they used as a store room; and numerous closets and sheds and cellars.

"I wonder how the Grundsells managed?" said Mrs. Cotton.

She referred to their immediate predecessors, who had purchased the house from the last incumbent some five years previously.

Mr. Grundsell had been a small, happy, cheerful person, popular in the Village. Not nearly as rich as Sam Cotton but perhaps happier. His wife, older than him by some years, had been something of a mystery at first. A heavy, dark, foreign-looking woman, who seldom spoke. However, nothing is hidden for long from the legion of charwomen and daily helps, and it became known — whisper it softly — that she drank. Seldom, but my, how deeply!

"A cupboard full of bottles," reported Mrs. Tizer. "Gin. And another pile — so big — buried in the paddock."

However, Mrs. Grundsell had not lasted. Perhaps she found the house too isolated. She spoke wistfully of Blackpool. Mr. Grundsell, who gave in to her on everything, gave in to her on this. One night of dark and storm, when no-one was about, he packed her and her belongings into their big, closed car and drove off. Or so he reported, when he mentioned it later. Marlhammer saw her no more.

Shortly afterwards, Grundsell decided to sell.

"Not surprised, really," said Mrs. Tizer. "A great big house, and him all alone in it."

That was how the Cottons had come to buy it. A handsome house, full of large, cheerful rooms, rooms still redolent of the line of sober, God-fearing clerics who had inhabited them along with their industrious wives, their contingents of servants, and their quiversful of children. (Against the edge of one bedroom door Sam Cotton had found their heights recorded, starting with Benjamin, a mere 2' 9" off the ground and running up, through eight others, to Ruth.)

A cheerful house, with one reservation.

Sam could not get used to the cellar.

Well, it was not really a cellar. It lay only two steps down at the end of a series of pantries, dairies, and wash houses. A sort of sunken cul-de-sac. It had been designed as a game larder. As you shone your torch upwards — the electric light did not reach so far down you could see the great steel hooks, deep-rusted now, in the beams of the roof. It had a floor of badly cracked concrete.

"Just the place for coke," said Mrs. Cotton. It was late summer when they moved in, but, warned by her experience of the winter before, she had ordered four tons. And she had got them — Mrs. Cotton usually got what she wanted.

And as autumn turned into winter and winter into spring, and as Sam Cotton made his nightly, dreaded pilgrimage, sometimes for one scuttle, sometimes for two, the huge pile diminished.

As it diminished, a curious fancy grew in Mr. Cotton's mind.

There was something evil in that cellar. And the evil lay, he was sure, in the far corner where the coke was piled deepest.

He got into the habit of calculating how long, at his present nightly rate of progress, it would be before he uncovered this corner. Two months ... One month ...

He said nothing directly to his wife, who was not an imaginative woman, and inclined to be impatient with her husband's fancies. But he did suggest, casually and tentatively, that they might perhaps take on a resident servant. At the moment they had only Mrs. Tizer, who worked like a giant by day, but deserted them at 6 o'clock.

"I could never stand anyone living in," said Mrs. Cotton. "They'd get on my nerves."

"We could afford it," said Sam.

"It isn't a question of money," said Bella. "And anyway, it's quite unnecessary. Do I ever ask you to do anything except get the coke at night?"

It was true. She was a splendid manager. Twenty years younger than Sam, and five times as healthy.

"I don't even ask you to wash up," she said.

"I wouldn't mind washing up," said Sam. But he had left it at that. It would have been too difficult to have explained. And it would soon be summer — and the last of the coke would be gone.

A fortnight ... A week ...

He had noticed lately that a crack in the floor seemed to lead directly into the corner. It grew larger as he uncovered it.

That there was something in the corner he was now certain. He had lived a great deal of his life by instinct, and now all his instincts told him so. As the pile of coke diminished, as he bent, night after night, to fill the two steel hods, nearer and nearer and nearer to that corner, the corner to which the crack pointed, a prickling sweat broke out all over his body. His heart thumped, and he felt curiously light-headed. He had never felt quite that way before, but it reminded him of an occasion when, as a boy, he had fainted from overwork and lack of food.

There *was* something in that corner. Something unavoidable, something deadly, that would become apparent when the last scuttle of coke was removed.

But how would it be if the last scuttle — the very last scuttle — was removed by someone other than himself? Like everything in life, it was simply a matter of calculation. The daily woman filled four scuttles during the day. He filled two at night. It was like one of those card games in which you had to arrange your play so as to avoid holding the last card.

When he had seen the coke the night before there had been, he calculated, about sixteen scuttles left. Four would have been taken during the day. He would take another two — then Mrs Tizer would take four more —

"You've been doing sums to yourself for ten minutes," said his wife. "What's wrong? Money?"

"Nothing's wrong," said Sam.

"Then hurry along and get the coke and we can get off to bed. I don't know about you, but I'm dog tired."

"We shall have to be ordering some more soon," said Sam, cunningly. "I don't suppose we've enough left for even three days."

"We haven't that," said his wife, briskly. "I lent a bit to Mrs. Tizer — she ran short. But you ought to be able to scrape up enough for tonight. They'll be delivering a ton in the morning."

With a curious leaden feeling which centred on the top of his stomach and the bottom of his chest, Sam Cotton walked heavily down to the cellar. It was as his wife had said. A pathetic remnant of coke and coke-dust covered the corner. The crack gaped, so wide now that he could almost put his fist into it. Two blocks of the cement flooring almost looked as if they had been taken up and carelessly laid down again.

Sam picked up the shovel and bent down.

It had come now, it had to be faced — as he had faced and outfaced other things in his hard life.

His heart was pounding so that it nearly choked him. One scuttle —

then the other. The coke which was left would exactly fill it.

He stooped again and scraped the shovel on the floor. A blinding red light, an uprush of dizziness. He was on his knees, then on his face, his nose an inch from the crack —

✠   ✠   ✠

"Murder," said the young doctor, savagely, to his partner. "Plain murder. Letting him go down, night after night, with his heart in that state, and grovel for coke and lift weights. But not the sort of murder she can be hanged for — more's the pity."

SCREAM IN A SOUNDPROOFED ROOM

I t was second nature in Orloff to watch people without appearing to do so.

So, as Ladislas Petrov walked slowly up and down the handsome, panelled room that was partly his old drawing room and partly his new library, Orloff took out a lighter, lit a cigarette, and put away his lighter, and polished his nails and examined the toes of his own boots. Though his eyes rested rarely on his host his attention was on him the whole time.

The precaution was unconsciousness, the fruits of the life that Orloff had lived: nearly forty years of it since, as a boy of ten, he had started by carrying messages for the anarchist underground.

How old had he been when he had first been flogged? Fourteen was it? Or fifteen? How old when first condemned to death, and saved by some quirk of the absolute monarchy? Saved to see that monarchy go down in blood and dust and bitter humiliation; saved to see himself, as Party Secretary, the effective ruler of the country that had once hung him to a steel ring and beaten him.

It was purely unconscious, because Orloff had no reason now to distrust or to fear Ladislas Petrov. Petrov was that rarity, a Communist leader who had succeeded in reaching retirement. Rich, no longer ambitious, politically secure, dangerous to no-one, he lived on in his handsome villa at Provst, a living exception to the rule that no revolutionary man dies in his bed.

"It is the joinery which is so clever," he said. "You see? Each edge dovetailed to the other, but the dovetails hide each other successively, so that in the end, no joint appears."

He stroked with his finger the clean poplar wood which, fashioned into bookshelves and pediment, ran the length of the wall.

The man who had fashioned it was in the room with them. He had completed his work on the bookcases and the presses and was finishing now the woodwork of the new door. Orloff had noticed the door as he came in. It was solid and very heavy, but so beautifully balanced and hung that it moved to a finger's touch. You would imagine almost that a breath would open or shut it. When it closed, it slid into the jamb with that soft kiss that meant fitting to a hundredth of an inch on every side.

"We have fine carpenters still in our country," he agreed.

"You must not say 'carpenter.' I made that mistake myself at first. A carpenter is a man who builds houses. He has a big saw, to cut beams, and a heavy hammer, to drive nails." Petrov made a pantomime of sawing and hammering and laughed at his own clowning. "This man is a cabinet maker. He is a craftsman, a precision worker."

Although the workman was within hearing and took in every word they said, both men spoke about him as if he were not there, or had no proper understanding.

Orloff turned his searchlight attention on him for a moment. He was a big, brown-faced, white-haired man with a smile. An unusually good advertisement for the regime.

"You pay him?"

"Nothing, but for each day's work I give him a month's privilege ticket. If he works here twelve days he will be able to live well for a year — is that right?"

Finding himself addressed, the man smiled and bobbed his head. A privilege ticket enabled him to buy, at low cost, the extra fats and meat and milk that, in the normal way, only senior party members could enjoy.

"It is good work. It makes a handsome room."

His eye was still on the man. On his face, his hands, his canvas sack of tools. Orloff's intelligence picked up one fact — two facts — but failed, for the moment, to translate them.

"I gave some thought to it," agreed Petrov complacently. "First, we designed the shutters." The shutters flanked the long, single window which looked straight across Lake Plerny. They were cleverly designed but did not entirely conceal the fact that the windows themselves were barred, like the windows of a cell, by steel bars. Even in retirement a revolutionary leader could not neglect certain safeguards.

It would be a difficult room to attack, thought Orloff. One narrow, barred window. One heavy door. He had no doubt that under the fine panelling was steel plate. The walls were so thick that they were almost soundproof. An easy room to defend. But why think of that now. There was no fighting nowadays. No opposition. They were getting fat. Fat and soft.

Petrov suddenly laughed. "We are all three cabinet makers," he said. "You realise that? All three in this room."

It was true, thought Orloff. Difficult to realise now, as you looked at old Papa Petrov. Difficult to see in him the fighter, the man who had held the post office for nearly a week in the first May rising, held it with a handful of men and boys, little ammunition and no food.

Even more difficult to see the ruthless prosecutor of the purges. The man who had placed his own brother on trial for treason and countersigned the order for his execution without emotion. The man who, when everyone else had cried, "Halt," had gone one step further — and then another. Who had shot, with the guilty Rabotkin, the innocent Kometsy. Who had said, as Kometsy was prosecuted and handed to the Security Police, "He is innocent now, perhaps. But he has the look of a man who may be guilty some day."

Orloff found himself thinking of things he had not remembered for many years, things he thought buried under the heap of the intervening time. Those had been days when every man carried his head loose on his shoulders.

Why did his mind come back to Kometsy? Perhaps because he had been the greatest, and the last, of the victims. And as an oak, when felled in a thicket, brings down a host of lesser trees, so had tumbled all Kometsy's friends.

His secretaries. His family. His department. His friends. His wife had taken poison. There was a brother, Andreas. Something about Andreas? He had escaped. By great good fortune Andreas had been in Washington at the time of the trials, and by better fortune had had his family with him.

So rapidly had these thoughts passed through Orloff's mind that he found Petrov was still laughing at his own stupid joke.

"I have made and unmade many cabinets in my time," he repeated.

But Orloff was still looking at the workman, who had just finished his work on the door jamb with a few strokes of a spokeshave. A first-class workman, indeed, thought Orloff, who knew something of most things. Not one to massacre his material and then hide the scars behind sandpapering and putty. His finished product was clean wood, cleanly worked.

"Was your father a carpenter?" he asked suddenly.

"Indeed, greatness," said the man, speaking for the first time, "and his father before him."

"I thought it might be so," said Orloff. "You do not often see tools like this now."

It was a gauger plane that had caught his eye. A lovely instrument of bright steel and brass. He picked it up and twirled the gauge screw which regulated with micrometer precision the depth and set of the blade.

"It would take you — what — a year — to buy such a tool?"

"More, greatness," said the man. "I work little for money. Many of these my father left me. Others came to me before — before the Liberation."

Orloff nearly smiled. He guessed that if the man had been alone he would have said something very different.

He was packing away his tools now, with careful hands, as a surgeon might lay aside his instruments. Each chisel with its edge hidden in a wad of oakum, the graded drills, the curious gouges, the small, thin, heavy, brass-backed saw.

When he had done he bobbed to the two men asking leave to withdraw himself from their presence.

Petrov smiled, and made a gesture of dismissal with his hand. The man opened the door and ambled through, then he turned, smiled again, and closed the door behind him.

The little sigh which it made hung on the air.

Petrov moved again to the window. Below the terrace wall the waters winked in the setting sun.

"When I die," he said, "I will leave instructions in my will for my coffin to be taken out and sunk in the middle of the lake. They say it is bottomless — an old volcano —"

"I think," said Orloff, in his hard, incisive voice, "that you should check up on that man. The sooner the better."

"That man?"

"The man who's just left. Who does he call himself?"

"I never asked him his name," said Petrov. "The local co-operative sent him."

"Even local co-operatives have been known to make mistakes," said Orloff, drily.

"Are you sure you're not —"

"— letting my suspicious mind run away with me? No. I'm not sure. But my suspicious mind has just told me two things which my eyes saw five minutes ago. Do you remember the gauger plane? It would cost you — in this country today — oh, thirty dollars. Would a man like that earn thirty dollars in a year?"

"But he told you," said Petrov. "It came down to him from his father."

"That sort of plane did not exist five years ago."

"I see," said Petrov. He walked across to the fireplace and touched the bell. "Are you sure?"

"I know about these things." said Orloff. "It is a precision instrument, first invented for the aircraft industry, in America. But it was not only the plane. Did you not see his hands?"

"I saw them," said Petrov. "But they said nothing to me. What did they show to you?"

"Fresh blisters. Blisters from this job he has been doing here in the past twelve days. In the palm, from the butt of his chisel. On the side of the index finger from the handle of his saw."

"Why not?" said Petrov. "He has used both chisel and saw. I have seen myself."

"A carpenter," said Orloff, contemptuously. "And the son of a carpenter. A man who had handled tools since he was in knee breeches. Those parts of his hands would be like leather. And a third thing —"

His voice was so sharp that Petrov stopped pacing and stood still, looking at him.

"Why has no-one answered your bell?"

"It is that old fool, Sebastian," said Petrov. "He is getting deaf. If he is not in his pantry he does not hear the bell —"

"Perhaps," said Orloff.

He walked across the room, his feet noiseless on the heavy carpet, and turned the handle of the new door. It turned quite freely. But the door remained shut.

He threw his weight back, once, twice. So little impression did he make that he might have been pulling against a tree.

"He has locked us in?"

"From the feel of it," said Orloff, "I should surmise that the door has been screwed to the jamb with half a dozen very long screws. You'd best try the telephone, though I should guess it is little use."

Petrov seized the instrument, listened a moment, jiggling it, and then put it back. "Dead," he said.

"Does your window open?" Orloff asked.

"The bars —"

"I had no intention of getting out of it. I wished to shout for help."

He had crossed the room as he spoke. Petrov came with him. Something seemed to have happened to the window. The catch could be opened, but their combined strength could not move the sash by a fraction up or down.

Quite suddenly the air in the room seemed stifling. Orloff ran to the mantelpiece, picked up a heavy iron candlestick, ran back, and swung it hard at the glass.

The next moment the candlestick had clattered to the floor. The glass was scarcely scratched.

"Bullet proof," said Petrov. For some reason he had dropped his voice to a whisper. "That man — could be have been Andreas?"

"It might have been," said Orloff. "It cannot be coincidence that his name was in my mind, too. I hardly knew him, but there was something in the look. Sit down, man, and stop sweating."

"What — how — what does he hope to do?"

Good God, thought Orloff, with a spasm of disgust, I was right. The old man's gone soft. There's no fight left in him.

"Sit down," he said again. "If he aims to suffocate us, the less air we use the better. It's a big room. Someone will come soon."

"Not before morning," said Petrov. "Not unless we can attract attention."

"A lot can happen in twelve hours," said Orloff. "If I am not back by nightfall, my own office will start to panic." For the first time that afternoon a very faint smile appeared round his lips. "They'll probably think I've crossed the Curtain."

"Stop talking," said Petrov. His voice was high. Like a woman about to plunge into the emotional depths of a tantrum.

Orloff looked sharply at him. Then he heard it, too.

Somewhere behind the bookshelves, behind the beautiful panelling, and the clever joinery: a deep, purposeful, purring, clicking, pendulum note.

"Maybe we haven't got twelve hours after all," said Orloff, resignedly. "Maybe not even one."

It was not too bad until Petrov started to scream.

THE SHEIK GOES SHOPPING

In a shuttered room on the first floor of an old, white, thick-walled house, overlooking the land-locked harbour, sat Hubert Palling, CBE, late of the Sudanese Civil Service, adviser now to the Sheik Abdul Rahman El Qwar, Slave of the Compassionate ruler of the Independent Principality of the Island of Ibbelin.

The house had been built by an Arab slave trader nearly two hundred years before, and was as well suited to the climate of the Red Sea as any building could be. (The Sheik's palace, though it had cost ten times as much, was not really as comfortable. The Political Resident's quarter on the Airport Road was a bad joke.)

Meeting Mr. Palling for the first time, observing his tall, thin, stooping frame and long horse-like face, you might have supposed him a man with a secret sorrow. Nothing could have been farther from the truth. For Mr. Palling was that rare and amiable creature, the completely non-attached and adult bachelor.

We find him in the act of opening a long envelope, slitting it with a slim paperknife and that degree of lingering care a man lavishes only on the communications of a loved one. The letter was from his brokers.

"Dear Sir," he read. "We were pleased to receive your enquiry as to the prospects for heavy industrial stocks in the next account. Provided that the selection is made carefully —"

"Yes, what is it?"

"It is the Lebanese interpreter, Sadawi," said the servant. "Perhaps I will tell him to go away and return in the evening?"

"Yes — no, I'm afraid we can't do that," said Mr. Palling. With a loving look at the thick, folded enclosure he rose to his feet. "I suppose I had better see what His Highness wants."

The car which was waiting for him was a new 300 horse-power Lotus Biarritz. It was hand-crafted in scarlet and cream, complete with automatic transmission, power-steering, air-conditioning, near-gold hub caps and a twelve-disc hi-fi record player.

52

The distance to the palace was about four hundred yards, mostly up a street composed of shallow steps which the Lotus negotiated with contemptuous ease.

"His Highness," said Sadawi, "is beset with devils. Nothing will please him. I buy him cars. No pleasure. I buy him aeroplanes. Still no pleasure. I buy him women —"

"Perhaps he has reached saturation point," said Mr. Palling.

To the left of the colonnaded entrance, secure within the perimeter of their ant-proof ditch, he observed five other cars, identical in all particles with the one in which he rode.

"Possibly," said Sadawi. He disliked Mr. Palling; but no more than Mr. Palling disliked him.

✠ ✠ ✠

The Sheik ceased pacing up and down his state apartment long enough to greet them.

"Ah, Mr. Balling," he said. "How good of you to come." (Like all Arab speakers, he experienced difficulty with the European 'P' and compromised with something much nearer to 'B' — a fact that had caused continual distress to Mr. Palling's predecessor, Mr. Pollock.) "You may leave us, Sadawi," he added, in tones which had become icy with displeasure. Whilst he was still within earshot, the Sheik added, "That man is a common swindler. I shall have to get rid of him. I discover that he has pocketed fifteen per cent — *fifteen per cent* — on each of my cars. Small wonder he wishes to buy me a seventh!"

"It had occurred to me to wonder why you needed quite so many," said Mr. Palling. "There are not many opportunities in Ibbelin for pleasure driving."

"I drive to the airport," said the Sheik. "I fly in my aeroplane. I return to the airport. I drive back to my palace. Such a life has its limitations. So many cars, so many aeroplanes, so many women. They are limited by one's capacity to enjoy them. Might I make a personal observation?"

"By all means," said Mr. Palling, who had never purchased an aeroplane or a woman, although he had once owned a Morris Minor.

"You continue to remain, if I may say so, extraordinarily happy."

"Certainly, certainly."

"Your predecessor, an admirable man in many ways, was addicted to drink. His predecessor to young girls. The one before that had the most curious vices ..."

✠   ✠   ✠

Mr. Palling found it difficult to express, upon a moment's notice, and as he was clearly being asked to do, his philosophy of life and happiness; so he simply said, "I find great interest in a modest flutter on the stock market."

"Explain, please."

Mr. Palling did his best. The fact that he spoke excellent Arabic was a help.

"All businesses are, you say, divided into parts."

"Shares."

"Into shares. And you purchase these shares in the market. One here, one there, until you have amassed more than half of all the shares. Then you are master of the business."

"Indirectly, yes. Of course, the board are the nominal masters. But the owner of more than half the shares can do as he pleases with them."

"Imprison them?"

"Well, no. But he can deprive them of their posts."

"There are several businesses I should like to have," agreed the Sheik. "I have been, as you know, but once in your country, for your Queen's coronation. There was a business which manufactured banknotes —"

"I doubt if the Government would wish to sell that one."

"Another then. It had a number of shops which sold merchandise. Each of their stores had a frontage of bright red with attractive golden lettering —"

"I rather think," said Mr. Palling, "that the owners of that one live in America and might be hard to get at. But if your mind is turning to stores, there are other groups in which you should be able to purchase an interest. If you would like an introduction to a reliable firm of brokers —"

"I will speak of the matter to my treasurer," said the Sheik, "and then we will talk of it again."

As Mr. Palling walked back to his quarters, refusing the loan of the fifth Lotus Biarritz, he encountered Derek. (He could never remember his second name.)

"Can I give you a lift?" said Derek. He was in shirt-sleeves and driving a jeep. "How is his Serene Highness?"

"Rather more cheerful now," said Mr. Palling. "No, thank you. I may be middle-aged, but I still have the use of my legs. How is the Agent?"

"Down in the mouth."

"Trouble with the Foreign Office?"

"The boys forgot to keep the ant-proof ditch topped with petrol, and the ants have eaten the squash court."

"Bad luck," said Mr. Palling, insincerely.

A few weeks later, at a moment when Mr. Palling was planning a small coup in phosphates, Mr. Stettler called.

Mr. Stettler was an American, a round, cheerful man who ran the Ibbelin Oil Concession with great efficiency and lived largely on Bismuth powders and soda water.

He and Mr. Palling found each other sympathetic.

"What have you been putting the old boy up to?" he asked.

"Nothing," said Mr. Palling. "I haven't spoken to him for a week."

"Then you'd better speak to him fast. He's selling out."

"Selling the concession?"

"He can't sell the concession," said Mr. Stettler, "because it's leased to my company for twenty-five years. But he's selling his royalties."

"All of his royalties?"

"I understand not. About a third of them. To a ready-money syndicate in Egypt."

Mr. Palling made a rapid calculation. "If he gets twenty million pounds a year —"

"Twenty-four," said Mr. Stettler.

"And sells a third – that's eight. He'd get about ten years purchase. I suppose that's eighty million pounds."

"He can't want another car," said Mr. Stettler. "So what's he planning to do with it?"

Mr. Palling, at the window, said, "Here comes Sadawi."

"Keep me in the picture," said Mr. Stettler.

The Sheik, once again, came almost directly to the point.

"There are certain other shops," he said. "Fewer than the red-and-gold ones, but in some ways more attractive. They have a blue frontage, and the sign is of hands clasped over the letters D and G in silver."

"Domestic and General Stores Limited."

"I believe that is the name."

✠ ✠ ✠

Mr. Palling consulted the brokers' monthly list which he carried in his inner pocket. "Issued share capital, five million pounds," he said. "They stand at about 85s. Of course, they'll go up as soon as it's known you're in the market for them."

"Then all must be done discreetly," said the Sheik. "I leave it to you. I should not wish to spend more, on this occasion, than twenty million pounds."

"Oh, certainly," said Mr. Palling.

His first move was to send a cable to his cousin, Mr. Detterling, a solicitor in London. Mr. Detterling showed the cable to his managing clerk. "The Post Office must have added at least three noughts by mistake," he said. "Lucky we didn't take Hubert at his word!" When they had both finished laughing he cabled back that he thought he might be able to get a few thousand shares at around ninety. On receipt of this answer, Mr. Palling perceived that further cabling would be a waste of time. He borrowed one of the Sheik's aeroplanes, flew into Aden, and booked a telephone call.

The radio-telephone link was excellent; Mr. Palling spoke clearly and forcibly to his cousin.

Mr. Detterling said, "I suppose you know what you're doing. I'm afraid none of my clients ever invest more than a few thousand at a time."

"Well, here's one that wants to. Can you handle it?"

"I don't see why not," said Mr. Detterling, slowly. "As a matter of fact, it's funny you should mention D and G. About a quarter of the shares were held by the old boy — the one who died last year. I was talking, the other day, to the solicitors who act for the estate. They were saying how difficult it was to float off a big block like that without knocking the price. I could make them an offer — they'd want to know who was buying."

"Tell them it's a Middle Eastern syndicate," said Mr. Palling. "But buy privately in the market, too. Nothing less than a clear majority's any use."

"I shall have to do it very carefully through nominees."

"Do it how you like," said Mr. Palling, conscious that the conversation was costing a pound a minute.

Mr. Detterling said to the managing clerk: "Well, don't sit there twiddling your thumbs. Ring up our brokers. And what's the name of that private nominee company we sometimes use? We don't get twenty million to spend every day. Do something."

✠ ✠ ✠

In Ibbelin the most resounding events of the great outside world echo but faintly. There are no telephones to sound their impertinent summons. Wireless communication depends on the vagaries of certain sun spots over the Arabian Desert; and the fortnightly post, which arrives by air from Aden, is, at its best, capricious.

The first real news that the Sheik received was when the Political Agent, Mr. Cherry-Bole, was announced.

"I wonder what he wants?" said Mr. Palling, irritably. He was in the middle of a lecture on Debenture Stock and resented the interruption.

Mr. Cherry-Bole, OBE, though an ornament of Haileybury and the Foreign Office, suffered from one drawback in his dealings with the Sheik. He spoke no Arabic. Mr. Palling or Sadawi had to interpret for him.

"Would you tell His Highness," he said to Mr. Palling, "that he would seem to have put the cat among the pigeons."

Mr. Palling did his best. His 'lion among the camels' was a resourceful improvisation. The Sheik looked blank.

"Hasn't he heard?"

"There was a seasonal interruption in the radio-link last week. And I don't think we have either of us had a letter from England —"

"I see," said Mr. Cherry-Bole. "I got a long screed in the official bag yesterday. That's what I wanted to discuss with His Highness. Apparently some solicitor called Detterling —"

"My cousin," said Mr. Palling, gently.

"Oh, yes, well, I've no doubt he was only doing what he was told. But he seems to have pulled off a bit of a coup. He bought a big block of founders' shares in D and G and his nominees went into the market and snapped up a lot more —"

"Yes?" said Mr. Palling.

"And — well — they seem to have snapped up over half the voting shares."

"I'm glad to hear it," said Mr. Palling, rubbing his hands together. "I'd no idea our little coup had been so successful. Our next move will be to reconstitute the Board."

✠ ✠ ✠

Mr. Cherry-Bole said, "That's just it. He has reconstituted them. On the Sheik's instructions Mr. Detterling sacked them all at the General Meeting last week. The chairman's Lord Clanrichetty, and he's got a lot of pull with the Foreign Office. He wants them to do something."

"I don't really see," said Mr. Palling, "that they can do much. They can only proffer advice to His Highness. Speaking personally, I should say they were well rid of Lord Clanrichetty."

"You know him?"

"I was in the same house at school."

"That's all very well. He's got rid of the *whole* Board. And he doesn't seem to have done anything about a new one."

"I see," said Mr. Palling.

"I think I'd better leave you to cope with this," said Mr. Cherry-Bole. What he really meant was: 'You got him into it, you can get him out.' He look his leave.

"And what would you advise?" said the Sheik. He seemed unperturbed by the crisis he had caused in the affairs of the third largest chain store in Great Britain.

"I suppose you ought to *have* a Board."

"You know people in England. Whom should I select? Mr. Churchill is no longer Prime Minister — ?"

"No, but I expect he's busy."

"You have, perhaps, some suggestions?"

"The most capable person I now," said Mr. Palling, "is my Aunt Enid. She has been running people all her life."

"Excellent," said the Sheik. "She shall be Chairman. Have you other relatives?"

"Her brother is a clergyman. An excellent man in his way. And perhaps it would be a good idea to promote the General Manager to the Board."

"Let it be done," said the Sheik. He added: "After all, it will only be for a short time."

Mr. Palling looked enquiringly.

"I have made all arrangements to go to England. I shall thus be able to oversee the matter myself."

☩ ☩ ☩

Three weeks later Mr. Palling again sat in his darkened upper room in the old slave trader's house, dealing with his correspondence. It was no longer an unmixed pleasure.

There was a reproachful letter from his stockbrokers (they appeared to consider that he should have let them in on the ground floor), a petulant letter from Mr. Detterling, whose decorous Lincoln's Inn office had been over-run by the Press, and a firm letter from his Aunt Enid. "A person called yesterday from the Share and Loan Department, whatever that may be," she wrote in her clear, Oxford College hand. "He told me that I had broken the rules of the Stock Exchange by converting my one-pound shares into five-shilling ones without *his* permission. I told him that I took no cognisance of the rules of an institution which appeared to me little better than a legalised lottery. He seemed surprised —"

"Oh dear," said Mr. Palling. "Oh dear."

At this moment Mr. Cherry-Bole was announced.

His superiors at the Foreign Office and the ants had combined with the Red Sea climate to engrave lines of settled apprehension on his face. At that moment he looked, thought Mr. Palling, more worried than usual.

"I had a long cable from the Foreign Office this morning," he said. "They seem to think the Sheik ought to come home. They can't order him, of course. He's an independent sovereign."

"Why shouldn't he buy a few stocks and shares? It's a free country."

"If he only wanted a few, it wouldn't matter."

"He's got twenty million to spend," said Mr. Palling. "Don't tell me the market can't absorb that."

"If he'd take advice and invest it properly, of course it could. It's the capricious nature of his purchases. Last week he made offers for Madame Tussaud's and the Zoo."

"How splendid. Do you think there's any chance he'll get them?"

"I shouldn't think so. The real trouble is that he's becoming a fashion. The Great British Public love him. If he buys, they buy. If he says no, that stock becomes practically unsaleable. Do you know he gave a Press interview the other day? One of the reporters asked him what principles governed his investing, and he said he'd never touch a share unless the certificate was printed in green. It's all having a very unsettling effect."

Mr. Palling knew just enough about the delicate workings of the Stock Market to appreciate that a few uncontrolled millions sliding about haphazard could have much the same effect as a piece of heavy cargo which had broken from its lashing inside a rolling ship.

"I'd better fly into Aden tomorrow," he said, "and have a word with Detterling."

✠ ✠ ✠

"Trouble?" Mr. Detterling's voice came thinly over the line. "Not really; I suppose it was a bit hot whilst it lasted. The people I was sorry for were the other shareholders in D and G".

"I suppose they've lost a packet?"

"I said I *was* sorry for them, I'm not now."

"I'm afraid I don't follow," said Mr. Palling. "We're a bit out of touch here."

"The shares are standing well over six now. The managing director's been a great success. He'd probably have got there in ten years or so, anyway. Your pal gave him his chance early, that's all."

"How does he get on with my aunt?"

"She's resigned and formed a rival company."

"My God!" said Mr. Palling.

"Very forceful woman. But she and the Sheik didn't really see eye to eye. You'll be seeing him soon."

"Is he on his way back?"

"And how!" said Mr. Detterling. "Bringing his sheaves with him."

"What do you mean?"

"Your three minutes is up," said an impersonal voice. "Do you wish to reserve a further period?"

"It's all right," said Mr. Detterling. "We've finished."

As Mr. Palling landed back at Ibbelin airfield Derek drove up in his jeep.

"Give you a lift, sir?" he said. "Just drove over to see if the wireless boys had got any news of the Sheik."

"And had they?"

"There's been a bit of a black-out since he left Paris."

"What's he doing in Paris?"

"I think the idea was to stay there a week and let the ship get ahead of him. Then they could both arrive together."

"What ship, for heaven's sake?"

"You don't mean to say," said Derek maliciously, "that you haven't heard? Well, you know that D and G own Grummidges?"

"Grummidges of Oxford Street?"

"Well, he bought it up."

"Bought a lot of stuff?"

"Not a lot, everything. Cleared it right out. That's what's on the ship. The manager had a fit. But he couldn't stop him. The Sheik was the boss. There's some marvellous stuff." Derek licked his lips. "Three grand pianos, enough carpet to cover the island, a rowing-machine, six motor mowers —"

"What's he going to do with a motor mower in Ibbelin?"

"He's bought lots of grass seed as well," said Derek.

✠ ✠ ✠

Porters were still sweating up under their loads. Mr. Palling arrived with the last of a consignment of electric sewing machines and pushed his way past a crate labelled "Boxing-ring, full size. Instruction for re-assembly within."

He found the Sheik in his first-floor room, brimming over with pleasure and proud excitement.

"You like them, yes?" he said.

"I haven't seen everything yet," said Mr. Palling, "but you've certainly got something."

"For all my friends, too. You choose some now."

Mr. Palling inspected the immediate selection. The choice seemed to lie between a more or less walnut cocktail cabinet lined with plate glass, and a complete set of the Everyman Library.

"More in the next room," said the Sheik. "Do not hurry your choice. You may have anything you wish — with one exception."

Mr. Palling look up sharply. There was a strange note in the Sheik's voice, too.

The door opened and Mr. Palling blinked twice. A very striking blonde girl walked in.

"I found her," said the Sheik simply, "in a cage behind the door of my shop. Her name is Bobby. Miss Bobby Parker."

"Pleased to meet you," said Miss Parker. She added: "I'm the only thing he didn't buy six of."

Mr. Palling gathered that, in addition to the other gifts so freely bestowed on her by Nature, she had a sense of humour.

✠   ✠   ✠

"What do you know?" said Mr. Stettler that evening. "She comes from a place called Bal-ham. That's in London, isn't it?"

"That's right," said Mr Palling.

"And do you know what she brought out of one of those six ice-boxes? A martini! Dry, and bee-outifully mixed. I'm going up to dinner there tomorrow night, and I don't know which I'm looking forward to most: tinned prairie chicken à la Maryland, or seeing Cherry-Bole being polite to the lady of the house."

"A new era dawns for Ibbelin," said Mr. Palling, truthfully.

CLOS CARMINE

Don Easton raised the tulip-shaped glass to the light and stared for a long moment into the crimson heart of the wine. It seemed sacrilege to drink it when you could get almost as much pleasure from looking at it.

He tilted the glass up and savoured the bouquet; fresh but already attractive.

"Of the vintage of 1953," said his host, Monsieur Desjardins, his eyes twinkling, his bald head gleaming.

"Too young," said a thin-faced man with a beard whom the others addressed as "Mon Colonel."

"On the contrary," said Monsieur Desjardins. "The wines of Burgundy are best drunk young, clear and fresh. It is only the more sophisticated wines of Bordeaux which improve with keeping."

Now another member of the party, an enormously stout, but hitherto silent, man, whose name Don understood to be Monsieur Serieux, cleared his throat. It was plain that he had an important contribution to offer.

"Wines," he said, "like women, are at their finest between the ages of 15 and 18."

He popped a wedge of hare pâté into his mouth, with the gesture of one re-corking a bottle from which a few drops of priceless wisdom have been reluctantly poured.

"Only claret, not Burgundy," said Monsieur Desjardins, obstinately.

The argument rolled on. Don had a sufficient knowledge of the French language to understand what was being said, but not quite sufficient confidence, as yet, to make a contribution.

Later, no doubt, when further drink had been consumed, the gift of Pentecost would descend upon him and his tongue be unlocked.

Meanwhile, there were worse ways of spending the middle of the day than sitting, in the open, in the late September sunlight of the Cote d'Or, eating the wonderful food of the Dijonnais and drinking the wine of Gevrey-Chambertin.

He realised that a question was being addressed to him.

"Have you," inquired Monsieur Desjardins, "been successful in your quest?"

"So far, not as successful as I had hoped," he said.

"Monsieur Easton," explained Monsieur Desjardins, "is an agent of travel. He seeks now to arrange for special and selected clients, little tours of the famous wine districts of France.

Don felt embarrassed at this abrupt intrusion of business into a social occasion. He need not have been. Frenchmen are gourmets twice a day, but they are businessmen all the time.

"It is natural," said the stout man, "that you should come first to the Cote d'Or."

"In particular," said Monsieur Desjardins, "he seeks to make arrangements with owners of the vineyards, so that small parties may stay, for a night or two, as paying guests in their houses. They would thus be at leisure to drink the wine, and observe the processes of the vendange."

The others considered the project carefully. The consensus of opinion was that in ordinary times, it would be well received.

"But why not now?" asked Don.

He had, indeed, been puzzled by the curious reserve of some of the people he had spoken to. He had put it down to his own lack of fluency.

"The times are not ordinary," said Monsieur Desjardins. "In the last two years — but the Colonel can tell you more about it than I can."

"In the last two years," said the Colonel, "there have been a number of well organised, vicious, and successful thefts from private houses, up and down the Cote d'Or. The houses of the vineyard owners have been particularly pillaged. It has made them distrustful of all strangers. A stranger may not be a thief. But he could be a spy for a thief."

"These have been jewel thieves?"

"Jewellery, gold, silver, objects of art, everything."

"I should have thought," said Don, "that thieves of this sort would most likely have been discovered through the receivers or disposers of the stolen goods."

The Colonel looked at him. For the first time something approaching a twinkle came into his eye.

"You are a criminologist?" he inquired.

"Well, no," said Don, conscious that he was being laughed at. "I have, in the course of my life, encountered a number of criminals. As I expect you have."

A roar of laughter split the table. When it had died down: "Monsieur le Colonel is Prefect of Police for the area," explained Monsieur Desjardins.

It was more than an hour later, when the plates had been cleared, that the conversation returned abruptly to the robberies. As the brandy came in, discretion went out. A name cropped up. "Clos Carmine."

It floated across the table to Don, who raised his head to listen. He tried to hear what was being said, but lost it in the intervening babble.

He turned to Monsieur Desjardins. "I heard mention," he said, "of the Clos Carmine."

By some trick of the talk, this fell into a moment of silence. Don found himself a target of eyes.

"You were inquiring —" said the Colonel, politely.

"It was just that I heard the name mentioned," said Don. "Clos Carmine, I was interested."

"We were recalling," said the Colonel, "that it was, at one time, widely suspected that the proprietor of the Clos Carmine was himself the organiser of the robberies under discussion. Indeed, so certain was I of the correctness of this information, that I risked, and nearly lost, my position in the police on the strength of that certainty."

The others murmured assent. The story was evidently known to them. Monsieur Desjardins refilled the Colonel's glass, sympathetically.

"Ten of my most experienced agents," he said, "searched the house from roof to cellar. Particularly the cellar. We found nothing. The proprietor, not unnaturally, made a strong protest. Political issues were involved. My head —" the Colonel rotated it solemnly "— was loose on my shoulders."

Don sipped his brandy. He was thinking. Indeed, he had reason to be thoughtful. It had not happened before, and was unlikely to happen again, that he should have heard propounded, and been in a position to solve, a criminal problem all in the course of a single luncheon party.

By merely opening his mouth, by speaking a single sentence, he could, as he was well aware, create a sensation. He could establish his own reputation beyond cavil. He could break up the party. He could send the Colonel scurrying back to his office.

But in the end he decided to do none of these things. It was not, as he told himself, any business of his.

Although he continued to tell himself so, it was no later than five o'clock that same evening that his car turned west off Route Nationale 74 into the minor road which wound upwards between the bluff, tawny hills; hills which are more truly and lastingly valuable to France than if they were, as their name suggests, made of pure gold.

All around him, in every fold and kerchief of the precious land, men, women and children were engaged in gathering the grape harvest. Twice he had to edge past slow lumbering ox-wagons. As the vineyards were giving way to oak and scrub, he came to the turning he remembered. High, flint walls were broken by an aged iron gate. He turned into the driveway, which followed the contour of the hill for nearly half a mile, and then the house of Clos Carmine was in front of him. In the Medoc it would have been styled a Chateau. But in truth it was no more than a large solidly built farmhouse.

When he tugged at the iron bell-pull, and heard the distant answering clang, memories came flooding back.

It was, perhaps, the coincidence of the weather. It was in just such September sunlight that he had first come to Clos Carmine.

It seemed absurd that he should only have spent in all a week there. A week? In retrospect, it drew out into a considerable section of his life.

Footsteps approached. The door was opened. A man was standing there, but in the shadow.

"Is Monsieur Carrier at home?" asked Don. "Or Madame Carrier, perhaps. Or the children?" (But it was 15 yeas ago. Of course, they would not be children now).

"Monsieur Carrier no longer lives here," said the man. He came forward from the shadows of the hallway. It was not a pleasant voice. And the face, now revealed, was not a prepossessing face.

"My apologies," said Don. "I trust that nothing has happened to him — or to Madame."

"I am afraid," said the man, with bare civility, "that I know nothing of their present circumstances. They left here shortly after the war."

"I see," said Don. "I am much obliged."

The man had no observation to make.

As Don turned his car, he heard the door clanging shut.

✠ ✠ ✠

"I had no idea," he said to Monsieur Desjardins that evening. "What a surly brute. You say he bought the Carriers out."

"In my view, he swindled them," said Monsieur Desjardins. "He was a shipper, in a small way. There were, as you know, two moderate vintages shortly after the war — 1946 and 1948.

"Monsieur Carrier borrowed money, on bond. The bond was foreclosed. He and his family were forced to leave. They live now in Lyons."

Don noted the address for future action. He spoke slowly, to conceal the fact that he was making up his mind.

Then he said, "Would you convey a message to the Colonel? He should visit the proprietor's cellar at Clos Carmine, and examine particularly the bins containing the bottles of the 1934 vintage. If he will trouble to remove all the bottles from the left hand bin, and insert his hand, he will discover the concealed latchet which opens a section of brickwork, set between oak newel-posts. Behind it there is a space measuring 8 foot by 10 foot square. Sufficient, I imagine, to contain the proceeds of the burglaries he was referring to. Or such of the proceeds as have not been dissipated."

Monsieur Desjardins was staring at him. Excitement struggled with incredulity in his eyes.

"Expert police searchers," he said, "have already subjected the cellar to careful scrutiny. They discovered nothing."

"The Gestapo of Dijon," said Don grimly, "subjected the cellar to very careful search in 1944. They discovered nothing either. Had they done so, I should not be talking to you now. For I was behind the wall."

Before he had finished Monsieur Desjardins' hand had gone out to his telephone.

✠   ✠   ✠

"Highly satisfactory, no doubt," said Janice, in the voice in which she scolded Don.

It was 10 days later, and they were getting ready to shut up the office in Marl Street.

"A receiver arrested, an unsolved crime neatly solved. But what did you get out of it?"

"Some useful contacts," said Don, dreamily, "And a bottle of Clos de Tart, 1945. A remarkable, memorable, prince of wines. The trip would have been well worth it for that alone."

"1945," said Janice, scornfully. "I don't call that old. My father told me that he once drank an 1872 wine."

"Claret," said Don. "Not Burgundy. The wines of Burgundy are at their finest between the ages of 15 and 18."

"Why are you grinning in that wolfish way?"

"Nothing," said Don, untruthfully. "Lock up, and let's all go home."

THE CURIOUS CONSPIRACY

When I qualified as a solicitor, one of the first clients I took on was Grandmother Clatterwick. I did so with some trepidation. I was a young lawyer and she was a formidable old lady, as tough and straight as one of the whalebone inserts in her own corsets. Surprisingly we got on well together. My mother, who died in the same year as my father, had been her youngest and favourite daughter, and I think some of the affection washed off on me.

As the years went by, it became a source of sadness to me to see Grandmother's estate diminish. Not that there was any question of her sinking into poverty. Her husband, Herbert Clatterwick, had been a strange silent man who had known nothing about anything except South American mining shares; but he had understood them well enough to make a comfortable fortune on the Stock Exchange, all of which was left to his widow, along with Hambone Manor and its park. Unfortunately the money was all unearned income and as taxation bit into it more and more deeply, pieces of the park had to be sold, wings of the Manor shut off, and servants dismissed or not replaced.

In the end Grandmother Clatterwick lived in the south wing, attended only by the faithful McGuffog and assisted by a couple of villagers who came up by day.

McGuffog had started life at the Manor as gardener's boy, had graduated through the pantry to assistant butler, and was now butler, gardener, and handyman combined. When I went down, as I did from time to time, to talk business and stayed overnight, McGuffog would wait on the two of us, through an elaborate meal. After dinner he would bring the coffee into the drawing room, place a log on the fire, inquire whether anything else was wanted, and retire to the rooms which had been fitted out for him over the stable. There were, in fact, a dozen bedrooms he could have used in the house itself, but when the last of the resident servants left, my grandmother's sense of propriety would not allow her to sleep alone in the house with a man. She was 75 at the time.

All these thoughts and memories of my grandmother were in my mind as we sat round the desk in my office that spring morning a week after her funeral.

The aunts were all there. Aunt Gertrude, a dry and intellectual spinster; Aunt Valerie, who had married Dr. Moffat and produced two ghastly children called George and Mary; and Aunt Alexandra, who had married a Major Lumsden and bought him out of the cavalry to listen to her talk.

"*Why* did she leave no will?" said Aunt Alexandra. "You were her solicitor. It was surely your duty to see that she made one. Isn't that what lawyers are for?"

"Don't be absurd," said Aunt Gertrude. "As if anyone, let alone her own grandson, could have persuaded mother to do anything she didn't wish to do."

"Does it make any difference?" said Aunt Valerie. "As I understand the law — you must correct me if I'm wrong, dear — her money is divided into four equal shares. Not that I mind for myself. I was thinking only of George and Mary."

Aunt Gertrude cackled sardonically. It was well known in the family that Valerie excused any personal selfishness by passing it on, second-hand, to her revolting children.

I took over to prevent a fight. "That's quite correct. The property passes to the children equally, per stirpes. That —"

"No need to explain," said Aunt Gertrude. "I haven't forgotten the Latin I learned at school" — and she shot a glance at her sisters which implied quite clearly that she suspected they had.

"How much will the estate amount to?" inquired Dr. Moffat.

"It's difficult to say. Estate duty will account for a slice of it. And the Manor will have to be sold."

"No-one will give a penny for it," said Aunt Gertrude. "A rambling old place in a shocking state of repair."

"What about stocks and shares and things like that?" asked Aunt Valerie.

I said, "Granny had been using up capital quite a bit during recent years. Not so much since we bought her that annuity — that cost capital too, of course. But there must be quite a lot left. And although we may not get much for the Manor there were one or two nice things in it. It's a couple of years since I've been down there, but I remember an attributed Morland in the drawing room. That was insured for £5,000. And I think there was an Etty in the dining-room."

"*I* was somewhat more regular in my visits," said Dr. Moffat reprovingly.

"For George and Mary's sake," said Aunt Gertrude under her breath.

"— and I was actually there a fortnight before her decease. It struck me that she had become rather eccentric. We had a good dinner, as usual, but what do you suppose we were offered to drink with it?"

None of us could guess.

"A very large bottle of raspberry wine."

I could hardly conceal my delight. My uncle is the complete wine snob. By this I mean that he reads books about wine, belongs to all the wine societies, has a cupboard full of wine lists and the catalogues of wine auctions, talks endlessly about vintages and *crus* — and has less taste and discernment than a camel. On one occasion when we had him to dinner I emptied a bottle of red wine, which I had bought for two francs fifty at a grocer's shop in France, into an old Château Margaux bottle which I happened to have, and received the warmest commendation of my choice. "Superb bouquet, my boy. One can almost taste the violets in it." I could visualise exactly his expression when he was offered a bottle of raspberry wine.

"Apparently," said Aunt Valerie, "she had been making quite a thing of it. McGuffog who had been helping her to brew it, told us that she had more than two thousand bottles of it in the cellar."

"Of raspberry wine?"

"Not all raspberry. There was raspberry, plum, and turnip wine, blackcurrant and redcurrant cordial, and elderflower champagne. And half a dozen other nauseating brews too, I don't doubt."

Major Lumsden was a silent man, as anyone would be who was married to my Aunt Alexandra, but he had a kind heart. He said, "Talking about that fellow McGuffog, are we going to do anything for him?"

"I was thinking about that," I said. "He looked after granny for more than forty years. If I could have persuaded her to make a will I'm sure she'd have left him something."

"But she didn't make a will," said Aunt Valerie sharply.

"All the same —" said the Major.

"As a matter of fact," I said, "I had a letter from McGuffog only this morning. I won't bother to read it all to you, although it's surprisingly well composed —"

"He must be reasonably competent," said Aunt Valerie. "After all, he used to manage a very large household. Larger than any of *us* had to deal with."

"Quite so," I said. "Well, this is the passage I wanted to read you: 'I realise that Mrs. Clatterwick didn't approve of will making. She often told me so. There couldn't therefore be any question of a legacy. However —' "

As I turned the page I was aware of five pairs of eyes on me. One pair sardonic, one kindly, the other three pairs frankly greedy.

" '— it did occur to me to wonder whether the family would agree to me taking over the unused stock of homemade wine. I co-operated with Mrs. Clatterwick in getting together what must, I venture to think, be a unique collection of vintages —' "

"If *that's* all he wants," said Aunt Valerie, striving to keep the relief out of her voice, "I should be the first to agree."

The others nodded. Major Lumsden said, "Don't you think that some sort of pension —" But he was quickly and decisively overruled.

"All right," I said, "I'll tell him. He can store it in the old stable. And I assume you'll let him stay on in his flat until the house is sold?"

"If the people who buy the house have got an atom of sense," said Aunt Gertrude, "they'll take McGuffog with the house. Servants like that don't grow on trees."

The winding up of an intestate estate, particularly the estate of an old and secretive lady, is not a quick matter. But as the months slipped by and the answers came in from banks and stockbrokers and insurance companies, I began to feel the first stirrings of unease. There was so much less in the estate than I had expected.

It was true, as I had told her daughters, that Grandmother

Clatterwick had been nibbling into capital for years. But when I finally persuaded her to put £40,000 into a life annuity, this had ensured her an almost tax-free income in the high thousands — enough, one would have thought, even for a Victorian old lady who liked to double the parson's stipend and to support charities with objects as diverse as the clothing of Eskimo babies and the moral rearmament of Hottentot girls.

Moreover, when I had bought the annuity I had made a very careful check of what money and securities were left, and the total was not far short of £20,000. Now, I could locate barely half of it.

The final blow fell in the early autumn when I got the schedule of the contents of Hambone Manor. I rang up the appraiser.

I said, "Why have you left out the Morland and the Etty?"

"I left them out," said the appraiser, "because they weren't there. The old man who looks after the place — McGuffog, that's the name — told me they were put up at auction about eighteen months ago. The Morland wasn't signed, so it only fetched two thousand. The Etty went for one and a half."

It was then I decided I would have to look into the matter personally.

Hambone Street lies in the miraculously still unravaged piece of Kent to the south of the A20. It has villages which still *are* villages, which possess things like village greens on which the local cricket team plays, village halls for the Women's Institute, and not less than three public houses for a population of four hundred and fifty. Lack of a rail service has helped to keep it the way it is, and I drove down by car on a lovely autumn morning when the leaves were just beginning to turn.

I found the Manor in sad decline. The grass was uncut, the hedges were straggling, and there were unfilled potholes in the driveway. This was disappointing. The estate had continued to pay McGuffog's salary on the understanding that he did some work on the grounds. It looked as though he had fallen down on the job.

However, there was someone in the house. Smoke was coming from one of the chimneys and the front door was open. I found Annie, one of the two village women, in possession. She had been told to keep the house as clean and dry as possible, and I could see she, at least, was doing a good job of it. When I asked her about McGuffog she looked startled.

"Didn't they tell you?" she said. "He passed away. They should have let you know, sir."

"I'm terribly sorry," I said. "When did it happen?"

"Two weeks ago it was. They laid him to rest on Sunday. A nice service. Vicar's been very helpful too. He left no family, you see. Only a cousin, or some such, who lives over in Essex. If you'd like a word with Mr. Stacey I saw his car in the yard. Likely he'll be over there now."

I walked across to the stable and introduced myself to the Reverend Stacey, who was coming down the stairs which led to McGuffog's flat. He was a cheerful young man with the well-scrubbed face and no-nonsense look that Theological Colleges turn out nowadays. He said, "I'm glad you're here. I thought of getting in touch with you. Not that there's much for a lawyer to do. All the stuff in the flat was borrowed from the house, you know. With Mrs. Clatterwick's agreement, of course. But it belonged to her, not to McGuffog. Almost the only things he left were the clothes he stood up in. Oh, and the remains of the wine."

"The remains?"

"He seems to have got rather fond of it. Rather too fond, perhaps." The vicar gave an unclerical chuckle. "People in the village used to hear him singing. Fortunately they couldn't make out the words, so they assumed it was Gaelic."

"*Can* you get drunk on raspberry wine?"

"I expect you can get drunk on anything, if you try hard enough. McGuffog certainly put his back into it. He took over nearly two thousand bottles of it —"

"Nineteen hundred and eighty-four," said Annie who had joined us. "I helped him store them in the hayracks in the stable."

"When he died there were just about fifteen hundred left."

I did some mental arithmetic. The period between my grandmother's death and McGuffog's was not much more than twenty weeks. Call it a hundred and fifty days. At three bottles a day he could just have done it.

Annie said unexpectedly, "I reckon he looked on it as a duty."

We both stared at her. She blushed and then said, rather defiantly, "Well, there's no harm in me telling you. They've both gone now. But they sometimes used to share a bottle in the evenings. I know, because I came back once and saw them. There was a bottle of raspberry wine on the table and they were taking a glass each. I reckon they used to do it most evenings, when they were alone. Being homemade wine seemed to make it all right. It wasn't really *drinking*, you see."

I saw exactly what she meant. If it had been real drink it would have been an orgy. As it was elderflower champagne or plum cordial it was simply a charming, old-fashioned ritual. I said, "I think it was a beautiful idea. You mean that McGuffog had such pleasant memories of those evenings with my grandmother that he thought it his duty to finish off the whole stock rather than let it fall into the hands of uncaring outsiders."

"Death cut him down before he could accomplish it," said the vicar. "Sad."

"Talking of outsiders, what have you done with the balance of the stuff?"

The vicar said, "The cousin from Essex suggested that we give it to the Women's Institute. They'll be selling it off at their jumble sale this afternoon. I was on my way there. Perhaps you'd like to come along."

While we were talking we had drifted into the stable — a fine old-fashioned accommodation for eight horses, with deep hayracks. Annie spotted something in the corner. She said, "There now. They've forgotten that one. It must have got hidden in the straw."

It was a claret bottle of the green-glass type used by some Bordeaux shippers for a few years after the War when supplies were scarce, but now uncommon. A label in Grandmother Clatterwick's spidery writing identified the contents as damson wine.

"Don't you think," I said, "that it would be a fitting gesture if we drank a last toast, a farewell salute to a gallant old lady?"

"An excellent idea," said the vicar, adding, "the later I arrive at that jumble sale the less I shall have to spend."

Annie fetched glasses and a corkscrew. It was while I was in the act of drawing the cork that a great many questions were posed — and a few answered.

The first thing that struck me was that the cork was remarkably firm. Amateur bottlers do not usually manage to sink the whole of the cork into the neck of the bottle. The next was that it was an old cork, stiff with age and impregnated with the lees of the wine. Now this was really curious. Not only was the cork clearly twenty or thirty years old, but it was equally clear that it had spent those twenty or thirty years *in that bottle.*

I carried the bottle to the door to examine it more closely. Imprinted into its side was the name of one of the four finest Châteaux in the Haut-Médoc.

I went back, picked up the tumbler which Annie had filled for me, and held it up to the light.

The vicar had already tasted his. "Remarkable damsons," he said.

I gave the tumbler a twist and watched the thick dark red liquid cling to the sides of the glass and slide away. Then I tasted it — and all my suspicions became facts.

The vicar, who had put his glass down, said, "Hold on a moment. I wonder if this will help us."

He went across to his car and came back with an exercise book. "I found it in McGuffog's flat. I was going to send it on to his cousin."

I opened the book. The writing I recognised as McGuffog's. I only needed a single glance at it. "When did you say that jumble sale was due to start?"

"It's started — half an hour ago."

"Where is it being held?"

"Take you in my car. It'll be quicker than explaining."

"Thank you," I said, "and if you'll excuse the expression, padre, drive like hell."

There were half a dozen cars parked outside the Village Hall, a crowd of women, most of them with perambulators and pushcarts, and a lot of children skirmishing round the flanks. We pushed in and the vicar introduced me to a tweedy lady whose name I never got. He said, "This is Mrs. Clatterwick's grandson." I admired his tact. It was a better introduction than "her solicitor." "He's interested in his grandmother's homemade wines."

The tweedy lady beamed at me. She said, "I'd have recognised you anywhere. You've got the family nose. Yes. It was kind of McGuffog's cousin to think of it. We've been doing quite a brisk trade."

My feelings must have been apparent. The tweedy lady said, "There's a good deal left, though. I had them all put together over there."

On and under the long trestle tables normally devoted to village teas stood the bottles, rank upon rank. "I had intended," I said, "to make you an offer for the lot. As a collection, you know."

"That's a nice idea," said the tweedy lady. "This gentleman is old Mrs. Clatterwick's grandson, Cynthia. He wanted to buy all the homemade wine. In memory of his grandmother. Has much of it gone already?"

Cynthia consulted a list. "Mrs. Parkin had a bottle. And Mrs. Batchelor had two. But the only other lot was Colonel Nicholson. *He* took six dozen."

I was making a rapid count of the bottles assisted by the fact that they were arranged in orderly groups of twenty-five. I said, "That's right. Fourteen hundred and twenty-five bottles —"

"They took *hours* to arrange," said Cynthia.

"What were you selling them at?"

"We had them down at sixpence a bottle," said the tweedy lady. "But we could give you a discount if you really are taking the lot."

"Far from it," I said. "A complete collection is always worth more than its individual parts." I wrote out a cheque for £100. "Who shall I make it out to?"

"A *hundred* pounds," said Cynthia, who had also been doing some arithmetic. "But that's nearly three times —"

"I'm sure my grandmother — and Mr. McGuffog — would have wanted it that way," I said. "I'll make all the arrangements for transporting the bottles. Please don't think of disturbing them. Leave it just as it is. If you'll excuse me a moment —"

Outside the hall I collared two intelligent-looking small boys. I said, "Would you like to earn half a crown?" The less intelligent boy nodded at once. The brighter one said, "What for?"

"One of you find Mrs. Parkin and one of you find Mrs. Batchelor — do you know them?"

The boys nodded.

"I want to buy back the bottles of homemade wine they bought here this afternoon. Here's five shillings each. See how cheaply you can buy them back — you can keep the change."

The two boys scudded off. I went to look for the vicar.

"Last lap," I said. "Can you take me to Colonel Nicholson's house?"

"Almost as quick to walk," said the vicar. "That path through the spinney there will bring you to his back lawn. Watch out for his dog, though. He's quite all right if you don't make any sudden movements."

I arrived at the colonel's front door followed by a Doberman pinscher. I refrained from making any sudden movements and rang the bell. It was the colonel himself who opened the door. No doubt about that. A tall man with guileless light-blue eyes and a silky white moustache. When I had introduced myself he said, "Ah, yes. Come along in. I was half expecting a visit."

He led me through into the dining-room. An agreeable apartment, full of polished mahogany and sparkling glass and shining silver. One of the bottles I had come for was standing on the sideboard. The cork had been drawn and there was a glass beside it.

"I don't normally drink wine at four in the afternoon," said the colonel. "But this was by way of being an experiment."

He brought out a second glass from the cupboard and proceeded to fill them both. I was glad to see that he did this properly, tilting the bottle slowly but firmly, with no sudden movements. The Doberman pinscher would have approved.

He said, "About nine months ago — it would have been around the turn of the year — I had the pleasure of having dinner with your grandmother. It must, I suppose, have been one of the very last dinner parties she gave. We drank a *remarkable* red-currant cordial. I made up my mind that I must at all costs obtain the recipe from her or from her man, McGuffog, who had, I was told, assisted her in brewing it."

His eyes twinkling frostily, the colonel picked up his glass, sniffed at it, tilted it delicately, and took a sip. I followed suit.

"Unfortunately she died before I could do so. And I did not like to intrude on McGuffog who seems to have led a somewhat hermit-like if happy existence for the last six months of his life."

"Musical, too," I said.

We drank again, and the colonel continued. "When, however, I learned that the wines were for sale I hurried down and purchased some. I fully intended, if they came up to my expectations as, indeed this one does, let me refill your glass — to go back and make an offer for the lot."

"Too late," I said. "I've bought them for the estate."

"I feared as much."

"And I'd like to buy back the six dozen you have."

The colonel considered the matter, stroking his moustache delicately with the tip of his little finger. Then he said, "I'll make a deal with you. You can buy back four dozen at the price I gave for them. I'll keep two dozen as a memento — that is, if you'll tell me the whole story."

"I'm not sure I know the whole story," I said. "A lot of it will be guessing. What I *think* happened is that my grandmother and McGuffog, both rather lonely people by that time, got into the way of splitting a bottle in the evening. But in order to avoid offending my grandmother's rather strict sense of propriety, it had to be something which sounded harmless and old-fashioned."

"Like raspberry wine?"

"Exactly. Unfortunately, the only thing they both liked and appreciated were good French and German wines."

"I wouldn't call it unfortunate," said the colonel, refilling our glasses. "Was it all as good as this?"

I took the exercise book from my briefcase and showed it to the colonel, who rifled through the pages.

"Glory be," he said ecstatically, "it must have cost her a fortune."

"Not a whole fortune — nine or ten thousand pounds."

"There's a page full of Private Estate bottled Trockenbeeren Auslese Hock. That must have set them back fifteen pounds a bottle. What did they call that?"

"I think that was called elderflower champagne."

"They seem to have chosen their stuff very well. I see they avoided the '47 clarets and stuck to the '45s and '49s. Sound judgment that."

"It would be McGuffog who did the buying. He'd had a good deal of experience."

"Ah," said the colonel. "*That's* what I was looking for. Domaine de la Romanée Conti. They've got some of the Richebourg '29. Do you think that could possibly be what we're drinking now?"

" '29 or '34," I said. "This is certainly one of the finest Burgundies I've ever tasted."

The third glass of a triumphant Burgundy induces contemplation and dispenses with the necessity for small talk. As we drank in silence I reflected on the real motives behind that curious conspiracy between Grandmother Clatterwick and Mr. McGuffog. Undoubtedly they both liked good wine. And undoubtedly the relabelling of a princely claret as raspberry wine and watching my Uncle Moffat turn his nose up at it must have appealed sharply to their sense of humour.

But I felt there was more to it than that. Like most very old and fairly rich people my grandmother must have been conscious of her next of kin like jackals sitting round a dying lion, licking their chops and waiting to get their teeth in. As each night the log fire flickered in the grate and another great wine sank in its bottle, must there not have been a feeling akin to triumph? Another ten pounds salvaged from Gertrude, Valerie, and Alexandra. Another crust out of the mouths of little George and Mary.

A further thought occurred to me. Might this not account for the heroic efforts of McGuffog after her death? His sensibility would not, of course, have allowed him to destroy such wine, but if it could all be consumed —?

The colonel seemed to have read my thoughts.

"I'm told," he said, "that McGuffog was averaging three to four bottles a day. I suppose that's really what finished him off."

"I fear it must have been."

"What a *wonderful* way to go!"

BLOOD MATCH

Last year, as students of the financial Press will remember, the old-established firm of Drake and Cowfold, linen-drapers and haberdashers (branches in North London and the Home Counties), "went public." That is to say, they published an advertisement which took up a whole page in *The Times* and the *Financial Times*, and contained a hotch-potch of unreadable information and incomprehensible figures, purporting to give the history of the firm from its beginnings as a draper's shop on Muswell Hill. Mr. Rumbold, senior partner of Wragg & Rumbold, solicitors, of Coleman Street, was one of the few people who troubled to read the advertisement through from start to finish. He read it very carefully, taking off his glasses from time to time and polishing them with a linen handkerchief, and when he had finished reading, he smiled.

His firm had acted for the Cowfold family for nearly a century, and he had in front of him a statement, sworn by the late Lavinia Marcus-Cowfold, which gave a rather more detailed account of the rise of that respectable firm of linen-drapers and haberdashers. It was not only more detailed. It was a good deal more candid. It dealt with a number of instances of fraud, two of blackmail, two of theft, one of rape and one of murder.

Albert Drake and Hezekiah Cowfold had opened their first shop together in the year of Queen Victoria's Golden Jubilee. Both had considerable experience in this line, and both had made money. The shop which they opened was an ambitious one. In their advertisements they described it as "The William Whitely's of North London" and, if this was an exaggeration, the shop certainly was imposing, being full of shining brass and polished mahogany, and little metal containers which ran along on wire and gave a pleasant "ting" as they arrived.

The partners were both typical Victorians, but were as different in outlook as two men could be. Hezekiah was a humanitarian. Albert was a buccaneer. To Hezekiah, shop assistants were souls to be saved. To Albert they were slaves. Differences of opinion were therefore bound to arise, and it is a tribute to their mutual tolerance that they got by as long as they did.

When the trouble came it was serious.

Hezekiah said, "That little girl, the one they call Millie, on the glove counter, she's going to have a baby. She says it's yours."

"Girls will say anything," said Albert.

"She's going to say it in court."

"What court, for God's sake?"

"The police court," said Hezekiah. "You realise she's only just fifteen now. If they believe her, you'll go to prison."

"Has she been to the police yet?"

"Not yet."

"I'll offer her five hundred pounds to keep her mouth shut. She'll take it."

"She may take it," said Hezekiah. "I won't. The partnership's at an end. You can have your shares for what they cost you. Nothing more."

Albert affected to consider the matter. Then he smiled and said, "I dare say it's better that way. As a matter of fact, I've been thinking of retiring. I'm nearer sixty than fifty. We'll go to our lawyers and sort it all out tomorrow."

Hezekiah was surprised. He had expected almost any other reaction. But then, Albert had often surprised him.

They both owned houses in Kent, and usually travelled home together. On this particular night there seemed to be no reason to vary their practice. They used the recently opened Blackfriars underground station. It was a damp Autumn night, with a thick mist rolling up from the river, and they strolled to the far end of the platform as they waited for the train.

When it arrived, Albert surprised Hezekiah for the last time by pushing him in front of it. No-one saw him do it. The exposed end of the platform was very slippery. The coroner, recording a verdict of natural death, described it, with considerable accuracy, as "a perfect death-trap."

Wars are always good for linen-drapers. The South African war was no exception. By the time it had dragged to its close, and the boys had come home again, and married the girls they had left behind them, and trousseaus had been bought and houses had been furnished, Drake and Cowfold (now describing themselves as general suppliers) had opened branches in Hornsey and Crouch End, and Albert was beginning to feel that he could do with some help.

He selected as a second-in-command one of the returning heroes. This was Captain Toby Transome, a Cowfold cousin by marriage, who came back from the wars with a South African tan, a military moustache, and a DSO, gained by the Captain, according to casual references he made to it, at the bloody skirmish of Elandslaagte. The Captain proved a good bargain. When the secretary of one of the leading West End Services Clubs came to discuss the bulk replacement of its table linen and cutlery, the deal went through noticeably more smoothly when he and the Captain discovered army acquaintances in common. Albert was so pleased that, three years later, he sold the Captain forty per cent of the shares in the company, carefully keeping sixty per cent, and control, in his own hands.

"When I die," he used to say, with the cheerful unconcern of a man who has no intention of doing so in the foreseeable future, "my shares will go to my son Maurice, and the firm will go from strength to strength under his chairmanship. And with your loyal help, my dear fellow," he would add. Captain Transome used to smile.

Like all consistently healthy men, Albert died very suddenly. He collapsed at the celebrations which attended the opening of a new branch on Highgate Hill. Captain Transome summoned a doctor, and as soon as he was certain that Albert was indeed dead (no suggestion of foul play this time; a hot day, a heavy lunch and the excitement of the occasion was the doctor's accurate diagnosis) he hurried back to the headquarters of the company at Muswell Hill.

Here he went straight upstairs to the office, and told the secretary to summon the staff. As soon as he was alone in the room, he turned his attention to the safe in the corner. He had long possessed duplicates of Albert's more important keys, and it was the work of seconds to open the safe and the deed box inside it in which Albert kept his private papers. He inserted into this box a long, brown, legal-looking envelope which he had extracted from a locked drawer in his own desk. The he re-locked the box and safe and went down to break the news to the assembled staff.

It was at this point, Mr. Rumbold remembered, that his firm had come into it. He recollected his father telling him about it. "When they wound up Albert's estate," he had said, "one of the first things they did was to look through his private papers, and they found this envelope. It was an option agreement. Captain Transome was to have the option to acquire half of Albert's shares, at a proper valuation, after Albert's death. The copy among his papers was signed by Transome. *He* produced a duplicate copy, signed by Albert. The signature was a bit shaky, but not so shaky that anyone felt like standing up in court and suggesting it was a forgery. And anyway, there was the counterpart locked away in Albert's private box in his own safe. Maurice Drake kicked up a devil of a row. It meant that Transome had control of the company, and he would have to play second fiddle. However, he accepted it in the end, or appeared to do so. The business was booming, and there were plenty of profits for both of them."

The corrupting effect of power has often been remarked on. Captain Transome was more corruptible than most. He married a widow from the shires, bought a town house in Hampstead and a hunting lodge in Leicestershire. His military past compensating, to a certain extent, for his commercial present, he was accepted by the more tolerant fringes of society and proceeded to enjoy to the full those last lush years of the Edwardian decade.

It was in 1911, during the blazing August of the Constitutional crisis, that a crisis of another sort developed at Drake and Cowfold. It was provoked by Maurice Drake.

He said to Captain Transome, who was paying one of his rare visits to the office, "I'm afraid I've got rather an unpleasant job to do."

"It's too hot for unpleasantness," said the Captain, mopping his scarlet brow with a handkerchief. "What is it? You got to sack someone?"

"In effect, yes," said Maurice. "I've got to sack you."

This took some seconds to penetrate. When the Captain finally decided that Maurice was serious, he guffawed loudly and said, "The heat's gone to your head, boyo. You can't sack me. I'm a majority shareholder. Actually, I could sack you."

"But you're not going to," said Maurice, "and you're going to sell me enough of your shares to give me control."

"Says who?"

"I say so."

"And if I tell you go to hell?"

"Then I shall publish the full and true facts of your career in South Africa. Such as, for instance, that you were not a captain but a very junior subaltern. That you took no part in the battle of Elandslaagte, or any battle for that matter, but spent the few months you actually were in South Africa looking after a supply dump in Cape Town."

The Captain looked ugly. He said, "No-one's interested in the details of the South African war now."

"The authorities would still be interested in the fact that you claimed a rank and a DSO to which you were not entitled."

"Prove it."

"Certainly. You had your photograph taken, in uniform, showing the badges of a rank you never reached, and the ribbon of a medal you never won."

The Captain looked up sharply. The space on the wall which this photograph had occupied was empty. "So you've pinched that old photograph, have you?" he said contemptuously. "As far as I can remember, it's so faded you can hardly see a thing."

"I was able to see one thing," said Maurice. "The name and address of the photographer who took it. I have a statement from him. He is prepared to produce his records in court, and say what you were wearing."

There was a long silence. It seemed to be hotter than ever. Transome's face was now more puce than scarlet. He said, "What do you want? What's the object of all this? It's a technical offence. The worst I could get would be a reprimand, or a fine."

"You know damn well that wouldn't be all," said Maurice. "You'd have to resign from your club. No decent hunt would allow you out. You wouldn't be able to show your face in society. You might be able to put up with that — I don't know — but think what Marcia would say." Transome thought about it. Marcia was his wife, a formidable woman with a tongue like the hunting crop she used so ruthlessly in the field.

"All right," he said at last. "What's your price?"

"Just enough shares to give me control," said Maurice, "and a reversion to the chairmanship when you go."

Transome looked as though he was going to have a fit, but he managed to mutter, "I agree." He did, in fact, have a stroke six months later, and died on Christmas Eve. In his certificate the doctor gave cirrhosis of the liver as the primary cause of death.

When the Germans invaded Belgium in 1914, and when patriotic crowds sang outside Buckingham Palace and young men rushed to an army which was far from ready to receive them, Maurice Drake kept his head. He decided that his talents would be more useful to England in the haberdashery and furnishing line than in the front line. "After all," as he pointed out to his chief cashier, "anyone can be a soldier. But it takes years of skill and practice to judge between two linens or price a bedroom suite." His chief cashier, who was ten years older than Maurice and suffered from a weakness in the lungs, said nothing at the time. Three months later, in the wet Spring of 1915, he managed to get himself accepted for active service. He reached France in time to be a victim of the first gas attack, at Ypres. This did his lungs no good at all and he was dead before the end of the year.

Maurice accepted the loss philosophically. He promoted the second cashier. "We shall all have to work a little bit harder," he said. When, in 1917, the second casher was called up too, Maurice very nearly went with him. He was well within the age for conscription. He managed, however, to persuade the local tribunal that the work he was then engaged on — he was specialising at the time in the production of army blankets and socks — was more important to the nation than the addition of one more infantry soldier to an army depleted by the Somme and preparing for Passchendaele. It was a narrow escape, however, and Maurice signified his gratitude by doubling his investment in the new War Loan.

After the Armistice, with business booming, it was clear that a major reorganisation of Drake and Cowfold was overdue. There were now eight branches in North London, and plans for opening three more in the Home Counties. The first side of the business which was going to need strengthening was the financial control. The second cashier, returned from Mesopotamia with a limp and the after-effects of amoebic dysentery, was quite unable to cope alone. He needed at least two assistants. But qualified accounts clerks cost money.

Maurice, casting his eye around the labour market, was one of the first to spot the potential of the newly emancipated woman worker. And it was agreeable both to his sense of economy and to his patriotism to offer a job, at a very modest wage, to a Mrs. Marcus, a young war widow, whose husband Commander Marcus, RN, had been killed at Jutland.

Mrs. Marcus worked methodically and well, taking upon herself extra jobs which no-one else wanted, writing up old ledgers, resuscitating forgotten accounts, sorting out the debris which five years of war had left in the cash department, and all for a tiny salary. After all, as Maurice reflected, she had her husband's pension to which he, as a super-tax payer, had contributed handsomely.

In the hard years of the middle and late Twenties, with the General Strike and the unemployment which followed it, the economical Mrs. Marcus proved invaluable to the company. And economies were necessary. Maurice sometimes used to wonder how on earth he could keep his two houses going. The town house in Kensington was not so difficult. It could be managed with a staff of three. But the country house at Leighton Buzzard, where his invalid wife spent most of her time, was a different proposition. Although reduced to the barest necessities, a companion and a personal maid for his wife, a cook, a man to drive the car and two gardeners, it still seemed to devour money. But what caused Maurice most distress was the iniquitous and ever-increasing burden of taxation. It seemed to him to be a sort of treachery that a Government which he supported willingly at election time with his vote should turn round on him later and try to rob him.

It was a fine summer morning in 1937, when England was beginning to shrug off the effects of the slump and the Stock Exchange index was slowly rising, that Mrs. Marcus sought an interview with Maurice Drake.

She had been with the firm for 17 years and, in her late thirties, combined natural good looks with the poise and composure of a woman who has made her own way. Maurice suspected that she had come to ask for a rise in salary and was prepared to offer her another £50 a year. After all, she had been head cashier now for six years.

She came straight to the point. "By my calculations," she said, "we have defrauded the Revenue, over the last six years, of something between forty-five and fifty thousand pounds. I imagine it went on before that but, since I wasn't head cashier then, I hadn't access to all the books."

When Maurice was able to speak, he said, "If anything of the sort has been going on — which I deny categorically — then it was the duty of the auditors to point it out to me."

"Auditors are accountants, not detectives," said Mrs. Marcus. "When invoices are concealed from them, when fictitious transactions are recorded between branches of the same firm, when certain cash receipts are entered only in a private ledger kept by you, and not produced to them at all …"

She continued for ten minutes, giving chapter and verse with appalling fluency and detail.

"All right," he said at last. "All right, what's your price?" Even as he said it, he seemed to hear the echo of a voice all those years ago.

"I'm not looking for control," said Mrs. Marcus briefly. "But I do think it's about time that fifty per cent share came back into the Cowfold side, don't you?"

Seeing the look of surprise on Maurice's face, she laughed. "You didn't know that my maiden name was Cowfold? Old Hezekiah was my grandfather. I've been interested in the doings of this firm for a long time — even before I joined it. I'd like the shares transferred into my full name, please — Lavinia Marcus-Cowfold. I intend, when I die, to leave them to my son. I have no doubt you will do the same with your shares. And talking of dying, I thought it wise — one never knows what accidents will occur — to leave a full account of the history of these transactions with my solicitor. To be opened at my death. Provided that it is *absolutely* clear that my death is due to natural causes, he has instructions not to publish anything."

✠   ✠   ✠

When Mr. Rumbold had read the advertisement right through, he turned back again to the beginning, where the names of the Board of Directors were set out. They included a Major-General, an ex-Lord Mayor and a peer of the realm. But, at the bottom of the list, he saw, in sinister proximity, the names of Michael Drake and Nicholas Marcus-

Cowfold.

He had no idea who would be the final winner in that long drawn-out match, but he rather doubted whether it would be the company. He picked up his pen to finish a letter he was writing, in his own hand, to a client.

"I agree the prospects of this company look excellent," he wrote. "But I should not myself feel inclined to invest in it."

THE SEVENTH MUSKET

Next to Julian Sanchez, who was so powerful that he was almost a regular Commander of troops, El Torino was the greatest of the bandit leaders in the west of Spain. His task, self-imposed, was to exist in the foothills of the Sierra de Gata and Sierra de Gredos, in the middle course of the River Tagus, and to exact from the French an ample and growing toll for the evils which his country and his family had suffered at their hands.

His father had been executed by shooting. His two brothers executed by the garrotte. His wife had died in childbirth, in the hills, during the unhappy winter in which the trouble had started. His son, a boy of fifteen, had been hanged by the heels in the market square of Toledo until the sun and the flies had finished him. (That was after El Torino had nailed the afrancesado Governor of Toledo to a board and auctioned named portions of him for charity.) His mother — he had no idea what had become of his mother. He hoped she was safely dead.

El Torino intercepted French messengers, cut off detachments, and even, after the most careful and detailed preparation, attacked and destroyed small regular posts. Above all, he occupied the attention of ten times his number of French soldiers, for which the English General was exceedingly grateful. Not that El Torino worried his head unduly about the English General. He did not love him as a brother, but he respected him as a master of war. And so, did he intercept a messenger, the message would go full speed northward to Frenada.

"For messages, like fish," observed Torino to his principal Lieutenant, "are doubly acceptable when fresh."

His Lieutenant, a man of few words, nodded.

Neither looked in the least like a brigand. El Torino had once been a lawyer, and still had the air of one, with his neat dark clothes and his pinched, ascetic face. His companion, a big man in black, might have been an undertaker.

They were seated among the rocks overlooking the village and bridge of Peraleda. The village was deserted. The bridge, to the naked eye, was unguarded.

"You were right," said the Lieutenant at last. "Here they come."

"I am frequently right," agreed El Torino. "But this was a simple matter. The summer campaign is impending. We know that messengers must pass. This is the only point at which they can with any convenience cross the river."

"They are fifteen minutes away." The Lieutenant screwed his eyes up against the glare. "A small escort. Chasseurs, by their plumes."

It was, indeed, almost an insultingly small escort for that time and place. But Edouard Philippe Chrétien Le Duc, Staff Major in the French Army of Andalusia, had his own theories about escorts, as about most things. He thought that large slow-moving escorts were often more of a danger than a protection. They took a lot of getting together, and the news of their assembly travelled fast. However large the escort, the guerrilleros, given time, could always collect three times the number. So where was your safety? On the other hand, as he had proved before, if you slipped off quietly at dusk, with twenty or thirty trusted sabres behind you, and rode with a loose rein, you could pass any danger before it had time to materialise.

Major Le Duc was riding at the head of his troop, regarding the Spanish countryside with the usual mixture of feelings that it inspired. Most of his fellow French soldiers had come to hate Spain. He hated it too, sometimes: for its starkness and sameness; for its lack of decent living; for its endless bleak hostility. Sometimes, too, he loved it, for the colour that it lent to everyday things, the salt of danger and urgency that it added to life. Had not five years of it made a man out of what had formerly been only a gentleman?

Why, were he to meet his brother François now — and with François, who could guess *where* one would meet him next? — he could stand beside him, proudly. François might be more accomplished, François might be high in the Councils of the Emperor, but it was surely something to set in the opposite scale if you were the only officer in the Army of Andalusia who could be trusted by Marshal Soult with a vitally important message, with the smallest of escorts, on a route where trouble seemed certain.

And trouble arrived; when the troop was exactly halfway over the bridge of Peraleda. It started at the moment when the leading troopers, with Major Le Duc, had already crossed, whilst the rearguard, under the Sergeant-Major, was cantering up to it. And it took a most unexpected form.

Beside the bridge-head stood a gallows — not, at that time, an uncommon enough decoration to merit a second glance. It was a single upright, with a cross-piece and what now looked like a long strip of dried seaweed hanging on a chain from it. At the moment that the last horse from the leading cavalry cleared the bridge, the gallows-post started to fall. It fell slowly, ponderously, and precisely across the bridge, and blocked it completely.

The rearguard clattered to a halt behind it. Even at this juncture it seemed nothing but a bizarre accident. The Sergeant-Major jumped from his horse and tried the obstacle with his foot.

Then there came a fluting whistle; then a single shot.

The Sergeant-Major put one hand into the front of his coat. With a foot up on the beam he looked, for a grotesque moment, as if he were going to make an oration. Then his knees hinged, he tumbled backwards over the low parapet of the bridge, and disappeared under the brown water.

There followed a brisk volley.

Both parties of horsemen broke for shelter. The half-troop who had not crossed went back. Before they could get out of reach two more men had been toppled from their saddles. The dozen men who had crossed were more fortunately placed, or seemed so. They were in the main street and the houses and enclosures offered shelter. They dismounted and scattered.

"Excellent," said El Torino.

"As planned," agreed his Lieutenant. "I do not think they will survive long. No doubt they will die bravely."

"No doubt they will die," said El Torino.

An hour later he stood looking down at what lay twisting painfully on the ground. It was Major Le Duc. He had suffered in the fighting among the horses, but he was not yet dead. The eleven troopers who had crossed with him were luckier. They were dead.

The Frenchman opened his mouth to speak and the two Spaniards craned forward. He said one word. It sounded like "François."

"His patron saint, perhaps," suggested the Lieutenant.

"Somewhere on him he will be carrying the message," said El Torino. "A search should reveal it."

"It would save time," suggested the Lieutenant, "if we were to ask him to reveal just where it is hidden."

"He might scruple to tell us."

"We could no doubt overcome his scruples," observed the Lieutenant, seriously.

☩ ☩ ☩

The township of Frenada, near the upland borders of Portugal, lay clustered in a hodge-podge of dusty browns and bleak greys under the April sky.

In the cramped front room of a house in the single cobbled main street that bisected the small square, Captain Lord Fitzroy Somerset sat on the corner of the table, swinging his neat legs. Out of the door — the hovel had no proper window — he could just see the church, dominating the square with its bat-infested dome and lop-sided cross.

He said, looking down at the other occupant of the room, "The Peer's in a shocking temper this morning."

Major Scovell looked up absent-mindedly. He was a tall man, who carried in his brown face the only outward hint that he had lived the last two years of his life in the open air, away from the grey aisles of the University Library where he had been reared.

He was fingering a thin strip of parchment which he was trying to flatten on to the table top. It had been so tightly rolled that every time his long sensitive fingers let go, it curled itself up again like a spring.

"Try pinning down the corners," suggested Fitzroy.

"An excellent idea," said Major Scovell. "I haven't any pins. What did you say about the Peer?"

"I said he was in a shocking temper."

"How do you happen to know?"

"The Peer," said Fitzroy, "is not a man who troubles to conceal his feelings. If he is happy, you may hear that great horse-laugh of his from Frenada to the Coa. If he is not happy — well, you know how it is — a sort of icy wind starts to blow —"

"And why should it be blowing this morning?"

"I didn't get the whole of it. But it's something about the guard muskets."

"Guard muskets?" Scovell looked vague. Many of the operations of war seemed quite meaningless to him. "Guard muskets? You mean those muskets they carry when they are on guard duty?"

"Yes. Special muskets. Clean slings, burnished barrels, and goodness knows what. There's a special set kept for Headquarters guard."

"And someone has lost one. Or sold it to the Portuguese."

"On the contrary," said Fitzroy. "As far as I could gather, the Peer discovered this morning that they'd returned one too many. What *is* that paper?"

"It was — is — a message. It was dispatched by General of Army Soult to Jourdan who is, in name, Supreme Commander, under King Joseph, again in name, of the five armies opposed to us."

"They don't show the deuce of a lot of co-operation," agreed Fitzroy complacently. "If they got together, under someone like the Peer, they could wipe us out in no time at all. Where did it come from?"

"It was wrapped round a split needle, which was inserted into the epaulette of a French officer. The officer fell into the hands of El Torino."

"Poor devil," said Fitzroy.

Major Scovell made no comment. He had gradually become hardened to that aspect of war in the Peninsula.

"It was brought to me," he said, "together with certain identifiable — er — portions of the officer in question, late last night. I am endeavouring to work on it now."

"In code?"

"Of course."

"But you can read it, can't you? You're a brainy devil."

"There is no question of brain. It is a matter of system." Major Scovell spoke as a patient adult to an excitable boy. "*All* messages are in the same cipher. The Great Paris Cipher. Which, between you and me, is a Great Paris Nonsense. Because once you have found out who's who in one message it's the same in all the others."

"Only the names are in code?"

"Names, numbers, military formations. There's quite a lot of it. But we've been at it a long time, too. There are precious few of them that we can't read. For instance if this message —" Scovell twiddled the tiny scrap thoughtfully between his fingers — "if it said that 1280 had withdrawn from 7720 with all his 660 under a threat from 1300, we should at once know that Soult had left Cadiz, with his siege artillery."

"I see," said Fitzroy. "Easy, isn't it? Under a threat from 1300?"

"1300," said Major Scovell with a wintry smile, "is the Peer."

☩ ☩ ☩

"You are quite certain that you laid out six muskets?"

"Yes, sir."

"It's not a matter about which you might have made a mistake?"

"No, sir. It's like this, sir —" The Quartermaster paused. He had known the General for a long time; had been with him in India. Sometimes he wanted explanations. At other times, very definitely, he did not.

Since the General said nothing he persevered: "We use drafts to make up the Headquarters guard. Convalescents on their way back from Belem, new recruits on their way up to the line. Sometimes there's plenty. Sometimes it's difficult to find even six."

"I see. And last night it was difficult?"

"Yes, sir. One big draft went off yesterday. Took most of 'em. Then that other lot that was due in yesterday was late. I couldn't put 'em straight on guard off the road. Seeing as how they were going straight on again this morning."

"But you found your six?"

"Yes, sir."

"Who were they?"

The Quartermaster delved painfully in the rag-bag of his mind. Even for a General who was notorious for counting every nail in the horseshoes of his cavalry this was coming it a bit strong.

"Two Rangers," he said at last. "A Rifleman, a dismount from the German legion. A gunner, and —" Think, think. The cold grey eye was on him. "Yes, and a horse-holder from the Hussars."

"I take it they are all in camp. They were none of them part of the big draft."

"That's right, sir."

"Parade them," said the General, "and find out how it was that they were issued by you with six special muskets when they went on duty, but handed in seven when they came off."

"Er— yes, sir."

"And send Colonel Waters here at once."

Colonel Waters was a jovial Welshman. His friends compared him to a chameleon. The things his enemies said of him were unprintable. He was the very able head of Army Intelligence. After three years he found that the Peer could still surprise him.

"I wish I could see why this extra musket, sir —"

"You heard the Quartermaster's report."

"Yes, sir."

"That there were seven muskets, not six — and that one of the guard seems to have missed his turn at sentry altogether."

"I might make more of it, sir," said Waters frankly, "if I had any idea how the guard was arranged."

"It was arranged like everything else in this damned Army," said the General, "too damned slackly. Six men parade in front of my Head-quarters at sundown. They're put there to guard it. One of them puts a musket on his shoulder for two hours and walks up and down. He's a guard. At daybreak they stop, and become soldiers again."

"I see, sir," said the Colonel.

Other Generals, in other armies, he might have pointed out, had numerous permanent bodyguards, who wore their own special uniform, and practised ceremonial drill until they did it perfectly. But apparently this General did not want it that way. Nor did he dress himself in gold braid, plumed hat, and long cloak. Everything simple. Everything utilitarian. A plain blue frock-coat, a short cape, a small cocked hat. A man with a musket outside his door. That was all he wanted. So be it. What was he complaining about?

"— no proper system of reliefs," said the General.

Waters was aware that his attention had wandered.

"You mean," he said, "that at the end of his two-hour stretch the guard walked off to the guard tent and woke the next man?"

"That's so. Leaving the Headquarters of the British Army unguarded for five minutes."

Colonel Waters pursed his lips. It wouldn't have done in the outposts, but Frenada was fifty miles from any known enemy.

"Except," went on the General, "that last night I surmise that it didn't happen that way. Not quite. Just imagine for a moment that you are one of the sentries." Colonel Waters did his best. "You have the turn from midnight to two. At five minutes to two a figure approaches you. You perceive that he is carrying a guard musket. You don't know him personally, but there's nothing odd about that. Most of the other members of the guard are strangers to you. He says, 'Two o'clock. Off you go to bed.' What do you do?"

A look of apprehension had come into the Colonel's eye. He was by no means a fool and he was beginning to have an idea where the conversation was going. "I fancy," he said slowly, "that I go off to bed."

"That's what I think, too. And two hours later, at four o'clock, this man goes along and wakes up the next man. Then he stacks his musket in the guard tent — because there's no chance at that hour of returning it to the store from which he filched it on the previous evening. And slips off to his bivouac where he finished the night."

"And the only signs he has left of his intrusion," said Waters slowly, "are one man who hasn't done his guard turn — which, of course, he will keep quiet about unless he is asked — and one extra musket."

"And for two hours he had the run of my Headquarters."

"Was there — was there anything particular, sir, that we should not have liked him to see?"

"On nine nights out of ten — no, on ninety-nine out of a hundred he could have my whole damned correspondence and welcome. No-one pays any damned attention to any damned letters I write, anyway. But last night, as it happens, was different. I wrote a letter to Beresford. It might interest you to see it. In the circumstances, I have not dispatched it yet."

He placed on the table a sheet of paper half covered with his own distinctive scrawl.

To Marshal Sir W. Beresford, KB, Frenada, 24 April.

My dear Beresford,

I have received yours of the 21ˢᵗ. I am very much obliged to you for the drivers and the dismounted cavalry. The former ... Waters skipped ahead. There didn't seem to be anything vital... *Artificers and pontoneers...*

"Try the last paragraph," suggested the General. Waters read it and tried unsuccessfully to conceal his feelings. The angular, decisive writing announced, *I propose to put the troops in motion in the first days of May. My intention is to make them cross the Douro, in general within the Portuguese frontier, covering the movement of the left by the right of the Army towards the Tormes; which right shall cross the Douro over the pontoons I have had brought up. I then propose to seize Zamora and Toro, which will make all our future operations easy to us.*

Well, there it was, in less than a hundred words, the secret that everyone in both armies wanted to know. The one vital piece of information that would enable the enemy to dispose his superior forces in such a way as to make manoeuvre impossible; make stalemate certain; defeat a possibility.

"Since Colonel Gordon went home," said the General — and if he allowed a shade of bitterness to creep into his voice, Colonel Waters could not wonder at it — "I have trusted no-one with my intentions. Beresford and Graham had to know first. I was confident of their discretion. No-one else was to know anything until they had to."

"I see," said Waters. He was still trying to grapple with the idea, the possibilities of disaster inherent in one extra guard musket.

"If what you fear is true, sir," he said at last, "the possibilities are that it could be an English traitor, or just a busybody who would go to the Opposition press with his news. Or it could be a professional spy."

"It's a good rule to suppose the worst," said the General. "Please assume the latter."

"Very well. Then suppose it really was a Frenchman on duty last night. He must be a Frenchman who speaks perfect English. I know of half a dozen. He must be able to pass himself off as an English soldier —

not within the Regiment — that would be very difficult — but in a mixed draft. Of the six men I mentioned not more than two could hope to do that."

"Two?"

"One we need not trouble about. He is in Russia — or dead. The other — yes. There's no denying it. It is right in his line. He's known to have been in Spain lately, and it's got just his touch of inspiration and daring. He's an odd fish. I knew him — oh, twenty-five years ago. François — something or other — Le Duc. We were at Eton together. He was brought up exactly as an English boy. I can only remember this, that in any parcel of scamps he was the maddest.

"He stayed on in England after the war started — professing sympathy for our cause and hatred of Bonaparte. He was of noble family, you see, so it was all quite natural. He even acquired a sort of semi-official standing at Whitehall. And all the time, as we know now, he was passing out a stream of deadly information. It went by fishermen and smugglers direct to Paris. In the truce of 1802 he went over to France — and stayed. He's been there ever since."

"You say that he's been lately in Spain?"

"Yes, sir. Scovell identified him in the Cipher a few months ago. He was tied up in some mischief near Cadiz, where he spent a month as a muleteer in General Graham's camp — and, incidentally, gave away the Tarifa landing."

"Better have Scovell in," said the General.

It took a few minutes to put Major Scovell into possession of the facts. If he was not as alarmed by them as Colonel Waters had been, this was because he had very little tactical knowledge.

"I know about the Le Ducs," he said. "A dangerous pair, I should say."

"Pair?"

"Yes, sir. There are two. Twin brothers, real identical, mirror twins. Edouard the elder, I believe, by a matter of seconds. François is an intelligence agent of the very first class. He crops up frequently in messages. He is —" Scovell referred to his list "— 1398 in the cipher. His brother Edouard is a Staff Major in the Army of Andalusia. One of Soult's promising young men. His name may have been mentioned in correspondence but he hasn't been identified yet."

"All right," said the General. "Let us suppose, for a moment, that it was brother François who impersonated the sentry outside my Headquarters last night. He's got what he came for. More than he could have hoped for. What will he do next?"

"Well," Colonel Waters considered, "assume that he came in under cover of the big draft yesterday. Surely he would stay with it until he reached the front. After that he would take the first opportunity to slip across to the enemy."

"Wouldn't be difficult," said the General. "We're losing men through the outposts every day. Most of 'em from damned carelessness and bad map-reading."

"I suppose we could immobilise the whole draft," suggested Scovell diffidently. "Turn them back to base for a month."

"Four hundred men!" said the General. "And what if we are wrong? It's nothing but surmise."

"You could hardly put four hundred men under guard for a month without giving a reason," agreed Colonel Waters. "And if you don't confine them under guard, what's to prevent this fellow slipping off again?"

"Would you know him if you saw him now?"

"Twenty-five years," said Waters doubtfully. "Even if he isn't disguised. Ten years of campaigning, a coat of bronze, and a pair of whiskers! I doubt if I'd know my own brother after that time."

Silence fell in the Headquarters Office.

"As I said," observed the General at last, "we are in the realms of surmise. Have you any evidence — any recent messages or information, to suggest positively that Le Duc might be contemplating a move like this?"

"We've had very little through in the last few weeks, sir," said Scovell. "This was sent to us this morning by El Torino. I had just finished deciphering it."

He laid on the table a clean sheet of paper on which he had transcribed the message. Under most of the code groups he had been able to pencil the name or word it represented.

The General cast his eye over it.

"Soult getting worried about Hill's position in Estremadura. That's excellent — or rather, it would have been if this damned thing hadn't happened. Soult rejects the suggestion of Jourdan that he should detach a Division and send it forthwith to strengthen the Army of the Centre. Damned odd sort of organisation where a junior General can reject the suggestion of his immediate superior! He suggests that 3004 — oh yes, I see, that's Suchet — should detach a brigade to help *him* in Andalusia. He concludes by recommending the bearer, 8931, to King Joseph's good wishes. I shouldn't think he'd have much of a reception carrying an insubordinate message like this — by God!"

The last exclamation was unconnected with what had gone before. The General was staring at the message. The two men looked at him.

"I wonder," he said at last. "It's worth a shot."

The two men continued to stare in bewilderment.

The General, on the contrary, for the first time that morning, seemed almost happy. A matter which before had been incalculable had been reduced, by one word, into the realms of calculation. The problem had become one of time and space, and the General was an acknowledged expert at such problems.

"All these French officers carry personal jewellery, don't they?" he said.

"Many of them," agreed Waters cautiously.

"Edouard was the eldest, you say? If there was any special piece of family jewellery — an heirloom — a signet-ring — he would be likely to have it?"

"I expect so, sir," said Waters, with a despairing glance at Scovell.

"Hmm. How long will it take the draft that left this morning to reach the Coa?"

"Three stages, sir."

"How far off is El Torino?"

"The message got here in a day, sir," said Scovell.

"Yes. Then it can get back in half a day, if the rider is prepared to kill his horse."

"The rider would have to find El Torino," said Waters. "That might take time for an inexperienced man. A Guerrilla leader does not leave a forwarding address."

"It will not be an inexperienced man," said the General. "For you are going yourself, Colonel. And here are my instructions — no, requests — to El Torino."

He started to scribble rapidly.

⊞   ⊞   ⊞

The draft, decided the young Lieutenant in charge of it, like all drafts, marched shockingly. It was difficult to say who was worst, the Johnny Raws, straight from England, or the Belem Rangers, professional convalescents whom a convenient bout of Guadiana fever kept out of every stiff piece of fighting. There were a few genuine convalescents, like himself. He was on his way back for the third time, to his beloved Rifle Brigade.

Three sergeants were engaged perpetually in whipping in. By God, they straggled worse than puppies in bracken. But no matter. The three-day march was nearly over. The midday halt, which they were enjoying at that moment, or would have been enjoying had it not been for the perpetual necessity of seeing that no-one in the draft did something stupid, was the last halt before the dispersal point which they were due to reach that evening.

It was at that moment that two horsemen came in sight. They were picking their way down a rough path beside the road. The Lieutenant thought he recognised the leading horseman. There was something about the black clothes, the prim carriage, the precise cast of countenance. Yes, indeed. It was El Torino himself. He had seen him too often to be mistaken. The stout man with him was no doubt his chief assistant or principal executioner.

"To what do we owe this honour?" asked the Lieutenant with a grin. He knew enough of the services of the great guerrilla to be rather more than polite.

El Torino reined in his horse.

"I am here to make market," he said, in execrable but understandable English. "We have much good fortune lately. Would your men care to purchase souvenirs?"

"I expect they would," said the Lieutenant curiously. But the word had gone round and the nearest men were already crowding the horses. The eyes of the recruits especially, were bulging.

From one of his saddle-bags El Torino took out a handful of glittering badges, numerals, epaulettes, buttons, and ribbons.

"Come and kill your first Frenchman," he said. "Send to your girl at home the hat-badge of a cuirassier — the buttons of a member of the Imperial Guard — the medals of an officer — take your pick."

The soldiers needed no second bidding. Most had money saved and El Torino was soon doing a brisk trade. Even the older soldiers joined the throng.

"Have you anything for me?" asked the Lieutenant at last, with a smile.

"But certainly," said El Torino. "For you I have reserved a most wonderful and special bargain." He turned to his follower, who unstrapped, with great ceremony, a small pouch which he handed to El Torino.

The crowd gaped up at the solemn man on horseback.

"What is it, sir, d'you think?" whispered one of the sergeants. "A diamond cross from a cathedral?"

"Open up," said the Lieutenant impatiently. "What is it? I won't buy a pig in a poke."

El Torino opened the pouch and extracted the contents. The crowd fell silent, for it was a man's hand, recently severed, but part-withered already, and yellowing.

On the forefinger blazed and winked a great signet-ring, a red stone cut in the form of a cross tilted on its side, surrounded by tiny, flashing brilliants.

"I fear that is beyond my purse," said the Lieutenant shortly. "You'll have to take that back to base, where the real money is."

A soldier was pushing and shouldering his way urgently through the crowd. A nondescript man with brown face and black hair. He wore the uniform of one of the line Regiments.

"Might I see the ring?" he inquired, as soon as he had reached the front rank.

With a short laugh El Torino tossed it, hand and all, to the soldier, who caught it expertly and turned it over. He seemed to fondle the hand as much as the ring.

"I will buy," he said, "if you will name your price."

El Torino looked down at him. "To you, little man," he said, "ten francs."

"*Francs?*" The soldier threw his head back like a boxer who meets an unexpected blow.

The Lieutenant found something in the scene puzzling. Suddenly he stiffened to attention and saluted. A very gorgeous Colonel was standing at his elbow. He had no idea where he had come from.

"Detail six of your men," said Colonel Waters, "under a sergeant, to form an escort. That soldier —" he pointed to the man who was turning the severed hand, over and over, blindly, in his own "— comes back with me to Frenada."

☩ ☩ ☩

"The Peer doesn't often explain his effects," agreed Colonel Waters. "But yesterday, being in a particularly handsome frame of mind he'd just signed half a dozen confirmations of Court Martial proceedings — he did explain to me how it was worked. Quite neat, I thought."

"It was luck," said Scovell. He had a scholar's distaste for luck.

"And what was lucky about it?"

"It was all luck. How could he know that El Torino could get hold of a piece of jewellery similar enough to deceive that — that spy?"

"Don't be so damned stupid," said Waters kindly. "That ring *was* the actual, genuine Le Duc family heirloom. And it was, I regret to say, on the actual hand of brother Edouard."

"More fantastically lucky still, then," said Scovell crossly. "How could he guess that this one messenger, out of all possible officers, should be Edouard Le Duc?"

"He didn't guess. He was told."

"Who by?"

"By you," said Colonel Waters.

He got to his feet and looked out into the square, where he could see the General, taking his constitutional. He was walking briskly up and down the cobbled street beside Mr. Larpent, the newly arrived Judge Advocate.

"That's the trouble with you specialists," continued the Colonel. "You've got your noses so close to the grindstone that you can't see the obvious. François was 1398 in your code. You said so yourself. Edouard was his twin — his mirror twin. Of course he had to be 8931, and that made him the messenger."

At that moment Mr. Larpent must have said something which amused the General. The dapper figure halted, the head went back, the famous nose cocked, the great high-pitched laugh screamed out.

Bats flew indignantly from the dome of the Church; the very cross seemed to shudder at that outrageous mirth.

THE INSIDE POCKET

The Major sat at his dining-room window and looked down the little valley. There was one other building in view, at the foot of the valley track. It was the bungalow which belonged to his nearest neighbour, Max Tarvin. The Major picked up a pair of Zeiss fixed-focus hunting binoculars, a relic of his war service, and swung them in a careful arc round the fields and hedges which formed the skyline.

8.30. Here he came; punctual to the minute. A cheeky little drophead coupé, painted canary yellow, had shot out of the bungalow garden and was coming up the road, raising a cloud of white dust. The Major frowned, keeping his glasses fixed not on the car but on the surrounding country. A squeal of brakes, a skid turn, and the car slid into the yard in front of the farm. Max bounced out, and trotted up to the door. The Major noted that he was wearing a white panama hat, with some sort of club colours round it, sunglasses and a blue blazer with two rows of broad brass buttons down the front.

"Come in," he shouted. "The door's unlocked."

Max pranced into the room. There was no other word to describe his self-confident high-stepping gait. He said, "Got your phone call. Here I am. Lots of visits to make. Can't waste time."

"I don't think you'll find it wasted," said the Major.

He had seated himself on the arm of the sofa, beside a low table. "When you worked for us, do you remember a lady called Elizabeth Frobisher?"

"Vaguely," said Max. "Vaguely."

"She was one of our clients you dealt with personally."

"Five or six years ago. One forgets."

"You won't have forgotten her. She took an overdose of sleeping pills. The coroner was kind enough to bring it in as suicide, but no-one believed him."

106

"Oh, *that* Mrs. Frobisher." A little of the self-confidence had faded from Max's voice. "What about her, eh?"

"Her brother has written me a letter. A rather curious letter. I think you had better read it."

He dropped an envelope on to the low table in front of him. Max sat on the sofa and picked it up. As he bent his head forward, the Major's right hand came up from behind the sofa, holding a heavy cylindrical wooden ruler. With it he hit Max a blow on the back of his neck. The crack as the spine snapped sounded curiously loud and sharp, like the breaking of a dry stick.

Max tilted forward over the sofa table. He was clearly dead. Without wasting a moment, the Major picked him up, slung him over one shoulder, and carried him through the house and out to the stable yard behind. There were two cars standing there; a heavy old-fashioned touring car with a luggage compartment at the back, and a lighter, speedier sports car.

The Major removed Max's blazer, hat and sunglasses, packed him into the luggage compartment of the tourer, and slammed down the lid. Then he tried on the hat and blazer. They fitted tolerably well. He picked up a rucksack which stood ready packed outside the back door and returned through the house, shutting and locking the back door behind him. He paused for a moment in the dining-room. There was a faint scuff in the carpet where Max's heels had slid forward. He smoothed it over carefully, then picked up the envelope, which in fact contained nothing but a blank sheet of paper, and dropped it into the wastepaper basket. Two minutes later, wearing Max's blazer, hat and glasses and driving Max's canary-yellow car, he was following a carefully chosen route, mostly on side roads, to Dover.

He parked the car at the hovercraft terminal, walked into the departure building carrying his rucksack, and purchased a single ticket to Calais.

"Just a passenger ticket," he said. "No car."

Having secured his ticket, he strolled across to the passage at the far end of the building. From the lack of hesitation in his movement it was clear that he was following a reconnoitred route.

At the end of the passage was the gentlemen's lavatory. It contained four cubicles and half a dozen stalls and was, like the terminal building, empty, since it was a full hour before the next hovercraft left. He went into the farthest cubicle, locked the door and opened his rucksack. From it he took a respectable brown felt hat, a light raincoat and a capacious briefcase. Max's hat, blazer and sunglasses went into the briefcase, followed by the empty rucksack, folded and pressed down on top of them. Five minutes later he was in the back streets of Dover, making his way sedately towards the Priory Station. He was in plenty of time to catch the 10.30 train to London.

He deposited the briefcase in the Left Luggage Office at Victoria, took a taxi to Waterloo, and was passing through the turnstile of the Rugby Football ground at Twickenham as the clock above the East Stand showed the time to be exactly one o'clock.

The event was the annual seven-a-side tournament which attracted sixteen of the top teams in the country. It was run on a knock-out basis, starting at noon, and not finishing until nearly seven o'clock. A feast of rugby football. The Major bought a programme and filled in the scores of the first three matches as they were announced over the loudspeaker.

Thereafter he passed an agreeable afternoon, watching the play from in front of the West Stand and chatting to acquaintances in the Terrace Bar. It was eight o'clock when he reached Victoria, recovered his briefcase, and took the train home. His local station was unmanned at weekends. A path across the fields brought him home by nine o'clock.

He had left a cold supper and two cans of beer in the icebox, and he was ready for them. It had already been a full day, and there was much still to do.

At three o'clock on the following morning, with a faint rind of moon in the sky, the Major drove the old touring car, using sidelights only, up the road which led into the North Downs and the woods which crowned them. At this point there had stood, during the war, a pre-OCTU training camp. It had been abandoned by the army in 1946 and occupied by squatters. When they had eventually been cleared out the huts had been pulled down, and all that now remained was a network of concrete tracks in an area of thick new woodland.

The Major turned in to one of these tracks, and then stopped. He stopped because, as he turned, his sidelights had picked out a notice which had not been there when he had last visited the place. It was headed with the name of the Borough Council, and said 'Preliminary Drainage Works. S. Trensham and Company.'

"So," said the Major to himself. "They have at last decided to develop the site. Pity."

It was a project which had been spoken of half a dozen times, and half a dozen times abandoned.

The Major sat for a full five minutes considering the matter. The first line of defence, the second line, the third line. The safety margins relevant to each line. He was like an engineer studying a new design, testing it, twisting it to look for flaws. At this point the most important single factor was time. It was already twenty past three. Dawn, in early May, would be a little before five-thirty.

Having thought matters through the Major evidently came to a conclusion. He re-engaged gear and drove forward, keeping to the concrete path, into the heart of the wood. When he stopped the car and got out he stood for a few minutes, listening, while the normal noises of the night re-asserted themselves. Then he sat down and pulled on a pair of wash-leather gloves, and a pair of long rubber overshoes on top of his ordinary shoes. His eyes were accustomed by now to the darkness and he could see the track he wanted. He opened the back of the car, pulled out Tarvin's body, which had already started to stiffen, slung it across one shoulder, and carried it down the track.

Some twenty yards on, in the middle of a small clearing, there was a sizeable chestnut tree. The Major dumped the body and knelt down, feeling for the poles which he had laid and covered with turf and leaves. The poles, woven with smaller crosspieces, formed a lid, which, when lifted, revealed a hole about six feet long, two feet wide and four feet deep. It had taken the Major three careful visits to dig it and conceal it.

He dropped Tarvin into the hole, went back to the car for a spade and started to shovel back the loose earth which he had left, also leaf-covered, near the foot of the tree.

When enough of the earth had been replaced to level the hole, he stamped it carefully flat and then covered it with a final layer of dead leaves, twigs and grass. The framework of the lid went back with him to the car. The sticks would serve as supports for his beans and peas.

✠ ✠ ✠

"Why should you suppose your brother has been murdered?" said Detective-Sergeant Michael Morath; six foot of black-haired forceful male, who pleased his superiors and trampled over everyone else.

Sonia Tarvin thought that he looked splendid. A bull of a man. She was not intimidated, because she was not a woman who was easily intimidated.

She said, "I knew about his business. It was — well rather a peculiar business."

"So I believe."

"He advised people on their financial affairs. Tax matters. That sort of thing. He knew a lot about it. He used to work for Bale and Reardon."

"The solicitors."

"*The* solicitors," said Sonia, putting satirical emphasis on the first word. "Alan Bale and Cyril-God-Almighty Reardon."

Although both of the senior partners had retired recently, their firm still had a monopoly of all the really important work in the County Town.

"You don't like them?"

"I can put up with Alan Bale, but Reardon — he's different. Let me be moderate and say that if it was a choice between Reardon and a skunk, I'd choose the skunk every time."

The Sergeant laughed. He found Sonia entertaining. Quite a lass, he thought. He said "Reardon seems to have put your back up. What's he done?"

"It's not what he does. It's how he looks at you, down his nose. When Max worked there, I went to one of their office parties. Bottom table, of course, with the riff-raff. After dinner Reardon deigned to speak to me. I could see him making up his mind to deign. He said, 'Miss — ah — Miss Tarvin. You are — ah — Max's sister. Enjoy yourself' and then he sailed off, like a Peruvian llama, to patronise the Mayor."

"And why should that make you think that he killed your brother?"

"I don't think," said Sonia. "I know. Reardon was one of his special clients. He used to pay him quite a lot of money for his — well — his advice, I suppose."

"Yes," said Sergeant Morath drily.

"My brother warned me. "Reardon's dangerous. If anything should happen to me, he'll be the man the police must concentrate on." And I happen to know that he was planning to see him, the morning when he disappeared. He'd several clients to call on, and *Reardon was the first*."

"How do you know?"

"Because he told me. He always telephoned me the night before and told me exactly where he was going. It was a sort of precaution. I wrote all the names down."

"*You* wrote them down, not him?"

He was a policeman now, thinking of Sonia not as a woman but as a witness. Her obvious bias would tell against her, but he had a feeling, a stirring of the primeval hunter's instinct, that there was something here that might be worth following up. He too disliked the great Cyril Reardon, although not as personally or as bitterly as Sonia seemed to. Since Alan Bale had been the partner who handled the litigation, he had not actually had occasion to cross swords with Reardon in court, but he had had one or two brushes with him out of it.

Peruvian llama. Not a bad description. What fun if he and the woman, working together, could bring the llama's nose down into the dust.

⚜   ⚜   ⚜

The Deputy Director of Public Prosecutions was a middle-aged lawyer called Benjamin with a full-jowled face like a Roman Emperor. He said, "In plain English, Max Tarvin was a blackmailer?"

"Yes," said Superintendent Sheehan.

"Who used to tip off his sister, as a matter of precaution, when he went visiting his victims."

"Yes."

"And the first man he was due to visit, on that particular morning, at 10.30, was this solicitor fellow, Reardon. A man he used to work for?"

"That's right. Tarvin worked for Bale & Reardon for five or six years, and I'd guess it was there that he picked up most of the dirt he used afterwards. He called himself a financial adviser, and there's nothing to show that the money people paid him wasn't a fee for advice rather than a payment for keeping his mouth shut."

"And he had something on Reardon."

"I think he must have done. Reardon had been paying him £100 a month. He was probably on to a tax fiddle, or maybe some breach of Solicitors' Accounts Rules."

Benjamin thought about it. He said, "I suppose you realise you haven't got the remotest beginnings of a case. For all that anyone knows, Tarvin is in France and has been there for the last month."

"It's possible," said Sheehan. "One of his victims might have thrown a big enough scare into him to make him feel he'd be safer across the Channel for a spell."

"Turn up some hard evidence, and I'll look at it again."

It was a curious coincidence that he must have spoken these words at almost the moment that the mechanical trench-digger of S. Trensham and Company turned up a human foot.

⌘   ⌘   ⌘

"It's open and shut," said Sergeant Morath. "Every day we dig out something new, and it's all helpful. Very soon we'll be charging him."

"Soon, soon," said Sonia Tarvin gleefully.

They were sitting close together in the candle-lit dusk of the restaurant.

"Identification wasn't any bother. Not once we'd got the dental and medical records. Then, thanks to you, we were able to get hold of all your brother's papers. There were letters from Reardon, they'd have made you laugh. I read them before I handed them over. He was down on his knees. Appointed your brother as his financial adviser. A regular salary. Silly old goat. But there was more than that. From his papers we've been able to identify all the initials on that paper we found in his wallet. The people he was going to call on that morning. Some of the times were different, but they were all there. We've questioned them. They keep up the story that your brother was an adviser. But they're squirming."

The Sergeant's right hand was lying on the table. Now he closed his fingers. It was the gesture of a boy who has trapped a small animal.

"But the biggest break of all was the footprints. We couldn't hope for anything around the edge of the pit, not after the driver of the excavator and his mates had trampled about, but when we lifted the top layer, very carefully, do you know what we found? After he shovelled back the earth, and before he laid on the leaves and grass, the silly old fool had trampled the soft earth down underfoot. If he'd left his visiting card behind it couldn't have been clearer. I guess that was what decided the DPP."

Sonia let out a long tremulous sigh of pleasure. Her hand rested for a moment on top of the sergeant's. She said, "When I see that old man crawl out of the dock humbled and broken and creep away to the cell that's waiting for him, then, I promise you, we'll have a private celebration."

The invitation could not have been more clearly expressed. The sergeant's left hand came up and clamped down on top of her small one.

✠ ✠ ✠

Cyril Reardon's first reaction on being charged with murder was incredulity. His second was indignation. When at last he understood that Superintendent Sheehan meant what he said, he demanded the immediate attendance of his old senior partner, Alan Bale.

No difficulties were made about this. The two men met in the privacy of an interview room, with the door locked and a uniformed constable outside it.

Bale said, "The charge relates to Saturday, 2 May. Can you remember what you were dong that day?"

"Of course I can remember," said Reardon. He was still indignant. "I went over to the reservoir for a last morning's fishing. Took sandwiches with me. Got home at four o'clock and packed up my stuff. I was going north that night to Scotland to join Laura for the last three weeks of her holiday."

"Did anyone see you?"

"Fishing? I doubt it. The reservoir's private property."

"Going or coming back?"

"I shouldn't think so. The path to the reservoir runs through the woods. The vicar called when I was finishing tea, and he gave me a lift to the station, which was kind of him."

"Time of your train to town?"

"Ten past five. I was catching the evening Highlandman from King's Cross at eight."

"Did you catch it?"

"Certainly. I had dinner on the train, and slept until the attendant brought me a cup of tea in my sleeper at seven o'clock next morning. We were passing Kirriemuir at the time."

"That seems clear enough." Bale was making notes. "Now, one important point. When this comes up for a preliminary hearing in front of the Magistrates, do you want me to brief counsel for you, or shall I do it myself?"

"Whatever you think. I know nothing about such matters. You were always our litigation man."

"It's not an easy decision. Counsel would do it better. On the other hand, I know old Parkin, who'll be taking it. That doesn't mean he'll grant us any favours, but it keeps things easy. If we weigh in with leading counsel at this stage, it'll simply put his back up. Time enough for that when we get to the Crown Court."

"You really think," said Reardon, and there was a shade of anxiety in his voice for the first time, "that they're going on with this nonsense?"

"I'm afraid they are," said Alan Bale sadly.

✠ ✠ ✠

Mr. Crackenshaw, the barrister who appeared for the Crown, was not a particularly nice man, but he was good at his job, which was bullying lay witnesses and obtaining convictions from lay magistrates. If he was only going to be opposed by a retired solicitor this made an easy assignment easier still.

The first day was given up to routine business. Plans and photographs were produced and proved, including close-up shots, highlighted and much enlarged of three shoeprints in the packed earth at the undisturbed end of the grave. The manager of the local shoe shop said that they were the marks of an exceptionally long shoe, about size 11½, and also, reluctantly, that he had sold more than one pair of shoes of that size, and with soles which could have made a similar pattern of marks, to Mr. Reardon. Max Tarvin's dentist and doctor identified the body and the Home Office pathologist told the court that death had occurred instantaneously from a fracture of a vertebra of the cervix not less than three and not more than five weeks prior to his examination.

Alan Bale sat with folded hands and asked the witnesses no questions. On the second day Mr. Crackenshaw's first witness was a Miss

Weldon who sold tickets at the hovercraft terminal at Dover.

He knew that she would need careful handling. He had seen a number of statements she had made, and he had noted how, under the skilful questioning of Sergeant Morath, she had grown gradually more certain in her identification. He said, "Tell us, in your own words, Miss Weldon, about the man who bought this single ticket to Calais."

Miss Weldon said, "Well, it was like this. When he came up I thought from his clothes he was quite a young man. The sporty hat and blazer and that sort of thing."

Mr. Crackenshaw nodded encouragingly.

"Then I was surprised to see he was really quite old. And he had a sort of — well — it's difficult to explain, but a sort of legal face. He only said 'Passenger ticket to Calais. Not a car.' Something like that. And I thought, funny, he's putting on a different sort of voice. I can't quite explain. I just thought his ordinary voice would be more posh, if you know what I mean, so I took more notice of him than I might have done otherwise."

"You took particular notice of his face?"

"Yes, I did."

"And can you see someone here who reminds you of him?"

"Well, yes, I can." Miss Weldon made an embarrassed gesture in the direction of the dock.

"I'd like to be quite clear about this," said the magistrate. "*Do* you identify the man who bought that ticket from you on Saturday morning as the accused?"

"Yes, I do."

Bale said, "You must sell hundreds of tickets every day of the week, Miss Weldon. How do you know that you sold this one that particular day to this particular man?"

"Well, I know it was Saturday, because I'm not on Fridays or Sundays. I only do alternate days."

"It might have been earlier in the week."

"The eleven o'clock hover only runs at weekends."

Bale said, "Oh," and seemed disconcerted. Then he said, "Nevertheless, you see a lot of different passengers every day. How can you be sure that this one was the accused?"

"Like I told you. Being curious, I had a particular look at him."

"There are quite a lot of people in this room with what you might call legal faces," said Bale with a smile. "The learned magistrate, counsel for the Crown, myself, among others."

"Well, it isn't any of you," said the girl. "It's him."

"You're sure?"

"Quite sure."

"And the more you press her," said Mr. Crackenshaw happily to himself, "the surer she'll get."

It was in the early afternoon that Sergeant Morath took the stand. Sonia was seated at the back of the crowded court in the space reserved for witnesses who had already given evidence. She was drinking in every word of the ritual proceedings which would destroy her brother's killer.

The sergeant gave his evidence well. He produced the statement which Reardon had made under caution after he had been charged and went through the timings in it. Then he turned to more immediate matters. He had been responsible for the removal of the body from the half-demolished grave, and superintended the photography, and had accompanied the body back to the mortuary, where the clothing had been removed and examined by him.

"Will you tell us what you found?"

"There was some loose money in the trouser pocket, or what was left of it. A handkerchief in the side pocket of the blazer, and in the inner pocket the wallet, which forms Exhibit Eight."

He indicated the handsome brown leather wallet on the table in front of the magistrate. It seemed to have suffered little damage from a month underground.

"And what was in the wallet?"

"Three pound notes, a driving licence and the paper which forms Exhibit Nine."

All eyes were on the folded sheet of notepaper.

The magistrate said, "This is the original paper, I take it. May I see it?"

"Certainly, sir."

The paper was handed up and the magistrate examined it. He said, "The first initials, C.R. 10.30. These are alleged to refer to a projected meeting with the accused at 10.30."

"In his statement, sir, the accused confirmed that he had made such an arrangement. He says that he waited until some time after eleven o'clock, and when Tarvin didn't turn up —" the pause was artistic and deliberate "—he went fishing."

"I see. And the other three sets of initials, at 12 o'clock, 3 o'clock and 5.30. These are other of the — er — special clients that Tarvin was planning to visit?"

"Apparently so, sir. We have spoken to all of them."

"And he failed to keep these appointments?"

"So they have told us, sir."

The magistrate examined the paper again, folded it and laid it on his desk. "In view of certain allegations which have been made," he said, "I direct that the other initials shall not be made public, and the people concerned, if they are to be referred to, will be called A, B and C."

As Mr. Crackenshaw sat down, Alan Bale rose slowly to his feet. He had the paper in his hand. He said "A, B and C, Sergeant. These are three other people that Tarvin was blackmailing?"

The brutality of the question seemed to take everyone by surprise.

"There's no evidence of it, sir."

"But that is your supposition?"

"A possible explanation, sir."

"I see. Has this paper been identified as coming from Tarvin?"

"It was found in his wallet, sir"

"And who found the wallet?"

"You might call it a joint effort, sir. I extracted it from the deceased's pocket in the presence of Detective-Constable Blakely; we placed it in an envelope, sealed it, and both initialled the envelope."

This was routine stuff and the sergeant produced it with relish.

"And what happened to the envelope when you had both initialled it?"

"Placed in a locked cabinet at the police station, sir."

"Then at all times since you removed it from Tarvin's pocket it has been under your control?"

"At all times, sir."

Bale looked down at some notes he had scribbled. Everyone seemed to be waiting for him to pull a rabbit out of the hat. He disappointed them. He said, "I take it you have questioned the various railway officials who could support the accused's story of his journey to Scotland and his movements afterwards?"

"We saw no necessity, sir. His movements after 5 pm are not questioned."

"Perhaps I could point out," said Mr. Crackenshaw, in the tones of a schoolmaster reproving a junior schoolboy, "that the charge in this matter is that, at some time *between* the hours of 9 am and 5 pm *on* Saturday 2 May the accused unlawfully killed Maximilian Tarvin."

"Oh, yes," said Bale. "Of course. Thank you."

The magistrate thought, "Poor old boy. He's getting past it. He hasn't even read the charge."

He said, "Are there any more questions, Mr. Bale?"

"Might I have the wallet?"

The clerk passed it up and Bale turned it over slowly in his hands. It was a fine piece of hand-crafted leather; old, but still in good shape.

Bale said, "Did it strike you as odd, Sergeant, that Tarvin should own a wallet like this?"

"No, sir. Why shouldn't he?"

"Did you not know that it is a relic of the war?"

"Of the war, sir? No, sir. What sort of relic?"

Bale was looking at it fondly. He said, "It was called an agent's wallet. Men on Special Service in enemy-occupied territory used to carry one."

The magistrate, leaning forward courteously, said "Your own exploits in that line, Mr. Bale, which earned you a majority and a DSO, are public knowledge. But can you be certain that this — it's a very ordinary-looking wallet — is — what did you call it? — an agent's wallet?"

"And even if it is," said Mr. Crackenshaw waspishly, "what relevance it has to the matter?"

"It seemed relevant to me, since it was a most unlikely sort of wallet for a man like Tarvin to own."

"People do retain such souvenirs," said the magistrate mildly. "My aunt has a lampshade made out of a prisoner-of-war escape map."

Ignoring Mr. Parkin's aunt, Bale said "The point is easily demonstrated. If you would examine the wallet more closely — please hand it up to the learned magistrate — you will see, sir, that the back flap appears to be solid. Actually it is composed of two very thin pieces locked at the top by a finely machined interior zip-fastener made of plastic. The space between them was designed for the carrying of the two or three vital documents — signal codes, alternative identity papers — which an agent might need, but which the enemy must never be allowed to find."

Everyone in the room was now following this with close attention. "Schoolboy stuff," said Mr. Crackenshaw irritably, but he said it under his breath.

"And how is this — this inner pocket — opened?"

"Very simply, sir. Using your thumbnail, push the catch on the outside of the wallet — the metal catch — that's right. The action releases the interior fastener."

"My goodness," said the magistrate. "So it does." He was as pleased as though someone had given him a new toy. "So you were right. It is —"

He stopped, because his fingers, questing through the opening which had now appeared at the end of the outer flap, had touched a paper. He drew it out.

The silence in the room was uncanny. No-one knew what to expect, and what happened next was a sort of disappointment. The magistrate unfolded the paper. It was a newspaper clipping. He said, "This seems to be an article on the benefit of foreign investment."

"Much the sort of thing that the deceased might be expected to be interested in," said Mr. Crackenshaw. The relief in his voice was obvious. He had hardly known what to expect.

"No doubt," said the magistrate. He had unfolded the clipping fully. "But this has been cut from the financial section of the *Sunday Globe* of 3 May."

There was a moment's silence, followed by something like a communal gasp, followed by a hubbub of voices.

The magistrate rapped for silence.

He said, "In order to give the prosecution an opportunity to consider this new evidence I will adjourn for forty-eight hours."

☩   ☩   ☩

"And, of course, the case was thrown out," said Benjamin.

"With apologies to Reardon," said Superintendent Sheehan. "What else could they do? Bale produced the production manager of the *Sunday Globe*, who said that nobody, even if they had been working on the paper itself, could have got hold of a finished copy of the financial page before ten o'clock on Saturday night, and the earliest copies weren't on the streets until 2 am. By which time Reardon was fast asleep in a train going to Scotland."

"One of Alan Bale's more remarkable efforts," said Benjamin.

Something in his voice made Sheehan look up sharply.

"You mean, he knew "

"About the cutting. Of course he knew. He put it there. And the wallet. If he picked up the paper at 2 o'clock he could have been back in his house well before three. He's got a fast car and is an excellent driver."

"But," said Sheehan.

He was trying to assimilate the idea.

"Yes?" said Benjamin encouragingly.

"That means that Bale killed Tarvin. Some time on Saturday."

"Early on Saturday. He spent the day at Twickenham. Difficult to say when he arrived. He was certainly there by one o'clock. I talked to him myself.

"Then he put the other bit of paper in, too. The one with the initials and times on it. Why?"

"You haven't really thought it out, have you?" said Benjamin kindly. "He supplied the wallet, which was probably a relic of his own service, and put the list in the outer pocket so that we should be bound to charge Reardon, and the cutting in the inner pocket so that we should be bound to acquit him. It also totally ensured his own future safety."

"I don't see that. We could still charge him."

"On what evidence? Of size 11½ footprints, where he takes a small 9? Of a girl who has positively identified the man who bought the ticket as Reardon? And indeed — do you remember — was actually invited to identify Bale and refused to do so? More. With Reardon you had strong evidence of motive. With Bale, none at all. The case would be laughed out of Court. If the Director allowed you to bring it. Which, I assure you, he won't."

Sheehan looked unhappy. He said, "I suppose you're right about that.

But — what beats me is — why did he do it? Like you said, he's got no real motive. Is he mad?"

"Mad. No, I don't think he's mad. I think he doesn't approve of blackmailers."

"You don't kill people because you don't approve of them."

"He killed at least two collaborators and one German SS man in occupied France. Probably he didn't approve of them."

"That was war."

"One must, of course, remember that," said Benjamin gravely. "But there may have been a further reason. I think he enjoyed the intellectual exercise involved. And that's the only thing that worries me. I don't really care about Tarvin. He was no loss. But removing people is a very addictive exercise. He may already be working on the next one."

✠ ✠ ✠

Alan Bale was sitting in his dining-room. On the table in front of him was a sheet of paper covered with hieroglyphics. An idea was forming in his mind. Clearly Miss Tarvin would have to go. A vicious woman. And if, as he suspected, she had taken over her brother's private records, what was to prevent her carrying on where he had left off?

He would have to wait, of course. Maybe a year. But it would be a year of enjoyable planning and scrupulous preparation.

The telephone rang. It was Cyril Reardon. He sounded excited.

"Slower Cyril, slower," said Bale. "Sergeant Morath did what?"

"He hit Sonia Tarvin. She was livid with him. Said he'd made a fool of her. She's got a vicious tongue, and you know what a temper he had. I don't suppose he meant to do any more than hurt her, but she hit her head as she went over, and never recovered consciousness."

"Dead?"

"Yes. I just heard."

"Well," said Alan Bale. "I am sorry. Really I am. I'm more than sorry, I'm heartbroken."

"Do you know," said Reardon to his wife, "I was quite surprised at the way he said it. He sounded as if he really meant it."

FREEDOM OF THE PRESS

It was at the Annual Fair on the Heath, on a hot evening in August, that Detective Sergeant Petrella first met Slippery Sam.

To the police of Q Division, the Fair, through the whole of its fourteen-day run, was a simple and unrelieved nuisance. It disrupted traffic, excited youth, upset licensing regulations, and attracted into the Division a floating population of undesirables with a hard core of really unpleasant characters.

Petrella avoided it unless duty took him there. Which it had on this occasion. He was strolling slowly with the crowd that filled the narrow avenue between two rows of booths. The ground underfoot was trodden to powdered dust, and thick upon the dust lay the paper and tin foil, the cartons and bottle tops, the detritus that the human race spews around it when it takes its pleasure. On all sides, men — sensible family men who would think twice about placing a shilling on an even chance in the Derby — were throwing away their money with crazed abandon on games of so-called skill and chance; games in which there was little skill, in which the chances were heavily weighted against them, and the prizes not worth winning.

Just ahead of him moved a trio of prosperous citizens, with thinning hair and spreading waistlines, who were out for an evening in search of their departed youth.

"Let's have a bang at bottle-popping," said the red-faced leader of the trio. "I'll bet half a dollar I knock down more than you, Toppy."

"You'll lose," said the middle one. "You never could shoot worth a damn. All you're good at is rolling pennies on to boards. That right, Charles?"

Charles said that was right. Old Hubert couldn't hit a haystack at five yards with a howitzer.

Hubert, more nettled, Petrella guessed, by being called old than by the slurs cast on his marksmanship, came to rest in front of a shooting-stall. The equipment consisted of four air-rifles, and for target there was a choice between a number of bottles, upside-down on wooden stakes, and a ping-pong ball precariously maintaining its balance on a tired jet of water.

"You hit that ball in six shots, Hubert, and I'll buy you a house, eh, Toppy?"

"Make it twelve," said Toppy, "and chuck in a car as well."

Thus goaded, Hubert slapped down a florin on the counter, examined the guns with a judgmatic air, and reached out for the newest-looking.

Reached out, but failed to make contact. A man's hand got there first, and whisked the gun away.

"That's a special gun," said the newcomer coolly. "Reserved for little me." He picked it up and started to load it. Little was right. He wasn't much more than half Hubert's size but there was an air of unregenerate impertinence about him which attracted Petrella. He thought of a sparrow and a thrush, at war over a snail.

"Special gun be jiggered," said Hubert. "I saw it first. You put it down at once."

"Go and boil yourself," said the small man distinctly.

Hubert said, "If you're asking to have your block knocked off, you've come to the right shop."

"Now, gents, " said the stall owner.

A lot happened then, more or less at the same time. The tough character took a step forward. Toppy grabbed him round the arms. A thin man with a lock of hair over one eye like Sam Weller's appeared from nowhere and grabbed Hubert. The small man dropped the gun and was seized by Charles. They were all too close together to do each other much harm, but Petrella felt it was time to intervene.

He bored his way ruthlessly into the crowd, using his toes and elbows as he had learnt at recruit school. When Petrella reached the storm centre, he wheeled sharply about and said, "You'd better drop it, all of you."

"And who the hell are you?" said Toppy.

"I'm a police officer," said Petrella, with great clarity, "and if any of you want to go on with this argument you can do it at the station."

He saw a uniformed constable pushing his way towards him, but the heart had already gone out of the opposition.

Hubert had recovered some of his poise. "I'm glad you're here, officer," he said. "This man made a quite uncalled-for —"

"Which man?" said Petrella.

"Why — bless my soul! He was here a moment ago. Where did he go?"

The sparrow had hopped off. Even Petrella, whose attention had not been distracted, had failed to see him go.

"Then these other gentlemen — my friends will bear me out "

"There was a tough character," said Toppy. "I don't see him now, but I got my arms round him, to prevent him butting in —"

"And then another man got hold of me," said Hubert.

"That's right," said Charles. "A tall thin man, with a bit of a cow's lick. Bless me, if he hasn't scarpered too."

"In that case," said Petrella firmly, "since all the relevant witnesses seem to have vanished, I'd suggest that —"

He was interrupted by a cry of pure anguish. Hubert's hand was clutched to his side. For a moment Petrella thought that the excitement and shock had brought on some sort of heart attack.

"My wallet," said Hubert faintly. "More than fifty quid, in notes "

☩   ☩   ☩

Back at Highside Police Station they held a post-mortem.

"There seem to have been three men in it at least," said Petrella. "The little man who provoked you over the air-gun —"

"Was *he* in it?"

"Certainly. These boys usually work in a group. Sometimes as many as half a dozen of them. Then there was the big chap who threatened to intervene, and took people's eyes off the ball. And last but not least —"

"The man who held me. The thin one, with the remarkable quiff of hair."

"Yes," said Petrella. "He'd be the actual operator. The only thing is, I rather think he may have been wearing a wig. I remember thinking at the time that his hair looked a little too good to be true."

"All I can say is," observed Hubert stiffly, "that if you knew how these people operated, and had all these suspicions, you might have intervened a little sooner and saved my fifty quid. I'm not insured or anything, and it's a very serious loss. The money in the wallet wasn't all mine."

Petrella could have pointed out that, in that case, a crowded fairground was a silly place to carry it. But he had long grown used to the fact that one of the functions of a policeman was to serve as a scapegoat.

"You can be sure," he said, "that we shall do everything possible to apprehend the people concerned."

Secretly, he thought it unlikely that he would see any of them again. If they belonged to a group operating in the Fair, they would move with it.

⌗ ⌗ ⌗

But as that autumn turned into winter, and winter into spring, he became less certain.

The indications were casual, at first. An increase in pocket-picking and larceny from unguarded premises. But as the coups became more ambitious, growing with their success, a pattern became discernible. It was the planning which was remarkable. Where the ordinary sneak-thief would seize his chance in some moment of confusion, the gang now operating relied on no such haphazard methods. They took the initiative. They manufactured their own chances, stage-managing each one with zealous application.

It was they who started the riot on the Highside Wanderers' football ground, and cleaned up more than twenty wallets from embattled partisans; who introduced hecklers in a meeting of Councillor Hayes's Ratepayers' Association and turned out the lights at a point when the meeting was becoming really heated; who arranged for a man to appear on the roof of a shop in the High Street, dressed only in woollen underclothes and a balaclava helmet. By the time the fire brigade arrived, a rich harvest had been reaped from gaping crowds of Christmas shoppers. And the man on the roof had disappeared.

In the files of Q Division, who were chiefly favoured with their attentions, a considerable dossier began to accumulate. Higher authority delivered itself of a series of sarcastic minutes, and the press began to sit up and take notice.

Petrella, who was one of the few policemen to have seen the principal operator at close quarters, had memories of a long sardonic clown's face and a pair of twinkling eyes. He called him Slippery Sam, and, for want of any more official identification, the name passed into general use.

"The trouble is," said Superintendent Haxtell, "that we're not used to dealing with criminals with imagination. Most of their methods are as old as the hills. They're in the books. All we've got to do is look them up. Then we come across something new, and we're scuppered."

"Perhaps he'll move on somewhere else," suggested Petrella hopefully.

Sam did not move. His next effort was a small one, but it had important results. It brought Councillor Hayes to Highside Police Station.

Councillor Hayes was one of those men, essential to the smooth running of democracy, whose dedicated task it is to keep officials on their toes. The particular object of his attentions had for some time been the police force. The malicious hinted that this particular object of his zeal dated from the time when a police constable had caused the Councillor to be summonsed three times in a fortnight for parking offences; but that was mere idle gossip.

"Your wife was shopping in the High Street when this occurred?" said Petrella.

"That's right. And this man — this fraud — was standing in front of Gummidge's window, with one arm tucked inside his jacket, and wearing a row of war medals — stolen, I've no doubt."

"And the little girl?"

"The little girl was crying. My wife's a very soft-hearted woman."

"I'm sure she is," said Petrella.

Councillor Hayes looked at him suspiciously. Then he went on, "The little girl wanted to be lifted up to look at the Christmas tree in the window. Her father — he said he was her father — couldn't lift her because he'd only got one arm. So my wife lifted her up."

"And had to put her bag down while she did so?"

"Of course."

"I see," said Petrella.

"But the man didn't go near her bag. He was on the other side."

"It would have been an accomplice who actually rifled the bag," said Petrella. "I suppose she didn't notice — "

"She didn't even know she'd lost the money," said Councillor Hayes, "until she opened her bag in a shop five minutes later. It was a serious loss. Very serious indeed. She was on her way to the bank to put away some of the funds of the Ratepayers' Association, of which I have the honour to be Chairman and Treasurer."

"That's bad luck on the ratepayers," said Petrella.

"Every penny of Association funds that my wife lost," said Councillor Hayes stiffly, "has already been replaced out of my own pocket."

⌖ ⌖ ⌖

"It was a stupid thing for me to say," said Petrella later to Superintendent Haxtell. "In fact I don't know why I did. He's a thundering nuisance but I'm sure he's quite honest."

"It wasn't very sensible," agreed Haxtell. He was fingering the pages of the current edition of the *Highside Mercury*, a weekly of broadly liberal views. "Did you know that Hayes was on the Board of the *Mercury?*"

"I haven't had time to read it lately."

"You should. There's a leader this week, it's headed —" Haxtell cleared his throat impressively "— *The New Fascists. Certain ominous symptoms of a fascist-type interference — whether officially inspired or not, the Mercury would hesitate to say — in the business of electing and conducting the apparatus of Local Government in certain London Boroughs including your own Borough of Highside and Helenwood* … What do you think of that?"

"It doesn't seem," said Petrella cautiously, "to have a verb in it. What's it all about?"

"As far as I can gather, it's something Gwilliam did. He had nothing much to do one evening, so he looked in on a meeting of the Ratepayers' Association. Old Hayes was well under way. He was winding up with one of his favourite rhetorical questions 'What do the police do?' And Gwilliam piped up from the back and said, 'Work eighteen hours a day for next to nothing.' This brought the house down, and wrecked Hayes's carefully prepared peroration. It's no laughing matter. A lot of people knew Gwilliam by sight, and the papers — particularly the *Mercury* — made out that it was an officially inspired job."

"Surely no-one believed that, sir?"

"People will believe anything if you tell it them often enough," said Haxtell. "And one thing we're not going to do is get ourselves mixed up in politics. You find this damned pickpocket, and put him where he belongs."

Petrella had a word with Gwilliam, whom he found quite un-repentant. "Silly old man," he said. "Why should he say anything he likes about us, and us not answer back? Are we children?"

"Because he's a newspaper proprietor," said Petrella, "and a Borough Councillor."

"If what I'm hearing's right," said Gwilliam, "he mayn't be that after the elections next month. Had you thought of that?"

Petrella had not thought of it. Borough Council elections were not a thing which interested him greatly, although he was aware that they took place from time to time.

"This year," said Gwilliam, "the Tories and the Socialists are both putting up candidates. And there's all the Independents who had seats before. They're not going to give them up just because a new lot are coming along. To say nothing of the Cranks."

The Highside and Helenwood Borough Council had, for many years, been run in part by a hard-working and public-spirited body of men and women who called themselves Independents, and in part by representatives of pressure groups, such as the powerful Ratepayers' Association, whose champion Councillor Hayes was; the Licensed Victuallers, whose object it was to open more public houses for longer hours; the Total Abstinence League, who sought to shut public houses down altogether; and the Friends of Dumb Creatures, who had scored a signal victory the year before in the passage of a bye-law forbidding the driving of horses and carts up Highside Hill.

With the advent of party politics it was clear, as Sergeant Gwilliam said, that there were not going to be enough seats to go round. And loudly though the existing Councillors complained of the strain and overwork of their job, curiously enough, when it came to the point, none of them seemed anxious to lay down the burden.

On the contrary, serious electioneering was soon in full swing. This meant unusually large crowds, and more work for the police.

"If this is taking an interest in politics," said Petrella to Gwilliam as, for the third successive night, they assisted the uniformed branch to cope with the rush, "you can have it."

"Did you see the *Mercury* this morning?" said Gwilliam. "They're attacking the railways now. Good strong stuff, too. *Ratepayers, unite! You have nothing to lose but your trains.*"

"I'm glad they're off the police for once."

"They'll be back again," said Gwilliam. "There's the Lord High Ratepayer himself."

The occasion was an eve-of-poll overflow meeting of the Ratepayers' Association at the local Oddfellows Hall. Councillor Hayes, wearing a large rosette, was descending from a car, accompanied by campaign secretaries and flanked by supporters. The subject matter of the meeting, according to the notices, was "Necessary Economies," and the size of the crowd bore witness to the fact that there is no more popular topic than the proposition that other people should spend less of your money.

"Looks pleased with himself, doesn't he?" said Gwilliam.

"Yes," said Petrella. "Hold on a moment — I'll be back."

It could easily have been imagination. The moment that Councillor Hayes entered the hall, the crowd had shifted and thinned as the latecomers streamed in after him. And under a lamp post Petrella had suddenly seen a figure he thought he recognised. It wasn't the face, which in any event was hidden under a broad-brimmed hat. But it was something about the slimness of the figure, the set of the shoulders, the jaunty cock of the head.

When he reached the lamp post, the man had gone. He saw him again clearly, twenty yards up the street. Then, as suddenly as he had come, he was gone again.

"Witchcraft," said Petrella.

He edged his way through the thinning crowd, and found an answer. At the point where the man had vanished, a back alley led off, down the side of the Oddfellows Hall. It was a dead end, which clearly served some emergency exit. And it was empty.

"Curiouser and curiouser," said Petrella. There was only one way out. It was a doorway, with big double doors to it, of the sort, he guessed, which would be closed on the inside by a long horizontal bar or riot bolt. He pressed against it, but without result. Then, on the smooth surface, he felt a cuphook. He slipped his finger through it and pulled. The doors came open towards him. The cross-bolt inside had been lashed in the "free" position with a handkerchief. Somebody had done some careful preparatory work at the Oddfellows Hall that evening. And Petrella had a feeling that he knew who it was.

Ahead of him a flight of concrete steps led upwards. There was nothing to do but follow them. On the first landing, which he guessed would be somewhere near the platform, was a door, and behind the door a crack of light.

Somewhere beyond, but muted by the interval of two walls, there came to his ears the roar of a crowd settling down to an enjoyable witch-hunt.

The door was marked *Committee Room*. Petrella considered various methods of tackling the job that lay ahead, but decided that there was no alternative to the direct approach.

He opened the door gently and looked inside. The thin man had his back to him. He was standing in front of a desk, all the drawers of which were wide open, and he was finishing packing something into a bulging briefcase.

Petrella's foot struck a loose board. The man turned, snapped his case shut, and with the agility of a professional clown, slid a chair into Petrella's path.

Petrella saved his neck by going on to his hands and knees. He was still effectively blocking the exit to the stairs. The thin man hesitated, then whipped round, opened the big door behind him, and went through it.

Petrella went after him.

The door opened direct into the auditorium, just below the platform. The thin man was scudding up the side aisle, walking, but moving as fast as most men would run. Petrella went on after him. The curious thing was that no-one else in the hall seemed to take any notice of them at all. Their attention was concentrated on a venerable gentleman with white hair who had risen from the audience to ask the speaker a question. The question was obviously an important one, and clearly also one of those helpful questions that speakers welcome, since Councillor Hayes was smiling broadly as he prepared to answer it.

The next moment, the smile was wiped from his face. Feeling Petrella's hand on his shoulder, the thin man dived to his left, past the earnest inquirer with the white hair. Petrella launched himself in a flying tackle, and the three men went down together.

At this moment all the lights in the hall were extinguished.

The reporter on the *Highside Mercury* had a seat near the emergency exit. He escaped first, slammed the door behind him to discourage competitors, and ran all the way to the office.

"Hold everything," he said to the Editor, for he was a young man, and impetuous. "It's the story of the year. Police try to break up Ratepayers' Meeting. I recognised the man who did it. Perella — Petrella — some foreign name. *And* then they turned the lights out. But not quick enough."

The Editor was a man of few words. "You're sure it was a policeman? Excellent. We're all ready to print, but we can clear the front page if we rush it. Better dictate it straight to my secretary. Ready?"

The young reporter took a deep breath. "One of the most scandalous outrages in the municipal history of Highside ..."

☖ ☖ ☖

The other members of the press, fortunately for themselves, did not make such a quick getaway. By the time the lights had been switched on and things had been sorted out, the true facts were beginning to become apparent.

The essential points were that Petrella was still attached to Slippery Sam and Sam was attached to a briefcase containing the not-yet-banked takings of the charity bazaar that Mrs. Hayes had opened in the hall that afternoon.

With sober satisfaction the agency representative sent an account of this police triumph to six morning and three evening papers, with further syndication to the provinces. He managed, through the good offices of the *Helenwood Gazette*, to arrange for a picture of the white-haired gentleman, who turned out to be Professor Lockhart-Murray, the Civics expert, shaking hands with a blushing Petrella.

"It is the first time," said the Professor, "that I have ever experienced the direct impact of our police in action. I was most impressed."

On the following morning at eight o'clock, the *Highside Mercury* was on sale.

By ten past eight, twelve people had telephoned the Editor who, as usual after press night, was still in bed. By half past eight the Editor was dressed and in his office, answering a telephone call from Councillor Hayes.

By ten o'clock the solicitors to the paper had been summoned into conference, that morning's issue of the *Highside Mercury* had sold out, and the telephone on the desk of the Deputy Director of Public Prosecutions was ringing. At two o'clock that afternoon Detective Sergeant Petrella called, by appointment, on a very great man indeed.

Romer, an Assistant Commissioner in charge of CID, had a long, bleak face, reminiscent of a hanging judge, and an eye that had impressed a generation of policemen and criminals alike.

"There's no doubt at all," he said, "that you personally could ask for very heavy damages for libel. You are mentioned by name. The allegation is a scandalous one, and in addition quite untrue. And the newspaper concerned behaved with great carelessness. In fact, they would settle out of court."

"I don't want their money, sir," said Petrella unhappily.

"Good," said the Assistant Commissioner. "Then I think a printed apology will meet the case. I shall have great pleasure in composing it myself." He paused for a moment and his forbidding face broke into a warm smile. "I'm glad to have met you," he said. "It gives me an opportunity to say that I think you behaved very creditably."

As Petrella stepped out into Whitehall, it was raining. So far as he was concerned, it could have been snowing. It would have made no difference at all.

MISS BELL'S STOCKING

It was widely known in Highside — in certain circles at least —that Miss Bell had a stocking. When such circles speak of a stocking, they are not thinking of that useful and often elegant arrangement of silk or nylon which covers the southern end of a lady; they mean a private store of ready money, in bank-notes or coin of the realm, secreted in a shoe-box or a dispatch case or a tin trunk, and placed, for greater safety, under the owner's bed.

D. S. Petrella knew about Miss Bell's stocking. He had heard about it from Square Peggs, the proprietor of the all-night café.

"She's barmy," said Peggs. "There's nothing in that. Most old bints go barmy, one way or another, after a certain age. It's their metabolisms." He paused to absorb a bismuth tablet, for his own digestive metabolism left much to be desired.

"I heard she keeps it in a cage."

"A cage?"

"It's the cage she keeps her old parrot, Joey, in. Got a false bottom." Petrella choked over his coffee.

"It's no laughing matter," said Peggs sourly. "*And* you know perfectly well what I meant."

"Yes," said Petrella. "Quite so. Just for a moment I couldn't help picturing — but never mind. Where did she get it all from?"

"She got it from her Pa — Colonel Bell. He was an inventor. Invented a gadget for cutting things off with. Very popular in Edwardian times."

"Cutting things off?"

"Fingernails, corns, cigar-ends, anything you like to mention. She showed me one once. In snakeskin, with a silver finish. *Bell's Collapsible Cutter*. What the Society man takes on a picnic to Cowes or Ascot. Use it to cut bread for sandwiches, a lock of your loved one's hair, or your nephew off with a shilling."

"Peggs," said Petrella, "you're making it up."

"Cross my heart, I'm not. I'd have bought one myself, only this was the only one she had left. Very useful in the restaurant trade, a collapsible cutter."

"Tell me about that stocking. How big is it?"

"Over five hundred nicker, I heard. Money her Pa left to her. She doesn't touch it. Lives on a pension, more'n she wants. Adds to it from time to time."

Petrella found nothing incredible in that. He himself had once had the job of clearing up the garret room of an elderly recluse who had died of slow starvation and, examining the ticking of his pitiful mattress before consigning it to the flames, had found it packed with bank-notes, savings certificates, and securities, mostly so filthy and so tightly packed together as to be almost indecipherable.

"I suppose a lot of people know about it," he said.

"These things get round," said Peggs. "You know how it is. I fancy I saw Gentleman Jackson calling there the other day. Nice line in motor cars parked outside. Hired by the day, of course. I thought you oughter know."

"Thanks very much," said Petrella. "Yes, indeed." He made up his mind that the sooner he paid a call on Miss Bell the better. For Gentleman Jackson was a character whose fame extended even outside Q Division, in which he chiefly operated.

Nature had endowed Mr. Jackson with thick, greying hair on top of that sort of clean-cut, long-chinned face that looks out at you from the heart-warming advertisements of Bank Trustee Departments: *Let the Eastminster Bank take the Cares of Executorship from your Shoulders.* Jackson was born to take cares from people's shoulders. It was his speciality. In the process he often took quite a lot of money from their pockets as well, but in such a distinguished and such a considerate way that his victims often felt quite reconciled to their loss.

"I'll call on her tomorrow," said Petrella.

✠   ✠   ✠

"You are a modern man, Sergeant Petrella," said Miss Bell, pouring China tea from a silver pot into a Rockingham china cup, "with modern ideas."

"I suppose so," said Petrella.

"And you think that I'm an old frump."

"Certainly not," said Petrella. "It's a very nice room."

"Overcrowded, I fear, and a lot of work keeping all the brass clean. But I wouldn't be without it."

Petrella scrutinised the room carefully.

"It would almost seem," said Miss Bell, "as if there were something you expected to find here but did not see."

Petrella blushed. "I'd heard," he said, "that you kept a parrot."

Miss Bell seemed genuinely surprised.

"I once had a stuffed mongoose," said she, "but it moulted sadly. Never a parrot, as far as I can recollect. And my memory is as good as ever it was."

"I'm sure it is," said Petrella.

"And I am sure you didn't come to talk about parrots."

Petrella told her exactly what he had come to talk about, and Miss Bell heard him out in silence, except for an occasional clucking noise which might have been encouragement or mild surprise.

At the end she said, "I was aware, of course, that Mr. Jackson was a fraudulent character."

"You were?"

"He told me that he was a solicitor. My father was always very careful in such matters. He possessed, and left to me, a volume called *The Law List*, in which all solicitors are arranged in alphabetical order. Only one Jackson appears, and he is practising as you can see, in Weston-super-Mare."

Petrella read the entry; and observed also that it was a *Law List* for the year 1898. However, as long as Miss Bell was forewarned, that was all that really mattered.

"I take it he is putting up some proposition to you."

"Certainly," said Miss Bell. "And a most interesting one. An Australian financier — he started life as a sheep-worrier, whatever that may be — has entrusted to him a large fund of ready money. I forget if it was fifteen thousand or a hundred and fifty thousand pounds. He had instructions to hand over to charity, out of it, five times as much as he can collect from donors in this country. If he collects a hundred pounds from me, then he immediately gives five hundred pounds to a worthy charity here. I am particularly interested in the Highside Branch of the International Goodfellowship Society, and I was gratified to find that this was on his list. Wasn't that a coincidence?"

"It was indeed," said Petrella. "Have you ?"

"I was cautious, of course. But he disarmed me. The money is not to be paid to him, but directly to the Society. He is calling on me tomorrow evening. He will bring five hundred pounds with him, as a sign of good faith, as he put it. Not that I needed a sign. We shall place it, together with a hundred pounds of my money, in an envelope, and I shall myself address it and post it — is that not businesslike? — to the secretary of the Society."

Petrella wondered exactly what the secretary would say when he received the envelope full of folded pieces of newspaper which, he had no doubt at all, Mr. Jackson planned to substitute at the last moment. He said, "It sounds an excellent scheme. But tell me — do you really keep such a lot of ready money in your own house?"

"Certainly," said Miss Bell.

"Whereabouts do you keep it?"

Miss Bell looked at him hard. "And what did you say your name was?"

"Petrella."

"That's a foreign name."

"It's Spanish, actually."

"You're an English policeman. Why should you have a foreign name?"

"I got it from my father."

"I see. And you are — I think you said — a detective sergeant, working in this district."

"Division."

"I beg your pardon, division." Miss Bell was busy with the telephone directory. She dialled a number which Petrella, from where he sat, identified as the number of Crown Road Police Station.

"Could I speak to the person in charge?"

"This is the Station Sergeant speaking, ma'am."

"Have you on your staff a detective sergeant called Petrella?"

"Certainly, ma'am."

"Is he a young man —" she regarded him, her head on one side. She seemed to be enjoying herself "— with blue eyes and black hair, and a somewhat juvenile air?"

"That sounds like him," agreed the Station Sergeant. "What's he been up to?"

"Nothing at all," said Miss Bell, and rang off. "My father taught me never to take people at their own valuation."

"If you're quite happy about me now," said Petrella tartly, "perhaps you could answer my question."

"Of course."

Miss Bell hopped up, and walked across to a large brass-bound, teakwood chest which stood underneath the window. It was the sort of thing that might have served for keeping logs in, except that it had an elaborate domed lid, which was shut.

"Open it for yourself," she said.

The lid was exceedingly heavy, but it moved up freely enough. The interior of the chest was lined with some sweet-smelling Indian wood; and it was empty. Petrella felt cautiously down the sides. They did not seem thick enough to contain any secrets.

"Now shut it again, and let me try."

Before she lifted the lid Petrella saw her do something to the handle. It was too quick for him to see precisely what she did, but this time the lid came up very easily, leaving behind it, in the top of the chest, a tray.

And it was full of bank-notes. Petrella looked at them curiously. They were of all ages. Greenbacks and brownbacks, Bradburys and Fishers, a few of the old white five-pound notes, and some of the recent issue as well.

Petrella found it difficult to tell how many there were in the chest, but there must have been at least a thousand pounds, probably more.

Miss Bell closed down the lid, which shut with a click, and returned to her chair.

"That was made by my father," she said. "He showed me the secret of the handle just before he died."

"Has it ever occurred to you," said Petrella, "how much money you're losing keeping it like this?"

"Losing?"

"Well, interest. Income."

"I have plenty of income. Why should I need any more?"

"You're not only losing income, you're losing capital as well. Do you realise that the pound note has depreciated in value so much that a pound in 1939 is only worth eight shillings now?"

Miss Bell looked at him pityingly.

"You're talking about the pounds in banks," she said. "The sort they give you in exchange for your cheques. I know all about them. Of course, they go down and down. It's something the banks arrange among themselves, so that when they come to pay you back the money you've been silly enough to lend them, they won't have to pay you so much."

"But —"

"How anyone could be taken in by so childish a trick, I can't imagine."

"But your money is just the same as theirs."

"Of course it isn't. Their money has gone down and down. Mine is just the same as it was when it was first put away. My pounds are still pounds."

"But —"

"And they're not only as valuable as they were when I first got them, there are more of them! Have you ever heard of that happening in a bank account?"

Petrella could think of nothing to say to that.

✠ ✠ ✠

At eight o'clock the following evening he was sitting in the front of a shabby tradesman's van that did not in the least resemble a police vehicle, although in fact it was equipped with a receiving- and transmitting-set. He was watching Miss Bell's front door.

He had seen the gentlemanly Mr. Jackson go in. Miss Bell had let him in herself; there was evidently no resident servant. The light was shining from the uncurtained bow window of the first-floor drawing-room. If anyone had approached the window to raise the lid of the great brass-bound chest, he was confident that he would have seen them. Miss Bell might, of course, have got the money out, ready, beforehand. In any event it would be better to stop Jackson on his way out, with the fruits of his nefarious sleight of hand actually on him.

So Petrella thought, and so he waited, patiently.

Mr. Jackson was also a man of patience. Seated in that charming, if old-fashioned, drawing-room, he had listened, with apparent interest, to Miss Bell's views on economics, the National Debt, bimetallism, the Gold Standard, and the appalling dishonesty of bank managers; but when nine o'clock struck, and then half past nine, he felt that it was time to proceed to business.

"Very interesting," he said. "Very interesting indeed. And now —"

He extracted from the inner pocket of his coat a bulky wallet. It was specially made of a plastic material which had the advantage, from his point of view, of being nearly but not quite transparent. When he laid it open on the desk, it could be seen to be divided into two pockets, each of which contained fifty five-pound notes. Or appeared to do so. The top and bottom notes on each side were absolutely genuine. The remaining ninety-six, if not quite genuine, were nothing so crude as torn-up strips of newspaper. They were a type of note which those who know the ropes can purchase at about ten for a pound, and which have a legitimate use as stage money, and a fairly legitimate use where an ostentatious show of wealth is required.

"There, dear lady," said Mr. Jackson. "My pledge is fulfilled. Count them if you wish."

"I am quite prepared to trust you," said Miss Bell, with a smile.

"Then let me add to them your contribution of one hundred pounds, place all in this envelope, and post it at once to the Goodfellowship Society. What a surprise for the secretary when he receives it. If we hurry, we shall just catch the last post."

Still Miss Bell hesitated. "I suppose I am justified," she said, "in making such a large contribution."

"Reflect," said Mr. Jackson, "that every pound you withhold must mean that five pounds of this money is withdrawn."

"Oh dear. When you put it like that it sounds almost as if I am robbing them."

"Think of the cause."

"Well —" said Miss Bell.

She did not hear it, nor did Mr. Jackson. But Simba, her old and crafty Persian cat, heard it, and removed herself delicately from the rug in front of the fire and jumped on to the back of the sofa to be out of harm's way. A stealthy creaking of the loose board in the passage. A hissing of breath.

Then the door opened, and two men shouldered their way abruptly into the room. The leader was a tall, thin man with iron-grey hair, a weather-beaten face, and two very long, very pointed incisor teeth, one on either side of the front of his mouth. He was known in criminal circles as Wolf Chops, and he was a very unpleasant character indeed. Behind him came a second man, half as high, but twice as broad. His name was Danny and he suffered from epileptic fits. Between fits he earned a precarious living by robbery with violence.

"You go and keep an eye open for trouble," said Wolf to Danny. "I can deal with this little lot, don't you worry."

Danny appeared to understand this. He backed out, bubbling a little as he went.

"To what do I owe the pleasure?" said Miss Bell.

Wolf addressed Mr. Jackson. "I don't want a bit of trouble from you Jacko," he said. "Your act's over. You can scarper. Or sit quiet and watch the fun. I don't mind which."

"Tell this man to go away, Mr. Jackson," said Miss Bell calmly. "I can't think how he got in at all. You must have left the door open."

"Really," said Mr. Jackson, in a voice from which most of the assurance had gone, "I think this intrusion is quite uncalled for."

Wolf took hold of the telephone, jerked it bodily out of the wall, and threw it on the sofa, narrowly missing Simba, who retreated with a hiss to the top of the bookcase.

"Tell him to go," said Miss Bell. "At once."

"I —" said Mr. Jackson.

"If you won't keep quiet, that's your lookout," said Wolf. His foot jerked up on to Mr. Jackson's bottom waistcoat button.

Mr. Jackson said, "Aaagh," as the air left him, and doubled over. This brought his chin into the right position for Wolf to hit it, which he did, with a fist covered in some curious device of leather and steel.

Mr. Jackson went over on his back, rocking the bookcase as he fell. Simba transferred herself nimbly to the pelmet.

Miss Bell sat bolt upright in her chair.

"That was unforgivable," she said, "to strike a man so much older than yourself."

Wolf hitched himself forward until he was within distance of Miss Bell. He was in command of the situation and felt comfortable. This old lady wasn't behaving quite true to form. Most old ladies, by this time, would have been screaming, or cowering in a corner with their hands over their heads; but the fact that she was doing neither did not make Miss Bell appear any more formidable to Wolf. He was a man of very limited imagination which, when one considers some of the things he had done from time to time, to people who were in his power, was probably just as well for him.

"Now," he said, breathing heavily in Miss Bell's face, "you saw what happened to him. So don't let's have any lip from you. Just open up, and we'll take it quietly."

"Open what up?"

"Now don't argue. You've got money here. In notes. A lot of it. I know, see. You hand it over, and we won't hurt you. You hold out on us and I'll call Danny in, and we'll pull you to bits. You know what this is?"

His free hand went down and came up again. In it was a curious weapon. Basically it was a potato. Embedded in it, with a quarter of an inch of blue steel exposed, was a safety razor-blade.

"A collapsible cutter," said Miss Bell, in a far-away voice.

"I call it a shiv," said Wolf. "And I'll give you the shivers with it. And anyone else who sees you when I've done with you."

"I won't —"

"Look, lady," said Wolf, and an earnest note had crept into his voice, "either you open up, or I open you up. It's as easy as that. One of them's got to happen."

Wolf was wrong. What happened next was that Mr. Jackson, having extracted a small, Italian-made, automatic pistol from his pocket, started shooting from where he lay on the floor. The first shot carried away a crystal cluster from the chandelier, the second embedded itself in the wall above the fireplace, and the third hit Wolf slap in the middle of the face.

The noise of the firing caused two immediate reactions. Danny, who had the simple instinct of self-preservation well developed, departed out of the scullery window by which he and Wolf had entered. Petrella jumped out of the van, shocked and horrified by this sudden development, for he had no idea that Jackson and Miss Bell were not alone in the house, and could not conceive why either of them should be shooting at the other. The front door was locked, but he circled the house, found the scullery window open, and went through it, missing Danny by about five seconds.

Upstairs he found Jackson sitting on the floor, his head in his hands; Miss Bell still rigid in her chair. And the quite-dead body of Wolf on the carpet.

"I am afraid," said Miss Bell, "that the telephone is out of order. If you wish to summon assistance, you will find another one in the hall."

Later, when he had got things sorted out a bit, Petrella had a final word with Miss Bell.

"In a way," he said, "it's your fault. This sort of thing is bound to happen if you keep a lot of money lying about. I really should be happier if you would put it in a bank."

"Certainly not," said Miss Bell. She was scratching the head of Simba, once more restored to her place by the fire. "I cannot pretend that I enjoyed it all but, viewed in a proper light, one can feel oneself to be spiritually enriched by such an experience. I hope that nothing terrible will happen to Mr. Jackson."

"I shouldn't imagine so. He could reasonably plead self-defence. Or at least the provocation will reduce it to manslaughter. He might have to explain how he was carrying a gun without a licence."

"It was merciful that he was," said Miss Bell. "And I am most obliged to him. Most."

Petrella later passed this message on to Mr. Jackson, who said, "It's a funny thing, no-one ever finding that wallet. If Wolf picked it up, why wasn't it on him? Perhaps the police ?"

"Certainly not," said Petrella. "Anything found would have been reported."

"You don't think the old lady ?"

"She did tell me that she had been enriched as a result of her experience."

"She said that?"

"Spiritually enriched."

"I see," said Mr. Jackson thoughtfully.

FIVE ON THE GUN

As man-to-man, the real difference between Captain Brumfit and Gunner Whillow was that Brumfit looked like a soldier whilst Whillow did not.

Brumfit was square, chunky, and had once been athletic. He had a red face, very slightly protuberant blue eyes and a fierce little moustache. He looked a killer.

As a matter of fact, having been just too young for active service in the last war, he had never killed anything except smaller animals and birds; and, as his conduct revealed, he had a second-class brain, little character and no morals.

Gunner Whillow, who was a member of the small Field Regiment, Royal Artillery, was in the Troop commanded by Captain Brumfit, and was definitely below him in the military hierarchy.

He was narrow shouldered, stooping and entirely unathletic, and went through life balancing a pair of steel spectacles on a large and pointed nose.

Nevertheless he possessed a brain of the first class — indeed, if brains could be accurately categorised, of the upper-first class — having specialised in Higher Mathematics at London University and being by training a geophysical surveyor, which is a very rare and splendid sort of surveyor. Amongst other accomplishments, if you were to name the Latitude and Longitude of two points he could at once inform you (having made proper allowance for the curve of the earth's surface) of the distance and bearing of one from the other. He could also multiply numbers of up to six digits in his head.

As anyone with any knowledge of the British Army will readily appreciate, Gunner Whillow was not given a job as Technical Assistant, or Command Post Operator, or Regimental Surveyor, where his specialised knowledge would have been of some use to him and to the Regiment, nor was he even placed in the Battery office, where his facility for adding up long columns of figures at sight might have shocked the Sergeant Clerk (who still added up everything on his fingers.)

To have given him a job of this sort would have been contrary to every tradition of an Army which prides itself on turning Greek Professors into Sanitary Orderlies and Physicists into Officers' Mess Cooks.

It will come as no surprise, therefore, to any old Gunners who may read this story, to learn that Whillow became "No. 5 on the Gun." For the benefit of non-gunners it should be explained that No. 5 represents the lowest possible form of life in a Troop of Field Guns. His duty is to kneel to the left rear of the gun and prepare the ammunition.

Even this sounds more exciting than it is, and you must dismiss any picture of No. 5 measuring out exact quantities of gunpowder or gelignite into a cartridge case. The Army has rightly guessed that this would be beyond the powers of the average No. 5, and has done most of it for him in advance.

The cartridge case, which is separate from the shell, and is put into the gun behind it, contains the cordite which will propel the shell on to its target. That is its sole function. When the shell lands it contains various further explosive devices which will cause it to detonate and damage the Queen's enemies but that is nothing to do with the cartridge. The sole job of the cartridge is to get the shell there.

Inside the cartridge is a quantity of cordite, which is done up into three bags. The bottom bag is red, and cannot be removed. The second bag is white, and the third bag is blue. These two bags are loose, and can be taken out by hand.

If you wish to fire Charge Three you leave all the bags alone. For Charge Two, you remove the blue bag. For Charge One both the blue and white bag.

It is as simple as that. Nothing to tax the intellect.

Even so, the Army is not entirely happy. Mistakes will happen, and it is a good rule to check everything three times; particularly since a mistake about a Charge may have serious results. For if a gun is duly elevated to fire Charge Three and, in error, you use Charge Two, your shell may drop as much as a thousand yards short and kill an infantryman — or even a Staff Officer — and it will be appreciated how carefully that must be avoided.

Accordingly a rigid drill is laid down. No. 5 prepares the ammunition, and hands it to No. 4, who is a slightly senior and more responsible person. No. 4 checks it, and shows it to No. 1, who is the Sergeant in Charge of the gun, an immensely responsible person. He sees that the correct coloured bag is showing and gives the order to load. Whereupon No. 4 shoves the cartridge into the gun, and that is that.

As Gunner Whillow knelt behind his gun, solemnly removing white and blue bags and blowing on his fingers, for it was early spring on Salisbury Plain, and the wind comes up fresh all the way from the Solent on to those sheep-nibbled, benighted heights, it must be supposed that he was doing mental arithmetic in order to keep his numb brain moving.

For it was on such a morning that the idea came to him of a safe, simple and satisfactory way to murder his Troop Commander.

As to why Gunner Whillow wished to kill Captain Brumfit it is perhaps sufficient to say that his motives seemed to him to be adequate.

Captain Brumfit, though no killer of men, was an accomplished slayer of ladies. There was something about him, either his protuberant eyes or his virile little moustache, that women found irresistible, and Whillow's pretty little wife had been seeing a good deal of both features ever since Captain Brumfit had spotted her at a Canteen dance.

Now, though reprehensible, this is the sort of thing that has happened before in history, and men have made love to other men's wives without getting killed for it, but Captain Brumfit aggravated his offence. To put the matter bluntly, he cheated. He used his position to ensure that Gunner Whillow would be safely out of the way and leave the field clear for him.

So Gunner Whillow found himself doing an extraordinary number of extra guards, piquets, fatigues and other jobs that confined him to camp, whilst Captain Brumfit seemed to spend more and more of his time down in the little market town at the foot of the hill, in one of whose many hotels Mrs. Whillow had a room.

On at least one occasion Gunner Whillow was actually on guard at the main gate of the Camp when Captain Brumfit came back from one of these expeditions. It was about 2 o'clock in the morning, and the Captain looked pleased with himself.

He waved a hand to Gunner Whillow as he went past.

Gunner Whillow contrived a sketchy salute.

During all this time the Troop, which formed part of the Depot Battery, was out on the ranges almost every day, and Captain Brumfit, as the only available Troop Commander, conducted and observed a good many of the shoots.

His method was to go out in a carrier to some safe spot about two thirds of the way up the line of fire, get out with a hand microphone and move to a point of vantage, then settle himself comfortably on his shooting stick and give the orders that would fire the guns.

In accordance with procedure he would first report his own position over the wireless and, at a later stage, the position of the target he happened to be engaging.

Since Gunner Whillow's gun was usually near to the Gun Command Post he would hear these positions as they came over the air.

To most people the string of figures meant nothing. To the eminent geophysical surveyor kneeling behind his gun they meant a good deal.

Sometimes they showed him that Captain Brumfit had stationed himself to the left of the line of fire — sometimes to the right. Occasionally they showed that he was actually in the line of fire, and on these occasions Gunner Whillow's concentration increased to an alarming degree.

He was like a big game hunter who sees the long awaited tiger come into the sights of his rifle but is prevented by circumstances from pulling the trigger.

For it was not enough that Captain Brumfit should be *in* the line of fire. He had to be exactly the right distance *up* it. Gunner Whillow had memorised several complete pages of the technical data in the Range Tables, and he knew, for each range, the precise drop that would be achieved were his gun to fire (accidentally, of course) Charge Two instead of Charge Three.

If you wait long enough, and patiently enough, almost any combination of circumstances will occur. And Gunner Whillow was infinitely patient.

It was at ten-fifty precisely, almost five weeks after the gate episode, that his sums at last came out right.

With scarcely a tremor he reached behind him and handed a carefully selected cartridge case to No. 4.

"Charge Three" ordered the Gun Position Officer.

No. 4 glanced mechanically into the cartridge case. It was a perfunctory glance, because he had known Whillow long enough to realise that he never made mistakes.

The blue and white bags were both there, all right, on top of the red.

No. 1, who was Sergeant Harris, and a confirmed bully, glared at the cartridge but could find no fault with it. "Correct."

"Load — Fire — Number One Shot."

It was a perfectly normal sequence, one which they had all repeated a thousand times before.

Some twenty seconds later they heard a loud "crump."

Then the wireless went mad. "Stop, stop, stop. Detachments Rear. No gun to be touched."

Some ten minutes later, when confusion was at its height, Gunner Whillow, unseen, quietly removed something from the inside of his battledress, pushed it down a rabbit hole, and kicked the top of the rabbit hole in with his boot.

And that was that.

The Court of Inquiry could make nothing of it. The gun had been checked and was found to be correctly laid. There were no faults in its mechanism. There were three separate witnesses that Charge Three had been fired. The spare charge bags were counted and found correct.

And yet there was the inescapable fact that a twenty-five pounder shell had neatly abolished a valuable Troop Commander.

Clearly something had to be done to restore confidence, and, in accordance with the best precedents, the Gun Position Officer was cashiered, the Sergeant in Charge of the gun was reduced to the ranks and No. 4, as Senior Ammunition Number, received a severe reprimand.

The Court felt that Gunner Whillow was too junior to be involved in its proceedings, which was a pity, because only he could have told them that the whole effect had been achieved by substituting a blue bag of wood shavings for a blue bag of cordite, and subsequently burying the cordite down a rabbit hole.

However, in the disruption caused by these proceedings Whillow managed to wangle an extra forty-eight hours leave, which he spent with his little wife.

THE JACKAL AND THE TIGER

On the evening of April 15th, 1944, Colonel Hubert, of Military Intelligence, said to the Director of Public Prosecutions, "The only mistake Karl made was to underestimate young Ronnie Kavanagh."

That afternoon, Karl Muller, who sometimes called himself Charles Miller, had been shot in the underground rifle range at the Tower of London, which was the place being used at that time for the execution of German spies.

"A fatal mistake," agreed the Director.

✠ ✠ ✠

Jim Perrot, late of the Military Police, wrote to his friend, Fred Denniston:

"Dear Denny,

"Do you remember those plans we talked over so often in North Africa and Italy? Well, I've got an option on a twenty-one-year lease of a nice first-floor office in Chancery Lane. That's bang in the middle of legal London, where the legal eagles are beginning to flap their wings and sharpen their claws again. Lots of work for an Enquiry Agency and not much competition — as yet. The lease is a snip. I've commuted my pension and got me a bit of capital. I reckon we'll have to put in about £2,000 each to get going. Denny's Detectives! How about it?"

And Denny's Detectives had turned out to be a success from the start.

As Perrot had said, there was no lack of work. Much of it was divorce work, the sad by-product of a long war. It was in connection with this branch of their activities, which neither of the partners liked, that they acquired Mr. Huffin. He was perfectly equipped for the role he had to play. He was small, mild-looking, and so insignificant that many businessmen, departing to alleged conferences in the Midlands, had failed to recognise the little man who travelled in the train with them and occupied a table in an obscure corner of their hotel dining-room until he stood up in court and swore to tell the truth, the whole truth, and nothing but the truth about the lady who had shared the businessman's table, and, later, his bedroom.

Jim Perrot's job was the tracing of elusive debtors. His experience as a policeman was useful to him here. Fred Denniston, for his part, rarely left the office. His speciality was estimating the credit-worthiness of companies. He gradually became expert at reading between the lines of optimistic profit-and-loss accounts and precariously balanced balance-sheets. He developed, with experience, a quite uncanny instinct for over-valued stocks and under-depreciated assets. Perrot would sometimes see him holding a suspect document delicately between his fingers and sniffing at it, as though he could detect, by smell alone, the odour of falsification.

One factor that helped them to show a steady profit was their absurdly small rent. When Perrot had described the lease as a "snip" he was not exaggerating. At the end of the war, when no-one was bothered about inflation, twenty-one-year leases could be had without the periodical reviews which are commonplace today. As the end of their lease approached, the partners did become aware that they were paying a good deal less than the market rent. Indeed they could hardly help being aware of it — their landlords, the Scotus Property Company, commented on it with increasing bitterness.

"It's no good complaining about it," said Perrot genially. "You should have thought about that when you granted the lease."

"Just you wait till the end of next year," said Scotus.

Denniston said, "I suppose we shall have to pay a bit more. Anyway, they can't turn us out. We're protected tenants."

When a friendly valuer from the other end of Chancery Lane learned what their rent was, he struggled to control his feelings. "I suppose you realise," he said, "that you're paying a pound a square foot "

"Just about what I made it," said Denniston.

"And that the going rate in this area is between five and six pounds."

"You mean," said Perrot, "that when our lease comes to an end, we'll have to pay five times the present rent."

"Oh, at least that," said the valuer cheerfully. "But I imagine you've been putting aside the fund to meet it."

The partners looked at each other. They were well aware that they had been doing nothing of the sort.

That was the first shock.

✠ ✠ ✠

The second shock was Perrot's death. He had been putting on weight and smoking too much, but had looked healthy enough. One afternoon he complained of not feeling well, went home early, and died that night.

Denniston had been fond of him and his first feelings were of personal loss. His next feeling was that he was going to need another partner and additional capital; and that fairly quickly.

He considered and rejected the idea of inviting Mr. Huffin to become a partner. The main drawback was that Denniston disliked him. And he was so totally negative. He crept into the office every morning on the stroke of nine and, unless he had some outside business, stayed in his room, which had been partitioned off from Denniston's, until half past five. The partition was so thin that Denniston could hear him every time he got up from his chair.

Not partner material, said Denniston to himself.

He tried advertising, but soon found that the limited number of applicants who had capital would have been unsuitable as partners, while the rather greater number who might have been acceptable as partners had no capital.

After some months of fruitless effort he realised two other things. The first was that they were losing business. Jim Perrot's clients were taking their affairs elsewhere. The second was that the day of reckoning with his landlords was looming.

It was at this point that Andrew Gurney turned up. Denniston liked him at sight. He was young. He was cheerful. He seemed anxious to learn the business. And he made a proposal.

In about a year's time, when he attained the ripe old age of twenty-five, he would be coming into a bit of capital under a family trust. By that time he would have a fair idea whether the business suited him and he suited them. All being well, he was prepared to invest that capital in the firm.

They discussed amounts and dates and came to a tentative agreement. Gurney took over Perrot's old room. Denniston breathed a sigh of relief and turned his mind to the analysis of a complex set of group accounts.

It was almost exactly a month later when Mr. Huffin knocked on his door, put his head round, blinked twice, and said, "If you're not too busy, I wonder if I might have a word with you."

"I'm doing nothing that can't wait," said Denniston.

Mr. Huffin slid into the room, advanced toward the desk, and then, as if changing his mind at the last moment, seated himself in the chair that was normally reserved for clients.

Denniston was conscious of a slight feeling of surprise. Previously when Mr. Huffin had come to see him, he had stood in front of the desk and had waited, if the discussion was likely to be lengthy, for an invitation to sit down.

He was even more surprised when Mr. Huffin spoke. He said, "You're in trouble, aren't you?"

It was not only that Mr. Huffin had omitted the "sir" which he had previously used when addressing his employer. It was more than that. There was something sharp and cold in the tone of his voice. It was like the sudden unexpected chill which announces the end of autumn and the beginning of winter.

"You haven't seen fit to take me into your confidence," Mr. Huffin continued, "but the wall between our offices is so thin that it's impossible for me not to hear every word that's said."

Denniston had recovered himself sufficiently to say, "The fact that you can overhear confidential matters doesn't entitle you to trade on them."

"When the ship's sinking," said Mr. Huffin, "etiquette has to go by the board."

This was followed by a silence which Denniston found it difficult to break. In the end he said, "It's true that Mr. Perrot's death has left us in a difficult position. But as it happens, I have been able to make arrangements which should tide us over."

"You mean young Gurney? In the month he's been here, he's earned less than half you pay him. And speaking personally, I should have said that he's got no real aptitude for the work. What you need is someone without such nice manners, but with a thicker skin."

Denniston said, "Look here, Mr. Huffin " and stopped. He was on the point of saying, "If you don't like the way I run this firm, we can do without you." But could they?

As though reading his thoughts, Mr. Huffin said, "In the old days, Mr. Perrot, you, and I earned roughly equal amounts. Recently the proportions have been slipping. Last year I brought in half our fees. At least those were the figures you gave our auditor, so I assume they're correct."

"You listened to that discussion also?"

"I felt I was an interested party."

Mr. Denniston said, "All right. I accept that your services have been valuable. If that's your point, you've made it. I imagine it's leading up to something else. You want an increase in salary?"

"Not really."

"Then —"

"My proposal was that I should take over the firm."

In the long silence that followed, Denniston found himself revising his opinion of Mr. Huffin. His surface meekness was, he realised, a piece of professional camouflage, as meaningless as the wigs of the barristers and the pin-striped trousers of the solicitors.

Mr. Huffin added, "Have you thought out what would happen if I did leave? Maybe you could make enough to cover expenses. Until your lease expires. But what then? Have you, I wonder, overlooked one point. At the conclusion of a twenty-one-year lease there is bound to be a heavy bill for dilapidations."

"Dilapidations?" said Denniston slowly. The five syllables chimed together in an ominous chord. "Surely, there's nothing much to do."

"I took the precaution of having a word with an old friend, a Mr. Ellen. He's one of the surveyors used by the Scotus Property Company. He's a leading expert in his field and his calculations are very rarely challenged by the court. Last weekend I arranged for him to make an inspection. He thought that the cost of carrying out all the necessary work in a first-class fashion would be between six and eight thousand pounds."

"For God's sake!" said Denniston. "It can't be!"

"He showed me the breakdown. It could be more."

To give himself time to think, Denniston said, after a pause, "If you have such a poor opinion of the prospects of the firm, why would you want to buy me out?"

"I'm sorry," said Mr. Huffin gently. "You've misunderstood me. I wasn't proposing to pay you anything. After all, what have you got to sell?"

✠ ✠ ✠

It was not Denniston's habit to discuss business with his wife, but this was a crisis. He poured out the whole matter to her as soon as he got home that evening.

"And I know damned well what he'll do," he said. "As soon as he's got me out, he'll bring in some accomplice of his own. They won't stick to divorce work. That's legal, at least. The real money's in dirty work. Finding useful witnesses and bribing them to say what your client wants. Faking evidence. Fudging expert reports."

His wife said, "He seems to be prepared to pay eight thousand pounds for the privilege of doing it."

"Of course he won't: that's a put-up job between him and his old pal, Mr. Ellen, of Scotus. He'll pay a lot less and be allowed to pay it in easy instalments."

"What happens if you say no?"

"I'd have to challenge the dilapidations. It'd mean going to court and that's expensive."

"If you used some of Gurney's money —" Mrs. Denniston stopped.

They were both straightforward people. Denniston put what she was thinking into words. "I can't take that boy's money and put it into a legal wrangle."

"And there's no other way of raising it?"

"None that I can think of."

"Then that's that," said his wife. "I'd say cut your losses and clear out. We're still solvent. We'll think of something to do."

It took a lot of talk to persuade him, but in the end he saw the force of her arguments. "All right," he said. "No sense in dragging it out. I'll go in tomorrow and tell Huffin he can have the firm. I'll also tell him what I think of him."

"It won't do any good."

"It'll do me a lot of good."

☩ ☩ ☩

On the following evening, Denniston arrived back on the stroke of six. He kissed his wife and said to her, "Whatever you were thinking of cooking for supper, think again. We're going out to find the best dinner London can provide. We'll drink champagne before it, burgundy with it, and brandy after it."

His wife, who had spent the day worrying about how they were going to survive, said, "Really, Fred. Do you think we ought "

"Certainly we ought. We're celebrating."

"Celebrating what?"

"A miracle."

It had happened at nine o'clock that morning. While Denniston was polishing up the precise terms in which he intended to say goodbye to Mr. Huffin, his secretary came into his room. She was looking ruffled. She said, "Could you be free to see Mr. Kavanagh at ten?"

Denniston looked at his diary and said, "Yes. That'll be all right. Who is Mr. Kavanagh?"

"Mr. Ronald Kavanagh," said his secretary. While he was still looking blank, she added, "Kavanagh Lewisohn and Fitch. He's the chairman."

Denniston said, "Good God!" And then, "How do you know that?"

"Before I came here, I worked in their head office."

"Do you know Mr. Kavanagh?"

His secretary said, "I was in the typing pool. I caught a glimpse of him twice in the three years I was there."

"Did he say what he wanted?"

"He wanted to see you."

"You're sure he didn't ask me to go and see him? He's coming here?"

"That's what he said."

"It must be some mistake," said Denniston.

Kavanagh Lewisohn and Fitch were so well known that people said KLF and assumed you would understand what they meant. They were one of the largest credit-sale firms in London, so large that they rarely dealt with individual customers. They sold everything from computer banks to motor cars and television sets and washing machines to middle-men, who in turn sold them to retailers. If Ronald Kavanagh was really planning to visit a small firm of enquiry agents, it could hardly be in connection with business matters. It must be private trouble. Something that needed to be dealt with discreetly.

When Kavanagh arrived, he turned out, surprisingly, to be a slight, quiet, unassuming person in his early fifties. Denniston was agreeably surprised. Such managing directors of large companies as he had come across in the past had been intimidating people, assertive of their status and conscious of their financial muscle. A further surprise was that he really had come to talk business.

He said, "This is something I wanted to deal with myself. Some time ago you did credit-rating reports for us on two potential customers." He mentioned their names.

"Yes," said Denniston, wondering what had gone wrong.

"We were impressed by the thorough way you tackled them. I assumed, by the way, that you did the work yourself."

Denniston nodded.

"You gave a good rating to one, although it was a new company. The other, which was older and apparently sound, you warned us against. In both cases, you were absolutely right. That's why I'm here today. Up to the present we've been getting the reports we needed from half a dozen difference sources. This is now such an important part of our business that the Board has decided that it would like to concentrate it in one pair of hands. Our first idea was to offer you the work on a retainer basis. Then we had a better idea." Mr. Kavanagh smiled. "We decided to buy you. That is, of course, if you're for sale."

Denniston was incapable of speech.

"We had it in mind to purchase your business as a going concern. We would take over the premises as they stand. There is, however, one condition. It's *your* brains and *your* flair that we're buying. We should have to ask you to enter into a service contract, at a fair salary, for five years certain, with options on both sides to renew. Your existing staff, too, if they wish. But you are the one we must have."

The room, which had shown signs of revolving on its axis, slowed down. Denniston took a grip of himself. He said, "Your offer is more than fair, but there is one thing you ought to know. You spoke of taking over these premises. There is a snag —"

When he had finished, Kavanagh said, "It was good of you to tell me. It accords, if I may say so, with your reputation. We are not unacquainted with Scotus." He smiled gently. "We had some dealings with them over one of our branch offices last year. Fortunately, we have very good solicitors and excellent surveyors. The outcome was a lot happier for us than it was for them. However, in this case it doesn't arise. Our own service department will carry out such repairs and redecoration as *we* consider necessary. If Scotus object, they can take us to court. I don't think they will. They're timid folk when they're up against someone bigger than themselves."

"Like all bullies," said Denniston. As he said it, he reflected with pleasure that Mr. Huffin had undoubtedly got his ear glued to the wall.

✠ ✠ ✠

It soon became apparent that Ronald Kavanagh was not a man who delegated to others things that he enjoyed doing himself.

On the morning after the deal had been signed, he limped into the room, accompanied by the head of his service department and a foreman. They inspected everything and made notes. The next morning, a gang of workmen arrived and started to turn the office upside down.

Kavanagh arrived with the workmen. He said to Denniston, "We'll start with your room. Strip and paint the whole place. They can do it in two days. What colours do you fancy?"

"Something cheerful."

"I agree. My solicitor's office looks as if it hasn't been dusted since Charles Dickens worked there. What we want is an impression of cheerful reliability. Cream paint, venetian blinds, and solid-brass light fittings. And we'll need a second desk. I propose to establish a niche here for myself. I hope you don't mind."

"I don't mind at all," said Denniston. It occurred to him that one cause of his depression had been that since Perrot's death he had really had no-one to talk to. "I'll be glad of your company, though I don't suppose you'll be able to spare us a lot of time."

"It's a common fallacy," said Kavanagh, sitting on a corner of the table, swinging his damaged leg ("a relic of war service," he had explained), "widely believed, but quite untrue, that managing directors are busy men. If they are, it's a sign of incompetence. I have excellent subordinates who do the real work. All I have to do is utter occasional sounds of approval or disapproval. It's such a boring life that a new venture like this is a breath of fresh air. Oh, you want to move this table. We'd better shift into young Gurney's office.

"As I was saying," he continued when they had established themselves in Gurney's room, "I have an insatiable curiosity about the mechanics of other people's business. When we went into the secondhand car market, we took over a motor-repair outfit. I got so interested that I put on overalls and started to work there myself. The men thought it was a huge joke, but they soon got used to it. And the things I learned about faking repair bills, you wouldn't believe. Oh, sorry I'm afraid they want to start work in here, too. Let's go to my club and get ourselves an early luncheon."

☒ ☒ ☒

Denniston found the new regime very pleasant. Kavanagh did not, of course, spend all his time with them, but he managed to put in a full hour on most days. His method of working was to have copies made, on the modern photocopying machine which had been one of his first innovations, of all of Denniston's reports. These he would study carefully, occasionally asking for the working papers. The questions he asked were shrewd and could not be answered without thought.

"Really," he said, "we're in the same line of business. Success depends on finding out who to trust. I once turned down a prosperous-looking television wholesaler because he turned up in a Green Jackets' tie. I'm damned certain he'd never been near the Brigade. Quite the wrong shape for a Rifleman."

"Instinct, based on experience," agreed Denniston. He already felt years younger. It was not only the steady flow of new work and the certainty of getting a cheque at the end of the each month, the whole office seemed to have changed. Even Mr. Huffin appeared to be happy. Not only had his room been repainted, it had been furnished with a new desk and a set of gleaming filing cabinets equipped with Chubb locks.

These innovations seemed to have compensated him for the setback to his own plans and he went out of his way to be pleasant to Kavanagh when he encountered him.

"Slimy toad," said Denniston to his wife. "When I asked Kavanagh if he planned to keep him, he laughed and said, 'Why not? I don't much like the sort of work he's doing, but it brings in good money. As long as he keeps within the law. If you hear any complaints of sharp practice, that's another matter.' "

"Mr. Kavanagh sounds terrific."

"Terrific's not quite the right word. He's honest, sensible, and unassuming. Also, he's still a bit of a schoolboy. He likes to see the wheels go round."

"I don't believe a single word of it," said his wife.

⊞ ⊞ ⊞

"Well, Uncle," said Andrew Gurney. "What next?"

Kavanagh said, "Next, I think, a glass of port."

"Then it must be something damned unpleasant," said Gurney. "Why?"

"If it wasn't, you wouldn't be wasting the Club port on me."

"You're an irreverent brat," said Kavanagh.

"When you wangled me into the firm I guessed you were up to something."

"Two large ports, please, Barker. Actually, Andrew, all I want you to do is to commit a burglary."

"I said it was going to be something unpleasant."

"But this is a very safe burglary. You're to burgle the offices of Denny's Detectives. Since the firm belongs to me, technically hardly a burglary at all, would you say?"

"Well —" said Gurney cautiously.

"I will supply you with the key of the outer door, the key of Mr. Huffin's room, and a key for each of his new filing cabinets and his desk. Mr. Huffin is a careful man. When the desk and cabinets were installed, he asked for the duplicate keys to be handed to him. Fortunately, I had a second copy made of each. Nevertheless, I was much encouraged by his request. It showed me that I might be on the right track."

"What track?"

Kavanagh took a sip of his port and said, "It's Warre '63. Don't gulp it. I suggest that you start around eleven o'clock. By that time, Chancery Lane should be deserted except for the occasional policeman. In case you should run into trouble, I'll supply you with a note stating that you are working late with my permission."

"Yes, Uncle, but —"

"When you get into Mr. Huffin's room, take all the files from his cabinets and all the papers from his desk and photograph them. Be very careful to put them back in the order you found them."

"Yes, but —"

"I don't imagine you'll be able to finish the job in one night, or even in two. When you leave, bring the photocopies round to my flat. You can use my spare room and make up for your lost nights by sleeping by day. I'll warn my housekeeper. As far as the office is concerned, you're out of town on a job for me. I think that's all quite straightforward."

"Oh, quite," said Gurney. "The only thing is you haven't told me what you're up to."

"When I've had a chance of examining Mr. Huffin's papers, I may have a clearer idea myself. As soon as I do, I'll put you in the picture."

Andrew sighed. "When do you want me to start?"

"It's Monday today. If you start tomorrow night, you should be through by the end of the week. I suggest you go home now and get a good night's rest."

✠ ✠ ✠

As his uncle had predicted, it took Andrew exactly four nights to finish the job. If he expected something dramatic to happen, he was disappointed. For a week his uncle failed to turn up at the office.

"Our owner," said Mr. Huffin with a smirk, "seems to have lost interest in us."

Andrew smiled and agreed. He had just had an invitation to dinner at his uncle's flat in Albany and guessed that things might be moving.

During dinner, his uncle spoke only of cricket. He was a devotee of the Kent team, most of whom he seemed to know by name. After dinner, which was cooked and served by the housekeeper, they retired to the sitting room. Kavanagh said, "And how did you enjoy your experience as a burglar?"

"It was a bit creepy at first. After nightfall, Chancery Lane seems to be inhabited by howling cats."

"They're not cats. They're the spirits of disappointed litigants."

"Did I produce whatever it was you were looking for?"

"The papers from the cabinets related only to Mr. Huffin's routine work. They showed him to be a thorough, if somewhat unscrupulous operator. A model trufflehound. Ninety-nine percent of his private papers likewise. But the other one percent — two memoranda and a bundle of receipts — were worth all the rest put together. They demonstrated that Mr. Huffin has a second job. He's a moonlighter."

"He's crooked enough for anything. What's his other job? Some sort of blackmail, I suppose."

"Try not to use those words loosely, Andrew. Blackmail has become a portmanteau word covering everything from illegal intimidation to the use of lawful leverage."

"I can't imagine Mr. Huffin intimidating anyone."

"Personally, probably not. But he has a partner. And that man we must now locate. Those scraps of paper are his footprints."

Andrew looked at his uncle. He knew something of the work he had done during the war, but he found it hard to visualise this mild grey-haired man pursuing, in peace, the tactics which had brought Karl Muller and others to the rifle range in the Tower. For the first time, he was striking the flint under the topsoil and it was a curiously disturbing experience. He said, "You promised —"

"Yes, I promised. So be it. Does the name David Rogerson mean anything to you?"

"I know he was one of your friends."

"More than that. During the retreat to Dunkirk, he managed to extract me from a crashed and burning lorry — which was, incidentally, full of explosives. That was when I broke my right leg in several places and contracted this limp which ended my service as an Infanteer. Which was why I went into Intelligence.

"I kept up with David after the war. Not as closely as I should have liked. He had married a particularly stupid woman. However, we met once or twice a year for lunch in the City. We were both busy. I was setting up KLF and he was climbing the ladder in Clarion Insurance.

About six months ago, he asked me to lend him some money — a thousand pounds. Of course I said yes and didn't ask him what he wanted it for. But I suppose he felt he owed me some sort of explanation. When he was leaving he said, with something like a smile, 'Do you play draughts?' I said I did when I was a boy. 'Well,' he said, 'I've been huffed. By Mr. Huffin.' Those were his last words to me. The next news I had was of his death."

Gurney said, "I read about that. No-one seemed to know why he did it."

"You may recall that at the inquest his wife was asked whether he had left a note. She said no. That was a lie. He did leave a note, as I discovered later. David had made me executor. My first job was to look after his wife. I soon saw that Phyllis Rogerson had one objective. To live her own life on the proceeds of some substantial insurance policies David had taken out — and to forget about him. I accepted that this was a natural reaction. Women are realists. It was when I was clearing up his papers that she told me the truth. He *had* left a letter and it was addressed to me. She said, 'I guessed it was something to do with the trouble he'd been having. I knew that if you read it all the unpleasantness would have to come out into the open, so I burnt it. I didn't even read it.' I said, 'If it was some sort of blackmailer, David won't have been his only victim. He must be caught and punished.' She wouldn't listen. I haven't spoken to her since."

"But you located Mr. Huffin?"

"That wasn't difficult. The Huffin clan isn't large. A clergyman in Shropshire, a farmer in Wales, a maiden lady in Northumberland. Little Mr. Huffin of Denny's Detectives was so clearly the first choice that I had no hesitation in trying him first."   ,

"Clearly enough for you to spend your company's money in buying the agency?"

"We were on the lookout for a good credit-rating firm. My Board was unanimous that Denniston was the man for the job. So I was able to kill two birds with one stone — always an agreeable thing to do. My first idea was to expose Huffin as a blackmailer. I felt that there would be enough evidence in his files to convict him. I was wrong. What those papers show is that a second man is involved — possibly the more important villain of the two. I see Huffin as the reconnaissance unit, the other man as the heavy brigade."

"Do you know his name?"

"The only lead I have to him is that Mr. Huffin used to communicate privately with a Mr. Angus. The address he wrote to was a small newsagent's shop in Tufnell Park, an accommodation address, no doubt. Receipts for the payments he made to the shopkeeper were among his papers. I visualise Mr. Angus calling from time to time to collect his letters. Or he may send a messenger. That is something we shall have to find out."

"And you want me to watch the shop?"

"It's kind of you to offer. But no. Here I think we want professional help. Captain Smedley will be the man for the job. You've never heard of him? He's the head of a detective agency." Rather unkindly, Kavanagh added, "A *real* detective agency, Andrew."

⌗ ⌗ ⌗

Captain Smedley said, "I shall need exactly a hundred, in ones and fives. That's what it will cost to buy the man in the shop. I'll pay it to him myself. He won't play silly buggers with me."

Kavanagh looked at Captain Smedley, who had a face like a hank of wire rope, and agreed that no-one was likely to play silly buggers with him.

"I'll have a man outside," Smedley said. "All the shopkeeper's got to do is tip him the wink when the letter's collected. Then my man follows him back to wherever he came from."

"Might it be safer to have two men outside?"

"Safer, but more expensive."

"Expense no object."

"I see," said the Captain. He looked curiously at Mr. Kavanagh, whom he had known for some time. "All right. I'll fix it up for you."

On the Wednesday of the third week following this conversation, Kavanagh got a thick plain envelope addressed to him at his flat. It contained several pages of typescript, which he read carefully. The look on his face was partly enlightenment and partly disgust. "What a game," he said. "I wonder how they work it."

After breakfast, he spent some time in the reference section of the nearest public library browsing among Civil Service lists and copies of *Whittaker's Almanac*. Finally he found the name he wanted. Arnold Robbins. Yes, Arnold would certainly help him if the matter was put to him in the right way. But it would need devilish careful handling. "A jackal," he said, "and a tiger. Now all we need is a tethered goat to bring the tiger under the rifle. But it will have to be tethered very carefully, in exactly the right spot. The brute is a man-eater, no question."

A lady touched him on the shoulder and pointed to the notice which said SILENCE, PLEASE. He was not aware that he had spoken aloud.

✠ ✠ ✠

During the months that followed, Kavanagh resumed his regular visits to the office in Chancery Lane, but Denniston noticed that his interest in the details of the work seemed to be slackening. He would still read the current reports and comment on them, but more of his time seemed to be spent in conversation.

In the old days, Denniston might have objected to this as being a waste of time which could better have been spent in earning profits. Now it was different. He was being paid a handsome salary, and if it pleased the owner of the firm to pass an occasional hour in gossip why should he object? Moreover, Kavanagh was an excellent talker, with a rich fund of experience in the byways of the jungle which lies between Temple Bar and Aldgate Pump. Politics, economics, finance; honesty, dishonesty, and crime. Twenty years of cut-and-thrust between armies whose soldiers wore lounge suits and carried rolled umbrellas — warfare in which victory could be more profitable and defeat more devastating than on any field of battle.

On one occasion, Kavanagh, after what must have been an unusually good luncheon, had devoted an entertaining hour to a dissertation on the tax system.

"At the height of their power and arrogance," he said, "the Church demanded one-tenth of a man's income. The government of England exacts six times as much. The pirate who sank an occasional ship, the highwayman who held up a coach, was a child compared to the modern taxman."

"You can't fight the State," said Denniston.

"It's been tried. Poujade in France. But I agree that massive tax resistance is self-defeating. Each man must fight for himself. There are lawyers and accountants who specialise in finding loopholes in the tax laws, but such success can only be temporary. As soon as a loophole is discovered, the next Finance Act shuts it up. The essentials of guerrilla warfare are concealment and agility."

Really interested now, Denniston said, "Have you discovered a practical method of sidestepping tax? I've never made excessive profits, but I do resent handing over a slab of what I've made to a government who spends most of it on vote-catching projects."

"My method isn't one which would suit everyone. Its merit is simplicity. I arrange with my Board that they will pay me only two-thirds of what I ought to be getting. The other third goes to charities nominated by me. They, of course, pay no tax. That part of it is quite legitimate. Our constitution permits gifts to charity."

"Then how ?"

"The only fact which is *not* known is that I set up and control the charities concerned. One is a local village affair. Another looks after our own employees. A third is for members of my old Regiment. I am chairman, secretary, and treasurer of all three. Some of the money is devoted to the proper objects of the charity. The balance comes back, by various routes, to me. A lovely tax-free increment."

"But," said Denniston, "surely —"

"Yes?"

"It seems too simple."

"But, I assure you, effective."

And later, to himself, Kavanagh asked, I wonder if that was too obvious. I can only wait and see.

✠ ✠ ✠

"There's something stirring," said Captain Smedley. "My men tell me those two beauties have got a regular meeting place. Top of the Duke of York's Steps. It isn't possible to get close enough to hear what they're saying — no doubt that's why they chose it — but they're certainly worked up about something. Licking their lips, you might say."

"The bleating of the goat," said Kavanagh, "excites the tiger."

The letter which arrived at his flat a week later was in a buff envelope, typed on buff paper. It was headed *Inland Revenue Special*

Investigation Branch. It said, "Our attention has been drawn by the Charity Commissioners to certain apparent discrepancies in the latest accounts submitted to them of the under-mentioned charities, all of which have been signed by you as treasurer. It is for this reason that we are making a direct approach to you before any further action is considered. The charities are the Lamperdown Village Hall Trust, the City of London Fusiliers' Trust, and the KLF Employees' Special Fund. You may feel that an interview would clarify the points at issue, in which case the writer would be happy to call on you, either at your place of business or at your residence, as you may prefer."

The writer appeared to be a Mr. Wagner.

Kavanagh observed with appreciation the nicely judged mixture of official suavity and concealed threat. A queen's pawn opening.

Before answering it, he had a telephone call to make. The man he was asking for was evidently important since he had to be approached through a secretary and a personal assistant, with suitable pauses at each stage. When contact had been made, a friendly conversation ensued, conducted on Christian-name terms. It concluded with Ronnie inviting Arnold to lunch at his club on the following Monday.

He then composed a brief letter to Mr. Wagner, suggesting a meeting at his flat at seven o'clock in the evening on the following Wednesday. He apologised for suggesting such a late hour, but daytime commitments made it difficult to fix anything earlier.

"I wonder if it really is a tiger," said Kavanagh, "or only a second jackal. That would be disappointing."

⌘　⌘　⌘

When he opened the door to his visitor, his fears were set at rest. Mr. Wagner was a big man, with a red-brown face. There was tuft of sandy hair growing down each cheekbone. He had the broad, flattened nose of a pugilist. He eyes were so light as to be almost yellow and a deep fold ran down under each eye to form a fence round the corners of an unusually wide mouth. His black coat was glossy, his legs decorously striped. He was a tiger. A smooth and shining tiger.

"Come in," said Kavanagh. "I'm alone this evening. Can I get you a drink?"

"Not just now," said Mr. Wagner.

He seated himself, opened his briefcase, took out a folder of papers and laid it on the table. This was done without a word spoken. The folder was tied with tape. Mr. Wagner's spatulate fingers toyed with the tape and finally untied it. With deliberation, he extracted a number of papers and arranged them in two neat lines. Kavanagh, who had also seated himself, seemed hypnotised by this methodical proceeding.

When everything was to his satisfaction, Mr. Wagner raised his heavy head, fixed his yellow eyes on Kavanagh, and said, "I'm afraid you're in trouble." An echo. Had not Mr. Huffin said the same thing to Fred Denniston?

"Trouble?"

"You're in trouble. You've been cheating."

Kavanagh said, "Oh!" Then, sinking a little in his chair: "You've no right to say a thing like that."

"I've every right to say it, because it's true. I've been studying the accounts of the three charities I mentioned in my letter. In particular, the accounts you submitted last month. They proved interesting indeed." The voice had become a purr. "Previously, your accounts were in such general terms that they might have meant — or concealed — anything. The latest accounts are, fortunately, much fuller and much more specific."

"Well," said Kavanagh, trying out a smile, "the Commissioners did indicate that they wanted rather more detail as to where the money went."

"Yes, Mr. Kavanagh. And where *did* it go?"

"It's —" Kavanagh waved a hand feebly toward the table. "It's all here. In the accounts."

"Then shall we look at them? These are the accounts of the Fusiliers' Trust. Previously the accounts only showed a lump sum, described as 'Grants to disabled Fusiliers and to the widows and dependents of deceased Fusiliers.'"

"Yes. Yes, that's right."

"In the latest accounts you supply a list of their names." The voice deepened even further. The purr became a growl. The tiger was ready to spring. "A very interesting list, because on reference to the Army authorities we have been unable to find any record of any of the people you mentioned as having served with the Fusiliers."

"Possibly —"

"Yes, Mr. Kavanagh?"

"Some mistake —"

"Thirty names. *All* of them fictitious?"

Kavanagh seemed incapable of speech.

"On the other hand, when we look at the KLF Fund we find that the names you have given do correspond to the names of former employees of the firm. But a further question then presents itself. Have these people in fact received the sums shown against their names? Well? Well? Nothing to say? It would be very simple to find out. A letter to each of them —"

This seemed to galvanise Kavanagh into action for the first time. He half rose in his seat and said, "No. I absolutely forbid it."

"But are you in any position to forbid it?"

Kavanagh considered this question carefully, conscious that Mr. Wagner's yellow eyes were watching him. Then he said, "It does seem that there may have been some irregularity in the presentation of these accounts. I cannot attend to all these matters myself, you understand. Income may not always go where it should. There may be some tax which ought to have been paid —"

Mr. Wagner had begun to smile. The opening of his lips displayed a formidable set of teeth.

"I had always understood," went on Kavanagh, "that in these circumstances, if the tax was paid, together with a sum by way of penalties —"

Mr. Wagner's mouth shut with a snap. He said, "Then you misunderstood the position. It is not simply a question of payment. When you sign your tax return, the form is so arranged that if you make a deliberate misstatement you can be charged before the court with perjury."

There was a long silence. Kavanagh was thinking, So this is how he does it. Poor old David. I wonder what slip-ups he made. I'm sure it was unintentional, but a charge of perjury. Goodbye to his prospects with the Clarion. And a lot of other things, too.

He said, in a voice which had become almost a bleat, "You must understand how serious that would be for me, Mr. Wagner. I'd be willing to pay any sum rather than have that happen. Is there no way —" He let the sentence tail off.

Mr. Wagner had taken a silver pencil from his pocket and seemed to be making some calculations. He said, "If, in fact, the sums of money shown as going to the beneficiaries of these three trusts ended up in your own pocket, I would estimate — a rough calculation only — that you have been obtaining at least ten thousand pounds a year free of tax. I am not aware of how long this very convenient arrangement has been going on. Five years? Possibly more? Had you declared this income, you would have paid at least thirty thousand pounds in tax."

"Exactly," said Kavanagh eagerly. "That's the point I was making. Isn't this something that could more easily be solved by a money payment? At the moment I have considerable resources. If a charge of perjury was brought, they would largely disappear. What good would that do anyone?"

Mr. Wagner appeared to consider the matter. Then he smiled. It was a terrible smile. He said, "I have some sympathy with that point of view, Mr. Kavanagh. Allow me to make a suggestion. It is a friendly suggestion and you can always refuse it. At the moment, the file is entirely under my control. The information came from a private source. It is known only to me. You follow me?"

"I think so. Yes."

Mr. Wagner leaned forward and said with great deliberation, "If you will pay me ten thousand pounds, the file will be destroyed."

"Ten thousand pounds?"

"Ten thousand pounds."

"How would the payment be made?"

"You would pay the money into an account in the name of M. Angus at the Westminster Branch of the London and Home Counties Bank."

"That should be enough for you," said Kavanagh. He was addressing the door leading into the next room, which now opened to admit Sir Arnold Robbins, the Deputy Head of Inland Revenue, and two other men.

Robbins said, "You are suspended from duty. These gentlemen are police officers. They will accompany you and will impound your passport.

It will be for the Director of Public Prosecutions to decide on any further action."

Mr. Wagner was on his feet. His face was engorged. A trickle of blood ran from one nostril down his upper lip. He dashed it away with the back of his hand and said, in a voice thick with fury, "So it was a trap!"

"You must blame your accomplice for that," said Kavanagh. "He saw the writing on the wall and sold you to save his own skin. There's not much honour among thieves."

When Wagner had gone, Sir Arnold said, "I apologise for not believing you.   I suppose the fact is that we give these special-investigation people too much rope.   Incidentally, I've had a look at Rogerson's file. It was as you thought. A minor omission, not even his own income. Some money his wife got from Ireland. She may not even have told him about it."

"Probably not," said Kavanagh. He switched off the microphone, which connected with the next room. "We've got all this on tape if you need it."

"Good.   And, by the way, I take it those donations of yours are in order?"

"Perfectly. Every penny that went into these charities has gone to the beneficiaries. I'll show you the receipts. The only thing I fudged was that list of Fusilier names. I'll have to apologise to the Charity Commissioners and send them the correct list."

As Sir Arnold was going, he said, "Why did you tell Wagner it was his accomplice who had shopped him?   Was it true?"

"It was untrue," said Kavanagh. "But I thought it might have some interesting results. It's going to be very difficult to get at Mr. Huffin. He really was only the jackal. He picked up scraps of information when he was doing his job and fed them to Wagner, who moved in for the kill. Wagner will be at liberty until the Director makes up his mind. I felt we should give him a chance to ask Mr. Huffin for an explanation."

⌘   ⌘   ⌘

"He didn't say anything," said Captain Smedley. "He just hit him. Huffin's not a big man. It lifted him off his feet and sent him backward down the steps. Cracked his skull. Dead before he got to hospital."

"And Mr. Wagner?"

"I had a policeman standing by, like you suggested. I thought he was going to put up a fight, but he seemed dazed. When they got him to the station, he just keeled over."

"You don't mean he's dead, too?"

"No. But near enough. And if he does recover from whatever it is — a stroke of kinds — he's in every sort of trouble. A good riddance to a nasty pair."

But that was not their real epitaph. That had been spoken by Colonel Hubert on the evening of April 15th in the year 1944.

JUDITH

Two hundred years ago Belling was an island. A hundred years later, with the draining of the fens, it had turned into a prosperous farming community. Fifty years after that, as its nearest neighbour, Woodhall Cross, developed into an industrial complex it became something between a large village and a small town. It had always had a church and a school. When the census showed that the number of its inhabitants had topped two thousand its upward progress was crowned by the award of its own police station.

Through all these changes and developments it had remained, as PC Hennessy often told the rector, a village at heart. "And thank the Lord," he would add, "a quiet village. A little noisy, perhaps, at the Annual Feast, but no-one minds a bit of horseplay once a year."

A Monday in early December was to change all that.

Mrs. Franklund lived in one of the three cottages in Binders Lane, on the northern fringe of the village. She had lost her husband shortly after the birth of her only child, Ellen. Ellie was a fair-haired mite, eleven years old, but looking much younger. She had attended the village school since she was six and had now been promised a place at Woodhall Grammar School. To take it up she had to pass a fairly stiff entrance exam. To make sure that she did so Miss Hooker, headmistress of the village school, had offered to give her an hour's extra tuition on Mondays and Thursdays. This would take place after the younger children had left the school, at half-past three.

Mrs. Franklund was grateful, but one thing worried her. As the year ran on towards Christmas, by half-past four dusk was going to be setting in. True, the distance between the school and her house was not much more than a quarter of a mile; up East Street, along the flank of Abbacy Copse, turn right at the top into Binders Lane and there you were. But alone! And in the dusk, with a mist coming up as it did so often from the fenland which encircled the village to the north. Ellie was the whole of her mother's life. Unthinkable to take chances with her.

In spite of a rheumatic hip which made walking difficult Mrs. Franklund would willingly have hobbled down to the school and brought Ellie home herself. Happily, an alternative had presented itself. Miss Hooker had extended her offer of extra tuition to Martin Amherst, eldest son of the rector. He was a stalwart boy of twelve. For a small addition to his weekly pocket money he had agreed to escort Ellie to her front door.

On this particular evening he carried out three quarters of his duty. The lane along the left side of Abbacy Copse curved slightly, but by standing on the verge of the roadway he could see Ellie almost up to the corner. When she was perhaps twenty yards from it he turned and ran. He was late for a most important date with Tim Pollard, who had acquired a video-taper which he proposed to use on the BBC programme which started at 4.30. It was now 4.35.

When Ellie was not home by twenty to five her mother comforted herself by remembering that, more than once, Miss Hooker had kept her back to finish a piece of work. But never for more than a quarter of an hour. By five o'clock that wisp of comfort had faded. She telephoned the school, but got no answer. There was just one more possibility. Might Ellie have gone back with Martin to the rectory? It had happened once before. She tried the rectory, but got no reply there either. The rector and his wife were out and Martin had gone straight to Tim Pollard's house.

Not knowing what to do, she did what most people in Belling seemed to do when in distress. She hobbled along to the cottage on her left where she found Judith Lyte in the kitchen, playing Animal Snap with her two younger children, Sarah and Jenny. Tea was waiting for the return of the older two, Becky and Mark. They were at Woodhall Grammar and had not yet got home.

As soon as she understood what the distraught Mrs. Franklund was trying to tell her, Judith rang the police station.

PC Hennessy was a great admirer of Mrs. Lyte. She was not only chairman of the Parish Council and one of the acknowledged leaders of the community, but was something else — something difficult to describe. He listened carefully to what she had to say, switched his telephone to 'answer', shouted to his wife to mind the front desk and set out into the thickening mist.

When he reached Binders Lane he found that Mrs. Lyte had telephoned the post office, as the quickest way of spreading the news, and a small search party was already on hand. The news had even penetrated the Pollard house and a white-face Martin had told them where he had seen Ellie last. He said, over and over again, "At the corner. She'd almost turned the corner," as though speaking the words somehow exculpated him.

Abbacy Copse was clearly the first place to search. It produced no sign of Ellie. On the other side of the copse and filling the space between it and the end of Binders Lane was an odd patch of waste land known as the Rectory Piece. It was part of the old glebe and the rector's predecessor had allowed half a dozen structures to be put up on it, the rents of which helped out his slender stipend. Two of them were solid, breeze block affairs, one used by Newton, the clearance contractor, to park his heavy machinery; the other by the rector himself for the storage of church furniture and oddments. The other four were smaller and were built of tarred timber. Since they were all securely padlocked they were, for the moment, ignored.

With the arrival of the bus bringing back children from the Grammar School and cars with men returning from their work, the search party grew and set out on what seemed to be a hopeless search of the fen. It was quite dark now and the mist was thicker than ever. After an hour had produced only frustration and falls into the dykes which criss-crossed the fields, the rector, in consultation with Ted Willows, called a halt. Ted was an expert on fen weather. "Like as not," he said, "we'll have a breeze by early morning. And the moon will be up."

The searchers retired for repairs and refreshment to the Bull, which was the unofficial centre of Belling. By one o'clock Ted had been proved a true prophet and it was under a cold moon, three hours later that the bedraggled body of Ellen Franklund was lifted from a dyke, four hundred yards north of the village. Her dress had been pulled off and then knotted round her neck. Her face was a mass of blood and bruises.

Hennessy then did what he should have done many hours earlier. He sent for help.

It arrived at half-past six in two cars. The first one contained Detective Inspector Waite and the County Pathologist. The second, Detective Sergeant Copsey and the Coroner's Officer. Waite was a smallish man, with the eyes and teeth of a fox terrier. He said, "I want all the men in the village — and when I say men I include boys of twelve or more —" As he said this he looked at Copsey, who nodded. He had just concluded a case in which three boys had raped a schoolgirl. "Get them together in whatever's the most convenient place."

"The church," said Judith and the rector nodded. "We could get five hundred in there, standing."

Very few people in the village had gone to bed and whilst the few men who had were being roused, Waite and the pathologist examined the child's body and paid a visit to Abbacy Copse.

At seven o'clock the Inspector climbed on to the step beside the pulpit and addressed the crowd which filled the aisles and transepts and had spread into the choir and sanctuary. He said, "Yesterday evening, at twenty-five minutes to five, somebody took Ellen Franklund into the wood up there —" He gestured over his shoulder and heard the murmur, "Abbacy Copse." "Is that what you call it? Well, that's where he took her. She may even have gone willingly. We think she probably knew the man." Heads turned and people started to look at each other as the significance of this sank in. "When he had her safely in the wood, I expect he terrified her by telling her what he'd do if she made a sound. Then he ripped off her dress, pushed her down on to the ground and got on top of her. When he had had whatever satisfaction he could get from her small body he got up, seized her by the ankles and swung her head, two or three times, against the trunk of a tree."

When he stopped speaking the silence was absolute. It was a silence of shock and held breath. Then he said, "We *know* that this is what happened. We have seen the blood and flesh on the tree and there are shreds of bark on the child's forehead. Now you know as much as we know. The rest will have to come from you. I and my sergeant will be questioning you. More than once perhaps. We shall go on until we have the truth." He added, in a more conversational tone, "I know that many of you work outside the village. Before you leave, give your names and a note of your destinations to my sergeant."

Probably only Judith Lyte really understood what the Inspector was doing. That he had painted the picture of Ellen's death in the coldest and most brutal words possible, in order to secure the co-operation of everyone who heard him. It had to be the whole-hearted sort of co-operation that would hold steady during the days — maybe the weeks — of questioning that were to come.

Most of the Inspector's attention on the first day centred on the six buildings on Rectory Piece. He did not suspect that they had played an immediate part in the crime. He had another reason which, for the moment, he kept to himself. The huts were subjected to minute examination. The team, which now included a forensic scientist, started at the south-east corner with the one used by Mr. Greenslade as a bicycle repair shop. North of that was the hut of Mr. Pollard, a photo-maniac. It housed an elaborate enlarger and other expensive photographic apparatus. The one above that was empty. Beyond that, the hut used by Mr. Coleman, an estate agent with a hobby of making mechanical toys. Next to it were two more elaborate structures; the depot where George Newton kept his heavy machinery and the rector's private store, where Sergeant Copsey spent a baffling hour inspecting presentation vases, broken monuments and three versions of the Christmas crib.

Binders Lane had to be acquitted. The three cottages in it belonged to Mrs. Franklund, Judith Lyte and old Mrs. Ambrose, who was deaf and bedridden. The far end of the lane was more promising. Fronting the road up which Ellen had walked to her death were the back gardens of four houses. The Inspector had good reasons for concentrating on them. He argued that a man coming from any of the houses behind them would have to pass many windows before reaching the copse, while a man coming from one of them had only to slip quietly down his own back garden and cross the road.

Further investigation had narrowed the possibilities.

The house owners, starting from the north end, were Mr. Marcus, Mr. Harris, the Misses Farrant and Mr. Vosper. Mr. Marcus had been in bed with pleurisy, with either his wife or his daughter Angela in attendance. Mr. Harris worked in Woodhall Cross and was vouched for by his secretary and others. Mr. Vosper had been at home all afternoon, allegedly writing letters. No-one had seen him until he joined in the search.

At the end of seven days of exhaustive and exhausting work the Inspector reported his conclusions to the Chief Constable. He said, "Having the advantage of knowing when and where this crime was committed, we've been able to acquit the great majority of the village, either by their own testimony or the testimony of their friends and neighbours. They were not my prime suspects. I was merely, as you might say, clearing the undergrowth. Nor was I looking for outsiders. There are only two bridges over the Skirm Dyke and a stranger would have been noticed at once. So I was able to concentrate on this proposition. That the crime must have been committed by someone who knew exactly what Ellen's programme was. Someone who had watched her walking back and had calculated that if her escort took his eyes off her he would have a chance. Therefore it must either be someone with a sound reason for hanging around Binders Lane — which means one of the owners of the huts in it — or someone whose house overlooks it."

The Chief Constable nodded his agreement.

"Taking the house owners first, we've been able to eliminate three of them." He explained the steps he had taken.

The Chief Constable said, "So Vosper seems the most likely."

"He heads my list. Then there are the hut owners. George Newton and the rector have got rock-solid alibis. But I can't eliminate any of the other three. Pollard, Greenslade and Coleman. They're all self-employed and being their own bosses they can slip out of their offices as soon as their day's work's over and get on with what really interests them — model cars or the like. In fact, Greenslade and Coleman admit that's just what they did. Pollard says he spent some time out in the fen looking for a hide for his bird photography."

"Pollard?" said the Chief Constable thoughtfully. "Wasn't it his son who lured young Martin away from his job as escort?"

"He's number two on my list."

"Vosper, Pollard, Greenslade, Coleman. It's not a long list, but it's still three too many."

"I agree," said the Inspector. "And that's where we come to the real difficulty. If there'd been one suspect, we could have justified asking for a warrant, gone through his house and his clothing and maybe picked up the clues we wanted. No chance of that now. Vosper, Greenslade and Coleman are bachelors. Pollard's a widower. Like most of the houses in the village they have wood-burning stoves. By now they could have destroyed every atom of the clothing they were wearing that evening."

"So you're stuck?"

"For the moment, yes."

"You realise that if he gets away with it he'll probably do it again."

"Next time," said the Inspector, "they may call us in at once. Before they've trampled over every helpful mark on the ground."

Constable Hennessy, who was in the Inspector's confidence, was able to report the gist of this to the only person in the village he felt able to confide in. Judith Lyte listened in silence. Then she said, "If the professionals are giving up, the amateurs must take a hand."

That evening she mustered her private army. It consisted of her four children: Rebecca, fifteen; Mark, thirteen; Sarah, eleven and Jennifer, nine. They showed no open surprise at what she said to them, although her idea was startling.

So far the search had proceeded along the upper level, the level inhabited by responsible adults, all willing to help, most of them speaking the truth. Now Judith had resolved to explore the lower level, the underworld where children lived and moved.

From studying her own family and their wide circle of friends she had concluded that the eyes and ears of children formed an astonishing information service which would tell you all you wanted to know, if you were patient, and if you could read its code.

It was not an easy code. Children had their private customs and taboos. They lied consistently and successfully. They talked sense and nonsense mixed. This was the network she was asking her children to tune into.

She said, "I'm convinced that some child knows something. Maybe they don't appreciate the significance of it. Maybe they're frightened to speak. I'm particularly interested in the girls. Girls talk to each other."

"Non-stop," said Mark.

"Boys are just as bad," said Rebecca.

They both attended Woodhall Grammar School. The two younger

ones were still at the village primary school. Thus she had spies in both camps and found, at the conferences which took place each evening, that she was being presented slowly with a conspectus of both schools; the loyalties and treacheries, the feuds and alliances, the double-cross and the treble-cross. A pattern as intricate as in any medieval Italian city.

"Look for abnormalities," she said. "Time's running out. We must do this before the end of term."

It was on the fifth evening, among a host of other trivialities, that Mark said, "If you want abnormalities, here's one for you. Billy Sherwood came to school today with a lovely black eye — a real shiner."

"Nothing unusual about that," said little Jennifer virtuously. "Boys are always fighting."

"What was unusual about it was that it was his older brother, Roger, who hit him. Normally they're pretty good friends. This time Roger lost his temper because Billy was teasing him about losing his girlfriend."

"Girlfriend?" said Judith. "For goodness' sake, isn't he a bit young for that sort of thing?"

The look on her family's faces showed Judith that she had committed the serious crime of being square.

"Most of the boys have girlfriends," said Mark. "What really upset him was that his steady had dropped him *for another girl*. She'd stolen her from her regular pash."

To re-establish her position Judith said, "You don't have to explain about pashes. After all, I was six years at boarding school."

"I think it's a bit more organised now than it was in your day," said Rebecca kindly. "All older girls are supposed to have one or two young adorers. They're called strings."

"I suppose you've got half a dozen," said Mark. "Did you know that she was the most popular girl in the school?"

"Pipe down," said his mother. "I want to understand this. Let's have it again, with names."

"Well, there was this girl Lucilla. She had two regular strings. Angela and Vicky. Vicky's a bit of a smasher herself, so she thought the time had come to stop being a string and pick up a couple of adorers. And the first one she collected was Patricia who had been Roger's steady. OK?"

"Say it all again slowly," said Judith. And when he had done this, "So Lucilla's left with only one string, Angela. Bad luck, no doubt, but —"

"It was worse than that, because Angela suddenly went right off her, too. In fact, she seemed to go right off everything."

"Meaning what?"

"Went broody. Seemed frightened to open her mouth."

"Has she got a surname?"

"Her name's Marcus."

"The girl who was looking after her father with pleurisy?"

"That's the one. She was allowed two afternoons off a week so that her mother could get out and do the shopping."

Judith felt like an angler who has fished long and patiently and sees the float disappear and feels the line grow taut. Too soon to be sure what it would lead to, but the catch was there. No doubt of it.

She said, "You've got just the one job now, Becky. Sack all your existing adorers and fasten Angela Marcus to you with hoops of steel."

"I'm not sure —"

"If you're as popular as Mark says, I'm sure you'll be able to do it. I suppose there's an accepted technique —"

"What you do is, you smile at her during morning prayers. If she doesn't look away, you get hold of her afterwards and ask her what her favourite hymn is — they've all got favourite hymns — and you go off to Miss Norton, who plays the piano, and ask if you can have it next morning. She's a decent sort and usually says 'yes'."

"And then?"

"When the hymn's being sung you smile again. If she smiles back, she's hooked."

"Can you do it?"

Rebecca giggled. "It'll be a bit of a rush job."

Two days later she reported that the first step had been taken.

"The hymn she chose did it. Lead, kindly light, amid the encircling gloom. Now I'm the light and she's the gloom. And then some! Yesterday behind the pavilion she told me her life story."

"But she didn't tell you what had upset her."

"No. But I'm sure she's going to. She's longing to tell someone."

That was on the Wednesday. On the Friday when Becky came home her mother saw that her face was white and that she looked as if she had been sick, or was going to be. She took her into the kitchen and bolted the door. Then she said, "Let's have it, love."

"It was horrible. If I'd had any idea what it was going to be, I couldn't have gone on with it. Before she'd tell me, she made me swear not to tell anyone. Then she agreed I could tell you, if you swore the same thing."

Her mother thought about this for some time whilst the other children, realising that something serious had happened, stopped trying to break down the kitchen door. Then she said, "Very well. You have my word."

"That evening, you know — when it happened — she'd left her father's bedroom to fetch something from the kitchen at the back of the house. She saw Ellie coming up the road and she saw Mr. Coleman step out, say something to her, and lead her by the hand, back into the wood."

"And said nothing about it to anyone."

"She couldn't. Her father works for Mr. Coleman and owes him money. If the police tried to get the story out of her, she'd deny it. I'm sure of that."

"All right," said her mother. "Now you can forget all about it."

"But what are you going to do?"

"I'm going to think about it."

✠ ✠ ✠

For three weeks she did nothing, except think. And her thoughts were confused and uncomfortable.

If she passed on Angela's story to the police, they would question her, and she would deny it. Would probably say that she'd made it all up. If she kept quiet, Coleman would have got away with his filthy crime. More, when a suitable interval had elapsed, as the desire built up, and the secret itch became intolerable, he would try again. Who would be the next — little Ellie?

As an estate agent he had every excuse for touring the countryside in his car, finding empty houses he could use. In the end a child would be dragged into one of them. On this occasion he would have more time to enjoy himself. Thinking about all of this she came to a conclusion.

Traditionally her two eldest went for the last week of the Christmas holidays to stay with her elder sister and sample the mild dissipations of the county town. On the night after they left, with the two younger ones safely in their beds, she was able to make the first move.

She went out just after midnight. On her way to Coleman's workshop hut she had only two cottages to pass and no observation to fear from either. Mrs. Franklund's was empty — the rector's wife had taken her under her wing and she slept at the rectory. Old Mrs. Ambrose's was as tightly shut as the eyes and ears of its occupant. The moon escaped the clouds from time to time and glinted on the trowel she held in her hand.

The door and tiny barred window of Coleman's hut were both in the front wall. The rear wall had no openings in it and weeds and undergrowth were encroaching on its base. She used her gloved hand to pull it away and scooped out the earth underneath. Six inches down she struck the concrete base of the hut.

After half an hour of careful work she had formed a sharp-sided trench, running the length of the wall. This she covered by allowing the weeds and undergrowth to fall back over it.

There was one other thing to do before she left. She went round to the front of the hut to examine the door. Its fastening was a metal flange that fitted over a staple and was held there by a padlock. She had brought with her a wooden peg and this she whittled down with a knife until she estimated it would fit snugly into the staple when the padlock was removed.

After that she went back to bed.

She had studied Coleman's movements. He left his office as late as six o'clock if he was busy, as early as four o'clock if things were slack and usually made his way straight up to the hut. As a bachelor he had little else to occupy him in the evenings. He was never away before eight and sometimes stayed there until ten o'clock. She would see his light go on and hear the clatter of his metal cutter.

Now she had to wait on the weather.

On the third night the wind got up, gusting from the south-west. She packed her shopping bag and set off to destroy Mr. Coleman.

First she re-fastened the metal flange, driving her wooden peg firmly into the staple. Then she arranged six paraffin-based fire-lighters end to end along the trench she had dug and put a match to them. When she was sure they were well alight she started back towards her house.

Already she could hear the crackling as the flames, driven by the wind, caught hold of the tarred wood of the wall. She saw the door shaking as though someone was trying, desperately, to open it.

The fire was building up now. Standing ten yards away she could feel the heat of it on her cheeks. At one moment she thought she saw hands clinging to the bars of the little window.

By that time the flames had reached the roof.

✠ ✠ ✠

Hennessy said, "When the fire people could get into what was left of the hut they said they could smell paraffin. According to Greenslade, Coleman had a paraffin stove and kept a small reserve of the stuff. He'd once borrowed some from him for his own stove."

"And you think," said Inspector Waite, "that he may have upset the stove and panicked when he couldn't get the door open. Why couldn't he?"

"I can only think the latch may have jammed. There was nothing left of the door to go by, but they did find the padlock inside the hut."

"And that's your idea of what happened?"

Hennessy took some time thinking out his answer to this. Then he said, "I can tell you one thing. It's not what the village think."

"And what do they think?"

"You must bear in mind, sir, that this is rather a primitive place. They think that what happened proves beyond question that Coleman was the murderer and that he's been punished for his crime."

"Punished by whom?"

"In their eyes, it was fire from heaven that destroyed him."

"And is that unanimous?"

"I'd say so, yes."

Hennessy was nearly right, but not quite.

The rector had been the first on the scene of the fire. Although it was clearly too late to do anything effective he had rushed down to Judith Lyte's house to use her telephone. He had met Judith coming out of her front door. The fire was now so strong that its flames lit up her face.

He said, "If poor Coleman was trapped inside, I'm afraid it's too late to save him."

"Much too late," said Judith.

It was not only the tone of her voice. It was the look on her face that troubled him. Calm, composed, triumphant. He had seen that look before. But where?

It was three years later that he found it, in the Louvre, in the painting by Raphael, of Judith leaving the tent of the tyrant Holofernes, carrying his head in a bag. She had that same look of remorseless triumph on her face.

VERDICT OF THREE

On that Wednesday morning, when the messenger from the Home Office arrived at my flat, I was reading the account splashed across the front page of *The Daily Telegraph* of my Uncle Alfred's suicide. It seemed that he had taken poison, at his house in Chessington Street. His body had been found by his sister.

I can't say that his departure caused me any sorrow. The fact that he was my relation had been a source of embarrassment to me from my school days onward. Alfred Laming was a man who delighted in taking the unpopular side in any public controversy and sometimes compounded his offence by being right. In 1939 he had declared himself a virulent supporter of Stalin and had been interned under Regulation 18B — until the arrival of the Russians in the war on our side had caused him to be released with apologies. After that he had enjoyed innumerable brushes with the authorities. The week before he killed himself, he had penned an open letter to the Home Secretary accusing him of systematic and malicious persecution. The details he gave sounded convincing, too.

I signed a receipt for the buff-coloured envelope and waited until the messenger had taken himself off before I opened it. I had a premonition of what it would contain. It was a three-line communication. It required me to present myself at No. 5 Richmond Terrace at eleven o'clock that morning and it was signed by the Secretary to the Cabinet Office.

It crystallised all my recent suspicions and apprehensions.

You cannot work in the innermost circles of government without sensing when something has gone wrong, particularly when that something may affect you.

I reasoned that it must be connected with the American note, because the American note was the most important piece of work which had ever been entrusted to me. It was only by chance that it had come my way at all.

The Prime Minister of that period had four Private Secretaries. (Nowadays he has six, but these are more spacious times.) We divided the work between us. The senior dealt with patronage and appointments. The next senior, Tom Rainey, with Foreign affairs. The two newest, myself and Bill Anstruther, with Home affairs. In the ordinary way, the drafting of a note from the Prime Minister to the British Ambassador in Washington, a note which was to form the basis of discussions between the Ambassador and the President of the United States, would have been Tom's job, had he not been shipped off to the hospital at the last moment with an inflamed appendix.

So the lot had fallen to me. I had taken the lift down to Registry Filing, had signed for the three green folders which were to form the basis of the note, and had taken them up, in the lift, to my room on the second floor of the Cabinet office building in Whitehall. I was by then no novice in the inner workings of government, but I must confess that those folders had opened my eyes.

They were verbatim accounts, taken down in the well-known handwriting of the Chief, of conversations earlier that year which he had held with the Prime Ministers of Canada, Australia, and New Zealand, whose presence in London had been carefully, and successfully, concealed. In them the steps to be taken, in certain circumstances, had been set out with brutal clarity.

When top people talk directly to each other, they do so without any of the euphemisms and half-truths which soften their public utterances. (I recalled some of the unpublished and unpublishable comments made by Churchill to Roosevelt at critical moments during the war.) I could well imagine the worldwide effect if a single one of the unvarnished sentences in those folders had been allowed to get into the wrong hands.

If I had needed any further reminder of their importance I had received it when, leaving my office for a quick lunch, I caught a glimpse of Patrick Regan at the end of the corridor. I'm not sure if he saw me, but I knew what his presence there signified. Patrick is a month or two older than me. I first met him when we arrived at our prep school at Broadstairs on the same day. He preceded me to our public school by a single term. During the war I lost touch with him. I was a plodding infantryman. He was in a number of irregular and dashing outfits suited to his Irish temperament. After the war, as I knew, he had joined MI5 and I didn't doubt that it was part of his job to patrol the corridors and make sure that no unauthorised eyes saw those three green folders.

Since it was a fine morning in late autumn and since there was plenty of time, I decided to walk from my flat, which is near Lords, to Whitehall. Before I left, I packed a few things into a suitcase. When you went into No. 5 Richmond Terrace it was not always certain that you would come out again. It has an underground exit which leads straight to Cannon Row Police Station.

As I walked down Baker Street and through the maze of little lanes behind Oxford Street, I was being followed — by a memory ...

✠ ✠ ✠

The School House fag was a cheerful shrimp of my own age called Edgecumb. Curious that I could remember his name and face when so many, more important, have been rubbed out by the passage of time.

"Ashford wants you in his study," he said. "I shouldn't hang about. He's in a frightful bait about something."

I sped along those stone-paved passages until I reached and knocked on the door of the large study at the end. Even now I sometimes see that door in my dreams.

A hoarse roar told me to come in.

A table had been pulled out from the wall and my three judges sat behind it. It was a hanging court. Ashford, in the middle, was head of the House. Captain of rugger, red in hair and temper. On his right a tall boy, called Major, a cross-country runner and one of the school racquets pair. The third was something of an unknown quantity, a boy called Collins who wore tortoiseshell glasses and was reputed to have a brain. He might, I felt, be inclined to take a more tolerant view of whatever crime I was supposed to have committed, but I hardly saw him standing up to the other two.

"I've been hearing stories about you," said Ashford. "You seem to think you can get away with anything. You may have been a big bug at your prep school, but in this place you're a worm."

To this evident truth no comment seemed possible and I made none.

"You were reported last week for cheek to head of the prep-room."

The head of the prep-room, a fat boy called Clover, had slipped on a cake of soap in the bathroom and fallen on his fat backside. I had been rash enough to laugh.

Result, six whacks with a gym shoe.

"I ought to have dealt with you myself that time. Then you might have thought twice about — this."

Ashford slapped down on the table in front of me a piece of paper on which was printed, in block capitals, the words: CLOVER IS A FAT ASS.

"But," I said, "I know nothing about that. Me? I never saw it before."

"Then how is it that Blackie saw you at nine o'clock last night putting something up on the house notice board?"

✠   ✠   ✠

"I should watch where you're going sir," said the policeman. "If you step off the kerb like that, without looking first, you'll be in trouble."

"Sorry, officer, " I said, "I was thinking about something else."

"Lucky he had good brakes —"

✠   ✠   ✠

Collins said, in his dreamy voice, "Blackie didn't actually say that. He said he saw him in front of the notice board."

Blackie was the youth who cleaned our boots.

Ashford glared at Collins and then swung around on me again.

"And anyway, what were you doing out of your dormitory at nine o'clock? You know the house rules."

"Barnes, the head of the dormitory, sent me down to get something for him. It was just before nine o'clock. He said if I hurried I'd be back in time. The clock was striking as I went down the stairs."

Major said reluctantly, "I did have a word with Barnes. He confirmed that bit."

"All right," said Ashford. "Barnes confirms that you went down, and Blackie confirms that you were hanging about in front of the notice board. What were you doing?"

"I did stop for a moment. I wanted to see if I was in the under-fifteen game."

"I think you're a liar. You had it in for Clover and you thought you'd get your own back in this — in this disgusting way."

"Isn't that man Alfred Laming your uncle?" said Major. "The man who wrote that letter to *The Times*. He sounds a bolshy sort of sod."

I admitted that Sir Alfred Laming was my uncle. I had read the letter, too. It was the one in which he said that Baldwin ought to be impeached for neglecting our air defences — a view which found quite a few supporters six years later.

"All right," said Ashford. This seemed to conclude the case for the prosecution. All that remained was to pass sentence. Major nodded.

Collins had taken off his glasses and was polishing them gently. He said, "By the way, when you looked at the notice board, was this paper on it?"

Imminent danger must have tuned up my mental processes to concert pitch, because I saw all the implications of that question as soon as it was asked. If I said "Yes," then why hadn't I reported it to someone in authority? If I said "No," then since all other junior boys were safe in their dormitories by nine, it left me as the last and most likely culprit.

In desperation I decided to tell the truth.

I said, "I'm sorry, Collins, but I simply can't remember. All I was looking at was the games list."

There was a moment of grim silence. Collins seemed to have lost interest. Ashford said, "You can wait outside."

In the corridor I found Patrick. His Irish blood made him a volatile boy, easily roused to extremes of passion and sentiment. He grabbed me by the arm and said, "Are they going to beat you?"

I croaked, "I don't know." We were both close to the door and had to talk in whispers.

"If they try to do it, you've got to appeal to old Flathers."

Flathers was Mr. Flatstone, our Housemaster.

"I can't do that," I said, aghast.

"You must. It would be totally unfair. They haven't got an iota of proof it was you."

"Hold it," I said.

I was listening unashamedly at the door. What I was afraid I was going to hear was the scrape of two chairs being put together, back to back. It would be my lot to kneel on one and hang my head down on the other.

Instead, I heard Ashford's voice. He said, "I don't quite see the point of it."

"It was a test question," said Collins. "The easiest thing would have been for him to have said that it *was* there and he saw it."

Major said, and there was unexpected deference in his voice, "I still don't see. How do you know he didn't see it?"

"He can't have," said Collins. "I took it down myself, at five to nine."

"Then why on earth," said Ashford, "didn't you say so before?"

"I was interested to see if he was going to tell a lie," said Collins. He sounded amused. "He jolly nearly did, too. But people usually tell the truth under pressure."

"I think it's going to be all right," I said to Patrick ...

✠ ✠ ✠

The Commissionaire at No. 5 greeted me with such a sombre look that I felt that he, at all events, had already found me guilty. He escorted me up in the lift and led me along to the room at the end of the corridor. I felt his hand metaphorically on my collar.

He knocked at the door and held it open. There were two men in the room. One was Lord Cherryl, the man who had headed the Inquiry into the Security Services. The other was Mr. Justice Rackham — a most appropriate name, as more than one journalist had pointed out, since he seemed to conduct his cases in a manner reminiscent of the Star Chamber.

Lord Cherryl said, "Please sit down. You must understand that this is an unofficial and preliminary inquiry. We have been asked by the Home Secretary to put some questions to you. No record will be kept of what is said. Nevertheless, although it is unofficial and off the record, you have the right to be represented by a lawyer of your own choosing, if you wish."

"I think I'd better find out what it is I'm being accused of first," I said. "That is, if I am being accused of something."

"It's your decision," said Lord Cherryl. There was a long moment of silence. I didn't say anything. Lord Cherryl turned to the papers in front of him.

"I'd like to clear up one or two preliminary matters first. When you left school in 1937 you went to Oxford, with an Open Scholarship at Balliol. You were there for two years and left in 1939, without taking a degree, to join the Royal West Kent Regiment." I nodded. "Whilst you were at Oxford you were a member of a group called the Barricade Club — a club which professed extreme left-wing views."

"They didn't only profess them," I said. "A number of our members fought in the Spanish Civil War. On the unpopular side."

"But since you joined the Armed Forces with such commendable promptitude in 1939 — at a time when Soviet Russia was our official enemy — it would seem that your feelings had altered."

"One tends to be volatile at the age of twenty."

"Of course. You fought throughout the war as an infantry soldier, attained the rank of Major, were wounded in the North African fighting and were mentioned in dispatches."

I had no quarrel with any of that.

"After the war you were called to the Bar, Gray's Inn, and joined Maurice Pastor's Chambers."

"As a pupil," I said, "I never actually achieved a tenancy."

Mr. Justice Rackham said, "That was the Maurice Pastor who was disbarred for sedition in 1950?"

I nearly said, "You know bloody well it was. You were Chairman of the Bar Council at the time and chiefly responsible for getting him chucked out." However, I still had myself in hand and simply said, "Yes."

"You gave up the Bar in 1950 and joined the Home Office under the special arrangements then in force for ex-servicemen. You were given accelerated promotion through the Principal grade and in 1952 were an Assistant Secretary in the Department of Establishment and Organisation."

"Officially, I still am," I said. "My next step was a posting, not a promotion."

"I was coming to that," said Lord Cherryl smoothly. "Two years ago you were offered, and accepted, the post of Private Secretary to the Prime Minister."

"Did it ever occur to you to wonder," said Mr. Justice Rackham, in his gravelly voice, "why you were selected for such a position?"

"Frequently," I said. "The only solution which occurred to me was that the PM himself had fought as an infantry soldier through the First World War."

This was an unkind side-swipe at Rackham, who was quite young enough to have served in 1939, but had preferred his career at the Bar. I wasn't feeling kind.   I thought this dissection of my early life impertinent and wished they would come to the point.

Lord Cherryl did so, with unexpected suddenness. He said, "Your duties would not normally have covered foreign affairs. It was only owing to the chance indisposition of Mr. Rainey, I believe, that you were charged with drafting a note for the PM to Sir Neville Stokes in Washington?"

Here it came.

"That's correct," I said.

"And in order to draft this note you were given access to three folders of documents of the highest security classification."

"I had them in my room for one complete working day," I said.

"And were they ever out of your sight?"

"Only when I went down to lunch in the canteen. When I locked them in my filing cabinet. I also locked the door of my room."

"Then you will no doubt be surprised," said Mr. Justice Rackham, "when you learn that photocopies of the documents in all three folders were in the possession of your uncle, Sir Alfred Laming, twenty-four hours later."

"But —" I said.

"Just to keep the record straight," said a third voice, "Sir Alfred isn't actually your uncle, is he?"

He had come into the room so quietly, and I had been so intent on what was being said, that he might have been there for some minutes without my noticing him.

I had seen him on one occasion only since I left school, but I recognised him at once.   The same tortoiseshell glasses, the same downward-turning mouth.   Time had taken away some of his hair and had put a stamp of authority on to his face, but it was the same stooped shoulders and unathletic figure.

"I called him my uncle," I said. "He was really only my mother's cousin."

Lord Cherryl did not seem too happy about this interruption but was clearly in no position to resent it. Collins pulled up a chair and added himself to the tribunal. He had a folder of papers which he put down as carefully on the table as if they had been new-laid eggs. He said, "Please don't recap for me. I'm fully in the picture."

"Then," said Lord Cherryl, "perhaps you would deal with Mr. Justice Rackham's question."

The interruption had given me time to get back some part of my wits.

"If I remember it correctly," I said, "he asked me if I was surprised to know that copies of these documents had found their way into the hands of my uncle. It would be an understatement. I am not surprised. I am flabbergasted."

"You can offer no explanation?"

"Before I say anything more, I should like to know exactly what happened to my uncle."

Lord Cheryl looked at Collins, who gave a very slight nod. I knew then that Collins was really conducting the interview.

"Home Security have had Sir Alfred under observation for some time. Yesterday morning he made an arrangement, on the telephone, to meet a man in the afternoon in Kensington Gardens."

"What man?"

Lord Cherryl didn't like being interrupted and he didn't like being asked questions, but after another glance at Collins he condescended to deal with this one. He said, "He is — or was, until that moment — the Third Secretary for Economic Planning at the Russian Embassy. As a result of what happened his credentials have been withdrawn."

Collins said, with a very slight smile, "He returned to Moscow by air yesterday evening. I don't imagine we shall see him again. I beg your pardon, Lord Cherryl, I interrupted you."

"As I was saying, Sir Alfred kept this rendezvous. He was in the act of handing over a packet when he was apprehended and taken into custody. He must have been prepared for such a contingency. He swallowed a cyanide capsule when he was in the car on the way to the police station."

"The report in the papers said that he died at home."

"We agreed to this minor variation with his sister. There seemed no point in distressing the family further by announcing that he was under arrest at the time of his death."

I was conscious, suddenly, of a very cold feeling.

The world, at that time, was balanced between a war which had just finished and a new war which might break out at any moment. Those particular documents would be embarrassing if they were published even now. At that time they could have been deadly. The prompt action of the Security Service had prevented the papers from getting into the wrong hands. But they would argue that Sir Alfred had read them and could probably reproduce them. *Was that why he was dead?* He had never seemed to me to be the sort of man who would commit suicide. He had far too great a sense of his own importance.

I had no illusions about MI5. Their motto was: *Salus Populi Suprema Lex.* A single life was unimportant where the safety of the State was in the balance. And if they convinced themselves that I was the only other outsider who had read those papers —

I became aware that Lord Cherryl had been speaking for some moments and the silence suggested that he had asked me a question and was waiting for an answer.

I said, "I'm sorry. Would you mind repeating that?"

"You must agree that the timing is significant. You had the papers under your control all day on Monday. When you had finished with them by six o'clock, you returned them to Registry Filing. Their records show that these papers have not been removed by anyone else since. Yet on the following morning we find copies in the possession of your uncle."

There was nothing to say but "No comment." I guessed this would be thought flippant, and said nothing.

Mr. Justice Rackham now took a hand. He said, in his Star Chamber voice, "Surely you can see the strength of the case against you?"

Again I said nothing.

"Unless you are going to suggest that there is some leakage in Registry Filing."

I knew better than to suggest that. The two middle-aged ladies who controlled our security filing system were of the utmost respectability. One was the daughter of an Admiral and the other was the sister of an Air Vice-Marshall. The only crime one could conceive either of them committing was assaulting someone they found being unkind to an animal.

"And in any event," said Lord Cherryl, "since neither of the officials concerned had, as far as we know, any connection with Sir Alfred Laming, even if, inconceivably, one of them had extracted these papers, they would have had no reason to hand them to him."

"Well?" said Mr. Justice Rackham.

At that point, regrettably, I lost my temper. I said, "It's no good saying 'Well,' as if I was an obstinate juryman. This tribunal may be unofficial, but I imagine it's meant to observe some of the elementary rules of law and procedure. All you're saying is that I *could* have taken these papers and no-one else *as far as you knew* could have done so. Therefore I've got to prove that I'm innocent. You ought to know better than that. You've got to prove me guilty."

Lord Cherryl started to say, "Where a strong presumption —" but Collins cut him off with a tiny movement of his hand.

He said, "The case against you isn't quite as watertight as you seem to be assuming. After all, there was a full hour when you were at lunch."

I rounded on him, in turn.

"There's no need to try and lead me into that trap. I know perfectly well that you had one of your watchdogs in the corridor during the whole time I was away."

"You mean —?"

"I mean Patrick Regan. I happen to know him. We were at school together. And I knew he was a member of your outfit."

"Yes," said Collins, with another of his ten percent smiles. "I remember you both, very well indeed."

It was difficult to explain quite how it happened, but from that moment the feeling of the meeting altered. The atmosphere lightened. The few remaining questions which Lord Cherryl put were couched in a much more friendly tone. Mr. Justice Rackham seemed subdued.

When I was shown out even the Commissionaire seemed to have caught the prevailing spirit. He positively smiled at me as he let me out. I walked down Whitehall gulping great lungsful of air and wondering what to do next.

Perhaps I was being subjected to the traditional hard-soft-hard treatment. Was the next thing a hand on my shoulder? Was I being kept under observation?

I suddenly felt that I didn't care.

I had a good lunch at my Club and then went for a walk. If I was being followed, I would give my followers some exercise.

I started from Central London, walked up to Hampstead, made a complete circle of the Heath, and came back down Fitzjohn's Avenue in the dusk. There were bonfires in the gardens and the smell of burning leaves filled the misty autumn air.

I was surprised to see a light on in my flat and had a word with the porter.

"The gentleman arrived half an hour ago. He said you were expecting him and I took the liberty of letting him in. I hope I did right, sir."

"Quite right."

I had guessed it would be Collins before I found him sitting primly on the edge of one of my armchairs.

"Do you know," he said, "there were moments this morning which took me back twenty years."

He sounded entirely friendly.

"Me too," I said with feeling. "Would you mind telling me what it was all in aid of? And would you care for a drink?"

I poured two drinks. Collins watched me in silence. Then he said, "Regan was arrested this afternoon."

I put my own drink down carefully on the table.

"We've had our doubts about him for some time. What we wanted was one clear piece of proof that he was lying. He'd committed himself, beyond the point from which he could retreat, to a statement that he had not been inside the Cabinet Office on that day, or any other day. We still don't know how he got in, without passing the security guard, or how he got out again. It's possible that he used the kitchen entrance and took a chance on not being spotted."

"He got into my room and opened my filing cabinet and photographed the papers? Whilst I was at lunch?"

"I don't suppose the locks gave him much trouble. We teach our people these tricks."

"And didn't realise that I'd seen him?"

"Even if he'd suspected it, he'd have taken a chance on it, I think. You assumed he was there on duty. You wouldn't necessarily have said anything about it. You very nearly didn't, either."

"That's right," I said. "I very nearly didn't."

"I'd concluded that he must have been there and that you might have seen him. I thought that if we went about it the right way you'd probably blurt it out. You were in such a bad temper by the time you got round to it that it convinced us all."

People usually tell the truth under pressure, said a voice from twenty years ago.

When Collins was putting his coat on in the hall he said, "Incidentally, did it never occur to you that it was Regan who put that notice up on the board? That was why he was so worried about you getting beaten for it. In those days he had a conscience, I suppose."

DECOY

"**B**orn?" said the Deputy Commissioner of Metropolitan Police. "Means nothing to me. What does he want?"

"He didn't say, sir. Just that he wanted five minutes of your time."

"If I had five minutes to spare, I can think of five things I could spend them on. If he's got something to say, tell him to put it in writing."

"Yes, sir."

When his secretary was at the door he added, "I suppose he hasn't got a Christian name."

"I understand it's Howard."

"Howard Bourne! Why on earth didn't you say so?"

The secretary nearly said, "Because you didn't ask." What she really wanted to say was that because he was in a brittle mood — the result of an hour with the Commissioner on Race Relations — there was no need for him to work it off on her. She was not a girl, but a woman of thirty-five, with a mind of her own, and she nearly said it.

"What shall I tell him, sir?"

"Tell him? Don't tell him anything. Just wheel him up."

Howard Bourne! The name took him back more than thirty years, when he had abandoned a dead-end career at the Bar to join the Metropolitan Police and they had walked the streets and alleys of Southwark together, creaking in their stiff uniforms and new boots. Since then, they had followed very different paths. He had climbed the dangerous slippery slope to the second highest position in the police hierarchy, ruining his digestion and overtaxing his mind to a point where he was rude to the best secretary he had ever had. How much more sensible Howard had been! Years of slow promotion in one of the South London divisions, followed by his final elevation to the rank of Detective Inspector in the Intelligence branch. By that time his name was one of the best known in the force, not only as a trusted and respected policeman but as a much-sought-after performer at police concerts and an inimitable raconteur.

He jumped up as Bourne came in, grabbed him by the arm, and pushed him into the visitor's chair. "What have you been up to, you old scoundrel?" he said. "Pegged at long last for imitating your superior officers, I suppose."

"Actually," said Bourne, betraying by his accent the Midland city be came from, "I hant been up to nothing. I'm on my way out."

"Already?"

"Age. They boot inspectors out younger than deputy commissioners. Maybe because they work harder."

"Could be. How are you fixed?"

"I'm fixed fine. I've got a wife and a house and enough garden to keep me busy."

"Then you're not thinking of taking up one of those posts in a private firm as security officer. After — how long is it? — ten years in the Intelligence section here, you'd be a natural for the job."

"I'd sooner grow roses. And I'll tell you summat about Police Intelligence. It's a two-edged business — times people tell you too much."

"I suppose that's inevitable."

It dawned on him that Bourne had not simply come to say goodbye — though that would have been natural enough — but that he had something he wanted to tell him and that he was finding it difficult to begin.

To help him, he said, "I imagine you must pick up all sorts of odds and ends — some true, some false."

"If they're true, they're useful. If they're downright lies, you can laugh at them. It's when they're half true, or you think they might be half true, that they worry you."

"And what particular half truth is worrying you?" said the Deputy Commissioner softly.

"Before I tell you what it is, I'll tell you two other things. The first is that if I hant been getting out meself I'd never have mentioned it."

"That sounds like running away, Howard."

"Call me any names you like. But what I've got to get across to you is that this isn't information. If t'were information you could do summat about it, get MS15 looking into it. But this is just a bad smell and a whisper."

"Point taken. Not easy to investigate a smell. But if there was a whisper someone must have done the whispering."

"That's my second point. If I tell you where I got it from you'll think even less of it."

He paused, clearly unhappy. The Deputy Commissioner sat very still. It was in just this way that, in his term of office, two major scandals had started. A smell and a whisper. He hoped to God this was not going to be the third.

Bourne took a deep breath and said, "I got it from a newspaper man. A chap called Jonathan Carver."

"The name rings a bell."

"He's a special correspondent with the *Sentinel*. Signs his own stuff. That's where you'll have seen his name. He was doing this investigation down on dockside. Race relations."

The Deputy Commissioner said, "Ugh!" And then, "Yes, I remember now. Didn't we give him some facilities in 'X' Division?"

"Right. If you know someone's going to kick you up the arse, always be polite to him first. Me being Area Intelligence Officer, I guess he thought I was the person to talk to. Not that he'd a lot to tell me."

"I understand that," said the Deputy Commissioner patiently. "He'd got hold of the tail end of some rumour and, being a sensible chap, he thought he'd pass it on."

Bourne nodded. He seemed even less happy than when he had started.

"So what is this tail-end rumour?"

"I'll tell you what it was, then," said Bourne.

As he started talking, the Deputy Commissioner touched the switch under the ledge of his desk which brought his tape recorder into action.

✠ ✠ ✠

"Where's the skipper got to?" said Detective Lampier.

Sergeant Blencowe, who was teaching himself to type, suspended operations and stretched his cramped fingers. It was a bitter morning in late January and the single-bar electric heater was doing little to raise the temperature in the CID room.

Sergeant Roughead, who was studying the court circular in *The Times* with his chair tilted back at a dangerous angle against a lukewarm radiator, said, "Covey told me he'd been sent for by the top brass."

Covey was the desk sergeant and was supposed to know where all members of the station were, and sometimes did.

Lampier said, "I remember the skipper once told me — it was when he was up in Highside — he had a message to go down to the Yard to talk about his pension. When he got there he found it was a cover story."

"A cover story for what?" said Roughead. He sounded interested.

"That's where he got a bit cagey. All he said was that it landed him up in some funny business in an East End boys' club."

"I've often told him," said Blencowe, "steer clear of the management. The things they want you to do, they always end in trouble."

"I don't know," said Lampier. "They've got the pick of the stuff up there. Computers, wireless sets, high-powered cars." A high-powered car was his idea of heaven.

"And typewriters that don't stick every time you try the letter E," said Blencowe, hitting the old machine viciously.

Chief Inspector Patrick Petrella, sitting on the edge of his chair in the Deputy Commissioner's second-storey office overlooking St. James's Park Underground station, would have felt inclined to agree with Blencowe.

It was the second time he had encountered Lovell. On the previous occasion, he had been Assistant Commissioner in charge of the CID. Now he was one step higher. As Deputy Commissioner, he was number two in the Metropolitan force. Petrella knew him for a formidable and devious character.

However, the interview had started in an unalarming way with a dissertation on the central organisation. "When I took on my present job," said Lovell, "my first reaction was that we had too many specialist sections, a round dozen private armies. I've managed to cut them down — against considerable opposition, as you may imagine."

Petrella felt that a sympathetic smile would be in order.

"We've run the Flying Squad, the Regional Crime Squad, and the Robbery Squad together. They were all really doing the same job and treading on each other's toes. We got rid of pornography altogether, by handing it over to the uniform branch. And I set up a new outfit, C11 — the Central Drugs and Immigration Unit."

At this point, Petrella began trying to fathom the object of the lecture he was being given. Out on the circumference, in the divisions, they had very little idea what was going on at the centre and it was certainly interesting and gratifying that he should be taken into the Deputy Commissioner's confidence in this way. It was also puzzling. A possible solution was that he was going to be offered an administrative post at the Yard. And yet — surely all this information could have been given him more simply and through less exalted channels.

As if divining what Petrella was thinking, the Deputy Commissioner abandoned generalities and came to the point with disconcerting suddenness. He said, "A corresponding disadvantage of creating these larger sections was that it put great power into the hands of the men at the top of them. I heard recently, from a source which I trusted, that there is a possibility that some officers near the top of my own brainchild, C11, were breaking the rules."

He didn't seem to expect any comment, which was as well because Petrella had nothing to say. He was aware that abuses of power had taken place from time to time. In recent years they had been dealt with very firmly by MS15.

The Deputy Commissioner had now swivelled his chair and was staring out of the window at the long white frontage of the new Home Office building. A man with a straggling beard was trying to get in and was being headed off by the Commissionaire. He watched for a few seconds and then swung back to Petrella. "You will notice that I chose my language carefully. I spoke of a possibility. It was no more than that. Until it becomes more definite I can't move. When it does, I can hand the matter over to MS15. They will do all that is necessary."

Petrella had no comment on that, either. He knew, of course, about MS15, which used to be A10 — the team which investigated wrongdoing in the force. It had been unpopular at the start, but its successes had earned for it a grudging respect. He had no doubt that MS15 could do the job — if there was a job to be done.

"When we set up the Central Drugs and Immigration Unit, it had two main functions. One was to keep an eye on immigrants once they'd been allowed into this country, rechecking their credentials and seeing that they settled down and behaved themselves. The other was co-ordinating our efforts to stop drugs coming in. You probably realise that once they're in there's nothing much we can do about it."

Petrella nodded. He had personal experience of the hopelessness of tracing the small middleman — and of the mess that drugs made of young lives.

"C11 concentrates on the Port of London and the river from Fulham down to Woolwich. That's mostly 'X' Division, with parts of 'H' and 'J'. That's their hunting ground. You'll find out more about it when you get down there."

This was the first indication of what he was going to be asked to do and Petrella stirred uneasily in his chair. "If C11 are breaking the rules, there are only two ways I can think of. They could be taking money for letting in drugs that ought to be stopped. Or for whitewashing immigrants who ought to be blackwashed. Or both. Maybe you'll be able to think of other ways. Now, for the people concerned."

The Deputy Commissioner had unlocked a drawer in his desk and took out a small file from which he selected several sheets of paper, stapled together. "The man in charge of the unit is Chief Superintendent Campbell-Jones. I don't think you need worry much about him. He's been on extended sick-leave for the last six months. That may be one of the reasons why discipline lower down is slipping. Number two is Detective Superintendent Lamont. These are details of his service and confidential reports on him and on all other members of the squad. I think, and hope, they have no idea that these dossiers have been compiled."

He pushed the sheets across the desk to Petrella, who picked them up, folded them, and put them into his inside pocket.

"When you've studied them and formed your own opinion on them, you will burn them."

Petrella nodded. He had pushed the papers over his heart, where they already seemed to weigh heavily. He wondered whether Judas, taking his instructions from Pontius Pilate, had felt the same oppression.

"You'll be attached to 'X' Division and I'll give you my authority — in writing, but use it discreetly — to make such enquiries as you wish.

You'll find that your main field will be Gulf Arabs and Pakistanis. The troubles in Iran on one side and Afghanistan on the other are inducing an increasing number to emigrate. Many of them are going to America but a surprising number are coming here. Incidentally, I understand that you speak Arabic."

"Tolerably. A bit rusty now, sir."

"And Urdu?"

"Enough to ask for a cup of tea."

"Luckily, many of the people you will be dealing with probably speak English. Many of them are people of substance. Your real objective will be known only to the Commissioner and myself. If you haven't reached a definite conclusion by — let us say by Easter, that will give you three months — we will call off the operation."

Whilst the Deputy Commissioner was speaking, he had referred from time to time to a list in front of him. As he proceeded, he ticked off the items on it. "You can take not more than two men off Divisional duties to help you. You will have to tell them, of course, what your real objective is. They must be completely reliable and had better be men who have never worked in that area before and are able to fade quietly into the background. Let me know who you pick."

"I can tell you that now, sir. I'll take Detective Lampier. That part of London is his natural background. If he stands still you can't see him. And if I'm allowed a second, it would be Sergeant Roughead."

"Raymond Roughead's boy? The one who went to Eton? I shouldn't have thought that he'd fade very easily into that particular background."

"I agree," said Petrella. "But I have a feeling he'll be useful all the same."

"It's your choice. Now, as to communications. You'll have a bat phone which will be linked with central control in my private office. Anything you want to say will come straight to me." There was only one more item on the list. Petrella wondered what it was. As the Deputy Commissioner ticked it off, he smiled. "You won't, I think, be displeased when I tell you that the officer currently in charge at Leman Street is Inspector Gwilliam."

"Taffy Gwilliam? Who used to be at Highside?"

"He tells me you know him well."

"Very well, sir. He coached me for my promotion exam. I remember when I asked him why he wasn't going in for it himself, he told me he was always sunk by vulgar fractions."

"He wasn't thinking about vulgar fractions when he jumped on top of the getaway car after the Branding's wage snatch — broke the side window with a piece of iron he'd picked up and knocked out the driver. He's an Inspector now."

"That's the best piece of news I've had today," said Petrella.

✠ ✠ ✠

"Glad to see you, Patrick," said Inspector Gwilliam.

"And am I glad to see you, Taffy," said Petrella. "A friend in need is a friend indeed."

"A funny sort of job you've been landed with, so I understand. Not that we've been told anything official. Something to do with the blackies — I beg your pardon, with coloured gentlemen."

"Yes. That's part of it."

"I've emptied a room for you here. It's at the top of the house, but the stairs lead down to a back entrance, which would be useful if anyone wanted to talk to you private-like."

"That's fine, Taffy. I'll need some sort of base. But the people I'm interested in will probably open up more if I see them at home, when they get back from work."

This seemed to worry Gwilliam. He said, "Yes. I suppose that's what you'll have to do. All I can say is, if you're out at night, watch out for trouble."

"What sort of trouble?"

"All sorts. When I remember the nice quiet times we used to have up at Highside I find myself wishing I was back there, with a sergeant's stripes on my arm."

"Tell me more."

"There's a crowd round here who seem able to make trouble out of anything or nothing at all. I call them the black mafia. Mostly West Indians, but a few from India and the Gulf. They seem to have set themselves up as champions for their black brothers. Give you an example. There was a Pakki who had a fish barrow. He was a perfect pest, setting it up in the main shopping street where no barrows were allowed. We were always moving him on and he was always coming back again, so in the end we had to run him in."

"And they made a fuss about it?"

"Fuss! You'd have thought we'd strung him up and burned his barrow. Protest meetings, banners, a deputation trying to get into the Mayor's office. We had to call in help from the other divisions to deal with it and that didn't make us popular."

"Then you're warning me," said Petrella, "to watch my step and not stir up any trouble. I'll watch my step."

It seemed to him that his distasteful mission was going to be even more difficult than he had imagined.

⌘ ⌘ ⌘

At the end of the first month he sat down in his office, which was not much larger than an exceptionally roomy cupboard, and tried to decide what progress, if any, he had made. In his real job, no progress at all. In his cover job, a certain amount.

Helped by the Community Relations officer, he had interviewed a number of immigrants from the Gulf, from Pakistan, and from India. Almost without exception, he had found them decent, hardworking folk. One thing that surprised him was the speed with which, after the obligatory residence period, many of them had obtained naturalisation certificates. It was explained to him that the important things were that they had learned to speak English — which most of them had, with extraordinary rapidity — and that they could find some respectable person prepared to vouch for them.

None of the people he talked to seemed to be particularly wealthy. "An advantage," said one of the women, who had two teenage sons. "People offer them drugs. If they had money they might buy them. Who knows? As they have not, they cannot."

A surprising benefit from poverty, thought Petrella.

His job brought him into touch with the Customs and Excise officers. He had thought they might resent him, but they turned out to be forthcoming and helpful. One of them, a serious young man with a degree in Economics, had opened his heart to him over a few pints of beer one evening.

"Of course we don't think you're butting in," he said. "We need all the help we can get in stopping drugs getting through. This area used to be a soft touch for the smugglers. They'd come in on the cargo boats as deckhands, or stokers, or assistant cooks. All they had to do was slip ashore, dump the stuff, and get back on board. Some of them made half a dozen trips before we caught them. That squad you've set up — C11 you call it — they've been helpful. They've stopped one or two of the holes. But as soon as you stop one, they open up another."

Gwilliam had confirmed this. "Drugs," he said. "And I don't mean reefers, I mean hard stuff. They're becoming as common as cigarettes and it's chiefly the young who go for them."

"And there's nothing we can do about it?"

"I wouldn't say nothing. We can always keep trying. No use sitting back and moaning about it."

"I'm not moaning," said Petrella indignantly. "I'm facing facts."

This conversation happened to take place on a Saturday morning, which gave Gwilliam an idea. "You've been working too hard," he said. "What you need is fresh air and a change of scene. Let's go along to Imber Court. The police are playing Blackheath. Should be some action."

Gwilliam, as Petrella knew, had played rugby football both for the police and the London Welsh and on more than one occasion for Wales. When they got to Imber Court, many of the people there knew him and made him welcome. It was a brisk February afternoon and they avoided the crowded stand and stood behind the ropes along the touch line. Petrella didn't know much about the game, but he soon realised that the efforts of the police team were concentrated on getting the ball out to the two players on the right wing — both powerfully built young men, but fast for all their bulk. From the shouts of the crowd, he gathered that one was called Ronnie and the other Mark.

"Ronnie Banks and Mark Watrous," said Gwilliam. "Worth an England trial, if you ask me. But they won't get one."

"Why not?"

"Got to play for one of the snob clubs to get an England cap. Quins or Wasps."

"I think that's nonsense," said Petrella. It seemed even more nonsensical a few minutes later when Banks, selling a lovely dummy, straightened up and went bald-headed for the line, arriving there with a Blackheath player clinging to each of his legs.

In the clubhouse afterward, where Gwilliam knew every other person, Petrella was introduced to the two heroes. They were, he guessed, some years younger than he was and he was surprised to learn that they were Inspectors. Gwilliam had produced pints of beer for all of them — the first of a succession of pints. As the evening went on, Petrella decided that there was more to both of them than mere brawn. Under his thatch of red hair, Banks had a pair of very shrewd blue eyes. Watrous, with his sharp teeth and pointed ears, looked like an amiable young wolf. He wondered what job they did when they weren't playing football, but it was no occasion for talking shop.

On their way home, many hours later, Gwilliam told him. "You wouldn't guess it," he said, "but they're both in MS15."

Petrella agreed that he would not have guessed it. He had pictured MS15 as being composed of serious and scholarly men who studied dossiers and compiled evidence against their fellow policemen.

"The Deputy Commissioner usually picks types who can look after themselves. Sensible, really. MS15 wasn't exactly popular, not to start with. It's accepted now."

"They've certainly accepted that pair," said Petrella.

✠　✠　✠

On the following Monday, when he was sitting in his office studying a list of names supplied by the Community Relations officer and wondering which of them he should visit first, Gwilliam poked his head round the door and said, "Got a visitor for you, Patrick. If I'd realised how small this room was, I'd have found you something bigger. Would you care to use my room?"

"This'll do very nicely," said the bulky man behind him. Petrella didn't need to be told who he was. He had been expecting his arrival any time for the past month and had not been looking forward to it.

In the continued absence of Campbell-Jones, Superintendent Lionel Lamont had headed the Central Drugs and Immigration Unit for more than six months. It was expected that he would shortly be given a step up and confirmed in actual charge. He was an impressive figure of a man as he squeezed through the door and settled down with a grunt on to the only other chair in the room. But not a very healthy one, Petrella thought. The effort of climbing two flights of stairs had suffused his face with red and he was sweating.

When he had got his breath back, he said, "I met your father once. When I was doing a job in Tangier. I trust he's well."

"Very well. He's retired and growing oranges."

"Lucky man." This opening gambit having been disposed of, a short silence ensued. Then Lamont said, "I suppose you're allowed to tell me what you're up to."

"Of course, sir."

"I understand you've been visiting around among our friends from the Gulf and India."

"That's really almost all I have done — so far. It's been a routine job — interesting, and, in a way, surprising."

"Surprising? How?"

"It was the speed with which most of them have settled down. Great credit to them, of course —"

"Of course, of course. And that was the whole of your job, was it?"

Petrella said cautiously, "There was a second leg to it. I was to find out anything I could about the import of illegal drugs and help — I won't say to stop it, but to keep it within limits. A heartbreaking job."

"Heartbreaking, indeed," said Lamont. He seemed easier now. As he talked, Petrella noticed a curious mannerism. He kept scratching with the nail of his forefinger on his trouser-covered thigh, as though there was something just above the knee and under the cloth that was irritating him. He said, "You've been in the force long enough, Inspector, to realise that we are an army of occupation in enemy country."

"Well —"

"Enemy country. I'm not exaggerating. And that means that we have to stand together. Any information should be shared."

"Of course."

"And we must help each other, even if we have to cut a few corners to do so."

It was the old appeal. Loyalty to one's own side and devil take the opposition. And there was no doubt Lamont meant it. He was leaning forward now and sweating so heavily that Petrella wondered for a moment if he was going to pass out. He said, "It's close in here, sir. I'll open the window."

"Don't bother," said Lamont. "I'm all right." He scrambled to his feet. "But remember what I said. You know where I live. If you've anything to tell me, don't hesitate. Come straight along." There was more than sincerity in this. An undercurrent, almost of desperation.

Petrella got to the door ahead of him, held it open, and watched him lurch down the passage and negotiate the first flight of stairs. Then he went back to his own room and from the window which looked down on the street watched Lamont get into his handsome car and drive away. He was badly worried. Lamont was a step ahead of him in rank. Must very soon be two steps. It was as though a captain in a regiment had been called on to investigate his own colonel. He shook his head angrily. He had dealt with him as fairly as his difficult position allowed. He had told him the truth and nothing but the truth. But not the whole truth.

A week before, there had been a single, very faint glimmer of light in the darkness. It had appeared when he was questioning a Pakistani fruit salesman called Jampatsingh. He had found him at home with his wife and family. The man had answered his questions but reluctantly. To prod him along a bit, Petrella had congratulated him on obtaining his naturalisation certificate, which had just come through. This had produced a spark of feeling. Yes, the man had said, it was satisfactory. Two men of standing in the City had been prepared to countersign his application.

His wife, who was sitting in the corner of the room, had added, "At a cost." She had said it very quietly, but Petrella had heard it. So had her husband. The look he gave her had promised trouble.

So. It seemed that naturalisation could be bought. For how much? And paid to whom?

It was time to get some help.

⌖ ⌖ ⌖

That evening, at six o'clock, Petrella bought a ticket for the back stalls at the Regal Cinema in Deptford High Street. There were four cinemas in the area, none of them much frequented, victims of television and bingo. Having left both of his assistants to their own devices for a month, from now on he had a standing date with Lampier each Monday at a different cinema. He found him waiting in the deserted back row.

"Very glad to see you, skipper. No-one knocked you off yet?"

"Knocked *me* off," said Petrella. "I'm a respectable copper working in a police station. It's you I was worried about."

"No need to worry. I'm one of the boys. You know that YMCA hostel I got into? Didn't take me long to find out that half the young Christians are juvenile delinquents and the other half are working hard to qualify."

Petrella had never doubted Lampier's ability to fall on his feet. He said, "Have you got anything useful out of your fellow criminals?"

"Nothing special. But I can tell you one thing. The amount of drugs that have been coming in lately makes your hair stand on end. Honestly, you can almost buy shmeck and charley at the supermarket."

"When you say lately, what exactly do you mean?"

"About the last six months."

Petrella thought about this whilst a young lady, in close shot, with a wobbling larynx sang to them about hills and thrills and daffodils. What Lampier had told him fitted in with an idea that was forming slowly at the back of his mind.

He said, "Have you picked up any gossip about Lamont?"

"I wouldn't say he was exactly a favourite character in our pad. Most of them know who he is and what his job is. One creep said he reckoned Lammy was on the hard stuff himself. But I expect he was just shooting his mouth off."

Petrella thought about Lamont's red and sweating face and the involuntary twitching of his hand. If true, it opened up a startling and disagreeable vista.

"What they talk about is that lovely car of his. It's a custom-built Mercedes D19. Can't be more than twenty of them in the country. List price seventeen thousand, five hundred pounds."

Petrella accepted this as gospel. Lampier's knowledge of cars was accurate and far-reaching.

As though aware that his bulletin of information had been disappointing, Lampier said, "There was one other thing. You know an old girl called Mrs. Jampot?"

Petrella, whose mind had been momentarily diverted to a

consideration of whether if the singer opened her mouth even wider they would be able to see her tonsils, came suddenly back to attention. "Jampatsingh" he said. "Yes. What about her?"

"She turned up at the shops one morning with a face like someone had run a lawn mower over it. The story was you'd tried to get some info out of her and when she wouldn't sing you'd worked her over."

"For Christ's sake!" said Petrella.

"When it was put to me, I said it was typical. The sort of thing the law did every day of their lives. I had to say that, naturally. Of course, I didn't really believe it."

"Well, thank you."

"I'm only telling you because I think you'd better watch out. There's a bunch of them work up a lot of feeling about a thing like that."

"I have been warned," said Petrella. He had noticed, recently, that when he went out for lunch, or for a drink in the evening, Gwilliam usually made some excuse to come with him. The reason for this was now becoming apparent. It seemed to him that the quicker he finished the job the better.

✠ ✠ ✠

Next morning, after some careful telephoning, he arranged to contact Sergeant Milo Roughead. That young man had experienced no difficulty in camouflaging himself. He had got in touch with one of his many influential relatives, an uncle on his mother's side, who was senior partner in a firm of stockbrokers. When Milo had left Eton, this uncle had offered him a job, which he had refused. He was delighted to learn now that Milo was abandoning the police and he was only too willing to take him on as a learner. Instead, therefore, of spending his days in the discomfort of the CID room at Patten Street, he sauntered out every morning from his mother's flat to a centrally heated, air-conditioned office. It made, he thought, a nice change.

He seemed to spend much of his time in the City bars and lunch clubs where congregated the gilded young in the service of Mammon. It was in the dining-room of one of these institutions that Petrella found him. "You mustn't think, sir," he said earnestly, over a preliminary drink, "that I'm wasting my time. When my uncle suggests that I ought to spend most of my day glued to my desk I tell him that what I'm doing is assimilating atmosphere."

"And does he believe you?"

"He's pretty tolerant. Actually, I suspect that he's angling for business from my father's side of the family. Would you like scampi? They do them rather well here."

"I'm sure I'd like them very much. But I'd also like to know if you've got anywhere at all with the enquiry I asked you to make."

This was said so coldly that it had the effect of turning a young financier into a detective sergeant.

"I've been asking around about that journalist chap. Jonathan Carver. No luck there. He's gone to America. No-one seems to know why."

"He went," said Petrella, "because he was frightened."

"But I did get hold of one thing, though I'm not sure what it means. I got it from a chap who's a friend of a chap I was at school with. That makes it a bit second-hand, but I think it's reliable. This chap is in property —"

"Which chap?"

"The first one. He says that more than a year ago Lamont bought an option in a dockside development. Not in his own name, of course. He did it through a private company, but these things get out."

"I suppose so."

"Secrets don't stay that way for long in this neck of the woods. The way I heard it, it was more a deposit. He had to put down a third of the agreed purchase price. But here's the odd thing. When the time came — about three months ago — for him to take up this option, he hadn't the cash to do it with. By that time the scheme had come good. If he could have completed the purchase, he'd have made a real killing."

"But he couldn't."

"He couldn't do it himself, and by that time his credit was so shaky that no-one would lend him the money. So someone else stepped in and picked the plums."

"Why was his credit shaky?"

"The usual thing. Someone starts a whisper and before you know where you are white's become grey and grey's become black. In his case, I gather, what started it was that he was finding it difficult to keep up the payments on that lovely German bus of his. Here comes the food."

Petrella paid little attention to the scampi — which were, in fact, excellent. A picture was forming of which he could see the outlines, but not the details. He said, "Have you heard of people taking money for backing applications for naturalisation?"

"That's a new one on me," said Milo. "But it doesn't surprise me. Two years ago it wouldn't have seemed likely, but since the October smash there are quite a few people around who wouldn't say no to a thousand in cash if all they had to do was say that some Indian character was an old friend and a thoroughly reliable type. What about cutlets?"

"Lovely," said Petrella. When the waiter had removed the plates and was out of earshot, Milo added, "Shoot me down if I'm out of order, but from what you told me your present job is to get Superintendent Lamont lined up for the high jump."

"*If* he's breaking the rules, yes."

"Well, it seems pretty clear that he's heading for bankruptcy. When that happens, he'll be slung out anyway. Why not just let it happen?"

"It might be an answer," said Petrella slowly. "But I'm beginning to think that it wouldn't be the whole answer."

Back in his office, he tried to straighten out his thoughts. A year ago Lamont had money. He had no idea what a third share in a building estate would cost, but it must have been a large sum. And it hadn't come from his family. No rich wife, no wealthy relatives — that much was clear from the dossier he had seen. So where had it come from? No prize for guessing the answer to that. From the pockets of a steady inflow of immigrants. Money to get them in. Money to fix their naturalisation. But — and here was the real puzzle — why had the money supply stopped, or, at least, diminished? Something had happened. Something that had brought Lamont close to breaking point. And if, into the bargain, he had started taking drugs, that wouldn't have helped him, either.

He saw that there was a note on his in-tray from Gwilliam. It said, "Someone telephoned and left a message for you. 'Tomorrow Plaz Fifteen hundred Red.' Means nothing to me. Perhaps it does to you."

Petrella understood it. When he got to the Plaza Cinema at three o'clock, it had only just opened and Lampier was waiting for him at the back of the deserted auditorium.

"I thought you ought to have this soonest, skipper," he said. "I couldn't reach Mrs. Jampot. She's being kept pretty well under hatches by her husband and his strong-arm friends, but I've been in touch with one of her sons. A boy called Sammy. What he said was that his mother hadn't forgiven her old man for beating her up — not by a long chalk she hadn't — and she'd like a chance to tell you one or two things about him. Things not to his credit — and if they got him into trouble, so much the better."

While Lampier had been talking, Petrella had been thinking hard. He said, "There's nothing I'd like more than a word with Sammy's mother, but I don't see how we're to arrange it."

"I might persuade Sammy to come to you, after dark, via your back door. He's a slim kid and I reckon he could manage it without attracting attention."

"That's an idea," said Petrella. "In fact, it's a damn good idea. His mother talks to him and he talks to me. Do you think you could fix it?"

"Do my best. I'll slide off now. I don't think this film's in my line. Something about female American coppers."

✠ ✠ ✠

On the evening of the second day, Sammy arrived. He made no noise when coming upstairs, opened the door without knocking, and slid into the room like a shadow. Then he started talking in broken English.

It was a monologue, not a dialogue. He had been told exactly what to say and had learned it by heart. Certainly the information he had brought shed light in a number of dark corners. But at the end, when Petrella started to ask questions, it was apparent that the boy had shot his bolt. He was apologetic. He had told all that he knew. If he had known more, he could have told more. Petrella thanked him and rewarded him appropriately. After the boy had slid out, as quietly as he had come, he sat back to think.

It was tantalising. Lovell had said that the rumours about Lamont were too vague and indefinite for him to take the logical step of moving MS15 into action. What he had now found out was both clear and definite, but it still lacked proof. He needed hard facts — names, dates, amounts of money, methods of payment. And he was sure that he could get this, or most of it, from Mrs. Jampatsingh, whom he had as much chance of visiting as of getting to the North Pole in bedroom slippers.

Two days, he thought. I'll give it two days. Then I'll report, in writing, and clear out. Which would, he realised, be a great relief to Gwilliam, who was becoming more and more worried about his safety.

On the following afternoon, when he was putting the finishing touches to his report, the telephone rang. The desk sergeant said, "I've got a call for you. It's from your uncle."

This seemed to Petrella to be improbable. His wife was six months pregnant and his only uncle, a man of some substance, had taken her and their son to Nassau for some winter sunshine. He said, "Put him through," and was not surprised to hear the apologetic voice of Detective Constable Lampier.

"Sorry to break the rules," he said, "but you ought to have this at once. According to Sammy, his mother has scarpered."

"Run away? Where to?"

"She's taken refuge with their priest. A very holy character indeed, respected by all. Even when her husband and his friends find out where she's gone, they'll think twice about dragging her out. However, it occurred to me that if you got round quick you might be ahead of the opposition."

"Address?"

"It's 4 Barnaby Street. If you're going, I'll come along, too."

"No," said Petrella. "There's no reason for you to join in. But if I should get into trouble, there's a report which I'm finishing now, which I'll leave on my desk. I want you to see that it gets to the Deputy Commissioner. Understood?"

Lampier understood what Petrella was saying and disapproved strongly of his going into danger unprotected.

Had he known, Petrella had no intention of going in unprotected. It seemed to him to be the moment to use his radio link with Central.

That afternoon he paid a visit to the Public Library. As he went, he was conscious of people watching him. Not all of them were hostile, some simply curious. In the reference section of the Library he found what he wanted. A map of scale large enough to show streets and individual buildings.

Barnaby Street was a dead end, running up to the railway. The seven cottages on the left, of which No. 4 was presumably the middle one, had back gardens the ends of which overlooked Barnaby Passage. This also was blocked at the far end by the railway and on the other side by the wall of a factory building. He would have been happier if there had been a second way out of the passage.

✠ ✠ ✠

It was eight o'clock when he let himself out of the side door of the police station. He was wearing a pair of rope-soled shoes and a dark pullover. It was a night of gusty wind, with spatters of rain as the clouds raced across the moon.

He reached Barnaby Passage without trouble. Such people as he met were hurrying home to warmth and light. There was no back gate to any of the gardens, but the fences were low enough to scramble over, the only obstacle being a line of rusty barbed wire along the top. Using his gloved hand, he jerked this away from the staples that held it and climbed over, leaving the wire hanging.

There was a light in the back kitchen. He rapped on the door, and after some seconds it was opened by a white-haired, white-bearded Indian, who regarded him placidly for a moment and then said, "Please to come in. You wish for Mrs. Jampatsingh, perhaps. She is in the back room upstairs. Go up, please."

It was not a large room and it was occupied to bursting point by the woman, her two daughters, her son Sammy, and much of their belongings. Petrella said, rather hopelessly, "I wanted to speak to you alone. Isn't there somewhere the children could go?"

"Where?"

A difficult question. But Sammy, who seemed to be enjoying the situation, said, "There is an empty room at the top. I will show them." He bustled his sisters out, turned round to grin, and went out, shutting the door behind him.

"We may not have much time," said Petrella, "so let me ask you at once the things I want to know. Your husband paid money to some businessman in the City to support his application. There must have been some writing involved."

"There was writing. I have part of it here."

She opened one of the bags on the floor and pulled out a half sheet of office notepaper. As she handed it to Petrella, he could see that the name and address at the top had been torn off, but there was a signature at the bottom.

"Thank you. Next thing: the drugs your husband had to bring with him, what were they?"

"Cocaine. In very small packets. We all had to hide them in our clothes. Even the children."

"And how much did the man here pay for them?"

She said bitterly, "Less than half as much as we had paid to the supplier."

A clatter of feet on the stairs. It was Sammy. He was still more excited than scared. He said, "Men are coming — they are at the front!"

Petrella said, "Then I shall have to go. Will you be all right?"

The woman said, "As long as we stay here, yes."

Petrella wasted no further time. Within seconds he was out of the kitchen door. Racing down the short length of the back garden, he threw himself over the fence. But quick as he had been, others had been quicker. The open end of Barnaby Passage gave on to the High Street — by its light he could see that five or six men were turning into the passage. It was the only way out and his slender hope lay in surprise. Keeping as far as possible in the shadow of the farther wall, he edged his way along until he was within a few yards of the men. Then he launched himself forward.

There were two men in front and four more behind them. There was no way round. He had to go between the front two. They were taken by surprise, but reacted quickly enough to grab one of his arms each. At this point, Petrella lost hope. In his mind was a picture of the policeman who had been hacked to death by a mob of West Indians. That was going to happen to him. It was going to happen now. Even if he wrenched clear of the two men who were holding him, the other four would stop him.

A car was coming down the High Street, headlights on and siren blaring. It executed a skid turn and headed straight into the passage. The four men threw themselves wildly out of the way. One of them screamed as the car hit him. The next moment the driver and passenger were out. Petrella caught a glimpse of a red head which he had last seen diving across the line at Imber Court and realised that his arms were free. Both his attackers had fallen back. One was holding his face in hands through which blood was dripping.

"Time to go," said the driver. Petrella found himself in the car, which had shot into reverse, pivoted as it reached the street, and roared off.

"Kill the headlights and siren, Mark," said Banks.

"Willingly," said Watrous, "if you'll stop driving at eighty miles an hour in a built-up area. I think," he added, "that our friend could do with a drink."

"Fair enough. We'll make for the Wapping Giant."

✠ ✠ ✠

Five minutes later they were installed in the back room of that riverside public house. There was a cheerful fire in the grate. To the landlord, who had shown them in and who seemed to be an old friend, Banks said, "Double Scotches all round, Joe. And see if you can keep other people out for a bit." And to Petrella, "You all right? You've been very quiet."

"I'm just beginning to believe that I might, possibly, be going to survive. And by the way, thank you."

"A pleasure. We enjoy dealing with this rabble, don't we, Mark?"

Watrous grinned and said, "Easy meat, if you've got a car like ours. Heavy-duty Land Rover. Wonderful little bus. Got a lock like a London taxi."

"I must confess I thought that when he got my message the Deputy Commissioner would turn out the heavy mob."

"We're an army in ourselves," said Banks modestly. "But you realise it had to be us. We're the only people at HQ who know what you're up to."

"Of course. Stupid of me."

"We've been kept in the picture because as soon as you've got the low-down on Lammy we shall have to take over."

"I've got nine-tenths of the low-down. Maybe the Deputy Commissioner will let me go for the last tenth, or more likely he'll tell me to hand it over to you now. Which I'll do very willingly. All I want is to get back to nice quiet Divisional work."

Both men laughed. Banks said, "Spill."

"It's a sweet little racket, with more than one string to it. A businessman wants to clear out of one of those Middle East or Indian trouble spots. He's told how to do it. Emigration made easy. He has to buy a specified amount of hard drugs and take them with him. Not all of them will get through, but a lot will. When he hands the drugs over, here, he will get back part of the money he paid for the stuff. Less than half, said that woman I was talking to. That's the first step. Later, maybe, he has to find the fee for quick naturalisation. I've got the name of one of the City sharks who was at that end of the game. Once he got his hands on the drugs, Lamont was well placed to dispose of them. That's how he lined his own pocket. Something seems to have gone wrong lately. Maybe it's not important, but I'd like to find out what it was and finish the job."

"And that's what you're planning to do?"

"If I'm allowed to. My report goes in tomorrow, and if I get the go-ahead I'll tackle Lamont at once. The sooner the better."

Watrous said, "Is it true he's a druggy himself?"

"I got that impression when I saw him. In fact, I thought for a moment that he was going to come across. Now that I've got evidence of one specific case, I think he'll crumble."

"He'll come apart in your hands," said Banks. "And the best of British Luck to you. I think you deserve one more shot of Joe's excellent malt whisky and then we'll drive you home."

✠ ✠ ✠

On the following morning, Petrella finished his written report and Gwilliam arranged for it to be delivered by hand at the Yard. He said, "I don't know what's happened, but the heat seems to be off you a bit. All the same, I shouldn't stray far from the station."

Petrella had no intention of straying. He was waiting for a message. It arrived, also by hand, on the following afternoon and came from the Deputy Commissioner's office. It said, "Carry on. You'll find Lamont at home tomorrow evening."

On the following evening, by ten o'clock, the sky had cleared and it was a bright, cold night under a moon that was nearly full. Lamont's house was a handsome building, standing in its own grounds, on the northern fringe of Blackheath. When Petrella knocked, it was Lamont who opened the door to him. He said, with the ghost of a smile on a face that was white as paper, "Have to be my own butler. I'm alone in the house these days. I've sent my wife away to her mother in the country. In a way, it makes things easier."

He had himself in hand, but his eyes were jumping.

"I gather from what I was told on the telephone that this is the end of the road. In a lot of ways it's a relief. I imagine you've got one of those recording gadgets with you."

"I switched it on when I came in."

"Come along to my office."

After that, Lamont spoke for ten minutes, in a level, almost uninterested voice, as though he was describing the experiences of a third party. At the end of it Petrella had an important decision to make. Now that everything had become clear to him, he didn't know whether Lamont or he stood in the greater danger. And the danger was there, no doubt about it, in the corners of the empty house, and in the deserted streets outside.

The police runabout, which Gilliam had lent him, was parked twenty yards down the road which ran along the side of Lamont's house. Twenty yards of possible ambush.

He was halfway there when the attack came in. The car, driving on sidelights, turned the corner and came straight at him. He was in two minds as to whether he might reach his own car, and the indecision nearly cost him his life. The other car was coming much faster than he had imagined and as he jumped to one side it swerved after him. He was nearly clear, but not quite. Something — it may have been the wing mirror — hit him and he went down. Lying there, he could see the Land Rover turning. He remembered Watrous saying, with his wolf's grin, "Wonderful little bus, got a lock like a London taxi." And unless he kept his nerve, the wonderful little bus was going to run right over him.

He was lying on his side and had to remain still and apparently unconscious until the very last moment. If he moved too soon or gave any sign of life, the car would come after him. There was no comfortable ditch to shelter him, just a stretch of grass.

Once again the speed of the car deceived him and he nearly left it too late. As he levered himself over in a frantic, last-minute roll, the rear wheel of the car went over his left hand.

Five yards up the road, the Land Rover jerked to a halt and Banks jumped out and ran back. He was holding what looked like an iron tyre-lever. With it, he swung a savage blow at Petrella's head. The only defence left to him was to move. He jerked his head to one side and the blow landed on his shoulder. Almost the last thing he heard was the crack of his collarbone breaking. Then the night was full of noise and lights and, incredibly, it was Gwilliam who was bending over him.

✠ ✠ ✠

When he regained consciousness, Gwilliam was still there and he imagined for a moment that he was on the grass by the roadside. Then he saw the white walls and the sun reflected from the polished floor and realised that he was in hospital. His hand had been heavily bandaged and there was some contraption round his left shoulder, but apart from this physical damage he felt surprisingly clear-headed. "What on earth are you doing here, Taffy?"

"I'm here because the Deputy Commissioner sent for me yesterday afternoon and put me in the picture."

"Then perhaps you wouldn't mind putting me in the picture."

"It was quite simple, really — insofar as anything that old snake thought up could be described as simple. He'd been warned by Howard Bourne — what a character, you ought to have heard him taking off the top brass —"

"Warned about what?"

"Why, that some of the leading lights in MS15 were running a private racket."

"Yes. Lamont told me about that. It's all on the tape. In his case, as the price of not reporting him, they took two-thirds of what he got. A third for Banks and a third for Watrous."

"What a pair." Gwilliam was finding it difficult to keep the admiration out of his voice. He could still see them scoring tries. "Well, Bourne didn't know the details. It was just something that newspaperman had picked up. But if it was true, no question, it put the Deputy Commissioner on the spot. Normally he'd use MS15 to investigate a rumour like that, but he could hardly ask them to investigate themselves."

"Difficult. So he put me in after Lamont and MS15 after me."

"That's about the size of it. That time, when you were on the wrong track, he sent them to help you. When you were heading for the right track, he sent them after you again. The difference in this case was that he sent half the Flying Squad after them."

"With orders to do nothing until those two beauties had nearly killed me."

"Well, you see," said Gwilliam apologetically, "he didn't know then what you'd got on that tape, so he wanted a water-tight charge. Attempted murder, with a dozen witnesses."

Petrella thought about it. He said, "Just how did that pair think they were going to get away with it?"

"Oh, I expect they had it all worked out. Once they'd got the tape off you and slung your body into Lamont's garden, all they had to do was shoot him and leave him with the gun in his hand. Assumption: you'd accused him, and he lost his temper and hit you — harder than he meant. Finds himself with a corpse on his hands and nowhere to turn. Takes his own life. End of story."

"End of story," said Petrella, shifting his position to ease the ache in his shoulder. "I'm beginning to think that what Blencowe told me was true. Steer clear of the management, he used to say. The things they want you to do always end in trouble."

DEAD RECKONING

The key to Gunner David Land's character is simplicity. He was simple and direct in a way which is commonly supposed to be confined to children. Also he was a Lowland Scot.

Davie got on to the Barchester bus at Parksbury, climbed to the upper deck, and secured the very front seat. The neat, worn, often-pressed battle-dress and spotless brass and webbing waist-belt proclaimed him an old soldier. The brass titles said Royal Horse Artillery — not horses now, of course, but thundering petrol- and diesel-driven monsters.

The face said nothing. It was brown with outstaring summer and winter on Luneburg Heath and Salisbury Plain. It was expressionless because his years in the ranks had taught him that a vaguely alert lack of expression was the best face to hand out to the world.

The bus was filling up with soldiers, for Parksbury is the home station and training-ground of all Gunners on the Plain and the Cathedral City of Barchester is where they spend their pay.

The conductor, when he sold him his ticket, did not spare Davie a second look. Nobody gave him a second look.

There was absolutely nothing to indicate that he was a traitor, engaged in trafficking his country's secrets to the enemy.

It had started with Badger Lees. Davie and Badger had joined the army on the same day in 1945, just in time to see the Wehrmacht go up in flames. Together they had signed on afterwards. They liked the life, they liked their jobs. Davie was a mechanic, Badger a wireless expert. They liked each other. Together they had outwitted simple young officers, and outfaced a dynasty of Sergeants-Major. Neither fate nor the War Office could prise them apart. They were inseparable.

And then, shortly after coming to Parksbury, in the simplest and most deadly way possible, it had happened.

Badger got money. Not in one glorious bang, by the death of an aunt

224

or the winning of a football pool, but insidiously, gradually, inexplicably.

At first it was a joke. On the day before pay-day, that lean period when the Canteen is empty and single cigarettes are at a premium, Badger had pulled a pound note — a whole Jimmy O'Goblin — out of his pocket and had stood them both a slap-up meal of eggs and bangers.

"Been robbing a till?" said Davie.

"That's right," said Badger.

Then it hadn't been so funny.

Badger had bought a motorbike. Not an army job; a real private, civvy motorbike, which he kept in a lock-up garage outside the Camp. He'd taken Davie out on it, too. But the plump carrier seat was designed for softer freight, and it wasn't long before Davie, standing outside the NAAFI, had watched his friend roar by with a bundle of something blonde and clinging which he had recognised, with dismay, as the daughter of the Officers' Mess Steward, a predatory young lady who had never before been seen out with anything humbler than a Quartermaster Sergeant.

Davie shut his eyes. He didn't like to think much about that period. There had been worse to come, of course. Much worse. But then it had been sharp and sudden. It was the gradual breaking-off that had really hurt.

The bus had ground its way up the highest point now. The golf course stretched away on the right. A quartet was forming up on the first green, two worried-looking men with stomachs and two over-coloured women. Davie hardly saw them. They lived outside his hard, male world.

The pay-off had come — how long ago? — almost a year ago. It had come with the arrival of a smooth-looking Sergeant of SIB who had asked a great many questions, and had seemed particularly interested in Badger and his motor bicycle.

And then, that Saturday evening, when Davie had been sitting on his bed wondering how to fill in the time, and Badger had come in and said, "Let's go up to the hut, Davie." No need to ask which hut. It was an old lecture hut, of which they knew the trick of the door, a quiet place for smokes and gossips, when Sergeants were looking for fatigues and only very green ducks hung around quarters.

In the half dark Badger had told him everything.

☩   ☩   ☩

It started, he said, almost by accident.

Did Davie remember that café they sometimes went to in Barchester? They used to call it the Ark, because the old man who kept it had a beard and a son called Ham.

Badger had gone in, one night, alone, and had got talking to Ham, a big red-faced lout who dressed smartly and knew a lot of answers. They'd talked about money. "You soldiers don't know money when you see it," said Ham. "What's your job? Wireless, isn't it? Know those new two-way valves?"

Badger said certainly he knew them. He took them in and out almost every day. If he hadn't been a bit lit he might have wondered how Ham knew so much about them.

"Did you know," asked Ham, "that you could get a fiver each for them?" And he told him where. A man who kept a garage on the London road, name of Bird. Badger knew the garage. The thought stayed with him.

About a week later he left camp with a new valve in his pocket and called at the garage.

The owner was in; a fat, jolly, greasy creature, who seemed to be expecting him. He hardly looked at the valve. He paid over five new one-pound notes and said that he was interested in variometers too. They worked out at eight to twelve pounds according to condition. A fortnight later Badger laid his hands on a variometer. It must have been in the very pink of condition because he got twelve pounds for it.

And so it went on. It wasn't always so easy. In the end even the Army, the great, prodigal, uncaring Army, began to get worried about the steady drain on its wireless stores. But Badger was skilful, and lucky.

It had gone on for nearly nine months. Then the trap shut, so smoothly and so quietly that he had hardly seen the springs move.

It was one evening at the café. He had been promoted now to the intimacy of the private room upstairs. That night another man had been there with Ham. A man who looked like a genial ape and whose name, it seemed, was Laddy.

Laddy said little, but what he did say was to the point. "There's a gadget," he said. "It's just been fitted to your service radar sets. It's called the No. 1 Attachment."

Badger said he knew it, but had no idea how it worked.

"Don't worry about how it works," said Laddy. "Just get it as it stands. There's a hundred pounds in it for you."

Badger had seen the red light then. This wasn't valves and transformers. This was the real thing. He was telling the truth when he said he knew little about it, but he couldn't help guessing, from the precautions that surrounded it, that it was pretty near top secret.

He argued first. Then blustered. It was like kicking a brick wall.

When he'd run himself down, Laddy had said: "You've got a month. At the end of that time the Army hears all about you."

"You'd be in for it as much as me if you did that," said Badger.

"How so?" said Ham innocently. "Have you been selling stolen goods to *us*? Can you prove any connection between us and Bird? Just you start to try. You might be able to get Bird into trouble, but he's used to that. He's well paid for it. It won't mean much to him."

Badger saw the point. He said he'd think it over.

"We're not going to talk about it again," said Laddy coldly. "And don't come here again, either. When you get it, phone up and arrange a meeting-place outside."

That had been six weeks ago, said Badger. He hadn't done anything. Chiefly because he hadn't been able to. The box had been too well guarded. Also because, somehow or other, he drew the line between scrounging and — the other thing.

Neither of them said the word, but it stood there, in the dusty darkness of the hut, like a presence: cold, with the cold of the axe-edge and the grease of the gibbet.

"What will you do?" said Davie at last.

"I haven't decided," said Badger. "I know what I want after all that talk, and that's a pint of wallop." And he had squeezed Davie's arm, just like in the old days, and they had walked to the inn on the London road and drunk themselves into a state where nothing mattered; and that night, or very early next morning, Badger had walked away from the Camp, a long way out on to the Plain, and had shot the top of his head off with a service rifle.

✠ ✠ ✠

Davie had done nothing and said nothing. But a month or two later, when some of the skirl had died away, he had gone to Barchester and visited the café.

It surprised him, whenever he thought of it, how exactly everything had been repeated. It was like a film seen twice. The same carefully casual opening. The same offer. Even the same prices. Thirty pieces of silver, no more, no less.

Any differences that existed were at Davie's end. He bought no motor cycle. He directed no attention to the Mess Steward's daughter. All the money he received he had rolled up and put in a cocoa tin, which he buried, by night, on the Plain. At the end of the fourth month he added a second tin.

He had even been able to forecast just when and how the screw would be put on. First it was an influx of civilians from the Experimental Station. He had noted the precautions which surrounded the gadgets they brought with them. No-one had precisely explained it to him, but Davie was an engineer, by birth and by training, and he had the engineer's extra sense which told him how things worked. After that it was no surprise when the special ammunition was issued, a propellant and a fuse so novel that only one set of Range Tables existed for them, and that one was written out by hand.

✠ ✠ ✠

The bus swung up over the second big rise — hardly a hill, a heaving-up of one shoulder of the Plain. From the top you could see, for the first time, the spire of Barchester Cathedral. It was to see it, just in that way, that Davie took the front seat.

He had put up more of a fight than Badger. They had had to get quite rough with him before he had knuckled under. Of course they had beaten him in the end. That was inevitable. And now he was on his way to them with tokens of final submission.

The bus slowed at the first traffic lights and Davie jumped off. There was a military policeman at the bus station and there was something in Davie's pocket that made it silly to take unnecessary risks.

The café lay behind the market. It was a hard, cheap, desperate place, little used by day, barely tolerable after ten o'clock at night when the public houses were shut and it offered another two hours of sanctuary and warmth and badly cooked, rather expensive food.

The downstairs room was empty, except for the girl behind the counter, whose face was as white and crumpled and as dirty as the dishcloth in her hand.

"Ham's upstairs," she said.

Davie thanked her politely and went up. At the door of the private room he took off his hat. They were both there, Laddy sitting behind the table, Ham lounging his great length in a chair under the window.

"Come in," said Ham. "No need to stand about. This isn't defaulters. Take a chair. No hard feelings."

Davie sat down.

"I hear you got something for us," said Laddy. He smiled. When he smiled he made his face look worse.

"I've got a sketch," said Davie. "It's a simplified working-plan. I made it from memory. After one of the instructors let me look at the blueprints. I think it's about right, though it's not to scale or anything. But that wasn't what I really wanted to tell you. I think I might be able to get hold of the thing itself."

Neither man stirred. And when Ham spoke, his voice sounded the same, or very nearly so.

"How could you do that?" he said.

"They used to take it back to Paulton," said Davie. "Every time. It never stayed in Camp. But lately they've given that up. It was too much trouble, I suppose. Now it stays in the Camp Q Store. But as a matter of fact —" Davie examined his square blackened nails apologetically "I can get in. We —" he nearly said, "Badger and me," but switched at the last moment "— a friend and me used to do it. We did it for fun, really."

"They'd spot it was missing at once," said Ham, but he said it thoughtfully. "There'd be such a flapdoodle no-one would be able to move hand or foot."

"Yes," said Davie. "And that's why I'd have to do it on a Sunday. No-one ever goes near the store on Sunday. I would get it out on Saturday night, and hide it somewhere outside, in the open. If you could get up on Sunday morning —"

"Then you'd put it back on Sunday night?"

"That's right," said Davie. "There's lots of ways up on to the Ranges if you know them. You don't need to go past a picket."

"You're telling me," said Ham. He lounged to his feet, went over to a cupboard, unlocked it, and took out a map. "I was born and suckled in Bunty's Folly. I know every blade of grass on those sodding Ranges. Let's think. A little pint-pot like you won't get very far from Camp, carrying the whole outfit. It must weigh most of a hundredweight."

"Here's where I thought," said Davie. He put his finger on a saucepan-shaped wood. "You can find it easy. There's a path runs up the left-hand side. It's not exactly a motor road."

"We've got an old jeep," said Ham. "It'll go anywhere the army can get."

"If you park it —" Davie picked up a pencil and marked a spot carefully inside the top left-hand angle of the handle of the pan "— just there. There's a little place you can back in and keep out of sight. I'll have it nearby. I can't say exactly where."

"Ten o'clock sharp," said Ham.

"You'll not be seen?"

"You do your own worrying," said Ham.

"And you'll bring the money with you?"

"You'll get the money all right."

"But you'll bring it with you?"

"All right," said Ham. "We'll bring it with us. Stop worrying."

Davie went downstairs, said good afternoon politely to the girl, and walked out into the street.

As he walked he thought about the two men. He had once watched the man called Ham in action. A drunken soldier had started to make a disturbance in the café. Ham had hit him. He had held him against the counter with one hand and hit him in the face with the other until his face was a mess.

Davie walked slowly, but steadily. He had an appointment with a great man. Unlike most great men, this one had no particular objection to being kept waiting. Five minutes or five days, it signified nothing to him. He had been standing for five hundred years in a niche outside the west front of the Cathedral.

More than two years before, on a hot summer's afternoon, he and

Badger had been in the Cathedral Close, lying on their backs on the grass waiting for the pubs to open. They had found themselves listening to a white-bearded clergyman who was lecturing a party of students. It was the sound of his own name that had caught Davie's attention. So he had strolled across to look, and the stone figure had taken his fancy at the very first sight.

He had said nothing to Badger, who would have laughed at him. Nevertheless, if he found himself with ten minutes to spare in his visits to Barchester he had got into the habit of sauntering, as if by accident, to the same spot and staring for a few moments at his namesake.

This time he went straight there; under the arch, across the cobbles, and over the smooth precinct lawn. The old stone man was waiting for him.

He was not quite like the others, kings, apostles and martyrs. A freak of time and weather had bitten into this one face a character all its own. Davie knew a little about him. He had been a shepherd boy, and then he had been a king. He had killed a giant, he had got the best of all his enemies; he had lost his best friend, and he had died in sorrow. All that could be read in his stern and beautiful face.

Davie stood for a long time staring up at the stone man above him. And when he turned away it was as if he was saying goodbye.

⊞　⊞　⊞

"Ten o'clock," Ham said to Laddy. "I hope our little friend is punctual."

It was a lovely Sunday morning. The two men sat in their small car. They had tucked it neatly into the extreme tip of Saucepan Wood. In front of them the Plain fell away, and without shifting in their seats they could see, through the thin screen of trees in front of them, a long stretch of valley, which dipped, then rose to the next wood.

At that moment Laddy gave a grunt. "I didn't know they made them work on Sundays," he said.

Ham looked up from the map he was studying.

Over the far crest had appeared a line of four self-propelled guns; squat and boxlike in shape, with none of the grace of a tank, and yet they moved over the ground with a curious, riding ease. Only, when they crossed a bare patch, a mare's tail of sand flung suddenly out behind each of them was a reminder of their soft-moving weight and power.

Ham picked up his field-glasses and studied them carefully. "That's our little friend's regiment," he said at last. "If the powers that be have suddenly decreed a Sunday exercise we may have to wait all day for him."

"Worth it," said Laddy. "Look out, they're coming this way."

"So what?" said Ham. "They can't shoot us for just being here."

The four guns dipped, like battle cruisers in line astern. They were following one of the many tracks scratched on the turf. Now they were near enough for the men in the car to distinguish figures. A very young officer was standing in the leading gun. He was frowning over the map, but the sight of Saucepan Wood seemed to reassure him for he gave a signal and the line veered slightly and came towards the tip of the wood.

"They're coming here," said Laddy.

"For goodness sake!" said Ham. "So what?"

As the guns approached, the noise of them swelled until they seemed to fill the wood with their deep roaring.

The leader reached the corner and turned; not like a car, in a running circle, but checking and pivoting on its belly as a tank turns. Then, straightening on to its new course, it followed the path down the side of the wood. It passed not six foot from where the two men sat. One of the gun-crew looked up and grinned. The officer was busy with his map again. A fine dust whipped suddenly across their windscreen. Then the monster was gone. The second and third guns followed precisely, twisting on the exact spot, like a well-drilled chorus.

The fourth gun varied a little from this routine. It checked a yard or two short of the turning-place, pivoted, and sliced through the corner of the wood. There was a rending crash as two small trees splayed out before it, a bush was caught in the track and tossed into the air. Then the great steel bow hit the car full and fair: it hardly checked: it rose a little, and passed on.

✠　✠　✠

"They had absolutely no *right* to be there," said the Troop Commander for the fiftieth time. "And if they had to choose a place to park, why pick one that's slap on the route to the gun position?"

"Nobody thinks it's your fault," said the Major soothingly.

"It's a mystery how they got there at all. They didn't check in at any of the pickets. If you ask me, it's damned fishy. And I hear the police found more than a hundred pounds in notes when they searched the — what was left."

"Rather them than me," said the Major.

"The man I'm really sorry for is Land," went on the Troop Commander. "It was a bit of a fluke that he should have been driving a gun at all. He's Troop Mechanic now. It was only because Higgins was on leave that he volunteered —"

"No-one blames him, either," said the Major. "All the same, it's nasty. Perhaps we could get him shifted."

"I wouldn't want to lose him," said the Troop Commander. "He's a very steady chap indeed. But you may be right."

The Dean of Barchester, some time later, received an oddly wrapped parcel through the post. He opened it cautiously and two cocoa tins rolled out. They contained just under two hundred pounds, all in one-pound notes, and a piece of paper with the words *From a Friend* printed on it. He is used to receiving odd donations, but would dearly like to know who was the sender of this one.

Since Gunner Davie Land is at Badhausen with his new regiment, the Dean is most unlikely to learn the truth.

SOURCES

"Audited and Found Correct," *Ellery Queen's Mystery Magazine*, February 24, 1982.

"Friends of the Groom," *Evening Standard*, April 7, 1953.

"The Blackmailer," *John Bull*, June 24, 1950, as "Blackmail Is So Difficult."

"Squeeze Play," *Evening Standard*, January 29, 1951, as "The Squeeze."

"Under the Last Scuttleful," *Argosy*, March 1955, as "A Corner of the Cellar."

"Scream in a Soundproofed Room," *Reveille*, April 26, 1955, as "The Cabinet Maker."

"The Sheik Goes Shopping," *Lilliput*, April 1957.

"Clos Carmine," *Sunday Dispatch*, date unknown but ca. 1955, as "Clos Carmine 1945."

"The Curious Conspiracy," *Accent on Good Living*, May-June, 1970, as "Grandmother Clatterwick and Mr. McGuffog."

"Blood Match," *Metropolis*, Autumn 1970.

"The Seventh Musket," *Argosy*, August 1954.

"The Inside Pocket," *Crime Wave*, ed. Swedish Academy of Detection, 1981.

"Freedom of the Press," *Argosy*, February 1958.

"Miss Bell's Stocking," *Argosy*, June 1958.

"Five on the Gun," *Evening Standard*, April 7, 1953.

"The Jackal and the Tiger," *Winter's Crimes 20*, ed. Hillary Hale, 1988.

"Judith," *Midwinter Mysteries 3*, ed. Hillary Hale, 1993.

"Verdict of Three," *Verdict of Thirteen*, 1979.

"Decoy," *Ellery Queen's Mystery Magazine*, September 1990.

"Dead Reckoning," *Adventure*, June 1955, as "The Man Who Sold Out."

THE CURIOUS CONSPIRACY

The Curious Conspiracy and Other Crimes by Michael Gilbert is printed on 60-pound Glatfelter Supple Opaque Natural (a recycled, acid-free stock) from 12-point Goudy Old Style. The cover painting and design are by Deborah Miller. The first printing comprises approximately one thousand copies in trade softcover, and two hundred seventy-five copies sewn in cloth, signed and numbered by the author. Each of the clothbound copies includes a separate pamphlet, Old Mr. Martin by Michael Gilbert. The book was printed and bound by Thomson-Shore, Inc., Dexter, Michigan.

The Curious Conspiracy and Other Crimes was published in April 2002 by Crippen & Landru Publishers, Inc., Norfolk, Virginia.

CRIPPEN & LANDRU, PUBLISHERS

P. O. Box 9315
Norfolk, VA 23505
E-mail: CrippenL@Pilot.Infi.Net
Web: www.crippenlandru.com

Crippen & Landru publishes first edition short-story collections by important detective and mystery writers. As of April 2002, the following books have been published (see our website for full descriptions):

Speak of the Devil by John Dickson Carr. 1994. Out of print.

The McCone Files by Marcia Muller. 1995. Signed, numbered clothbound, out of print. Trade softcover, sixth printing, $17.00.

The Darings of the Red Rose by Margery Allingham. 1995. Out of print.

Diagnosis: Impossible, The Problems of Dr. Sam Hawthorne by Edward D. Hoch. 1996. Signed, numbered clothbound, out of print. Trade softcover, second printing, $15.00.

Spadework: A Collection of "Nameless Detective" Stories by Bill Pronzini. 1996. Signed, numbered clothbound, out of print. Trade softcover, out of stock.

Who Killed Father Christmas? And Other Unseasonable Demises by Patricia Moyes. 1996. Signed, numbered clothbound, out of print. A few signed unnumbered cloth overrun copies, $30.00. Trade softcover, $16.00.

My Mother, The Detective: The Complete "Mom" Short Stories by James Yaffe. 1997. Signed, numbered clothbound, out of print. Trade softcover, $15.00.

In Kensington Gardens Once . . . by H.R.F. Keating. 1997. Signed, numbered clothbound, out of print. Trade softcover, $12.00.

Shoveling Smoke: Selected Mystery Stories by Margaret Maron. 1997. Signed, numbered clothbound, out of print. Trade softcover, third printing, $16.00.

The Man Who Hated Banks and Other Mysteries by Michael Gilbert. 1997. Signed, numbered clothbound, out of print. Trade softcover, second printing, $16.00.

The Ripper of Storyville and Other Ben Snow Tales by Edward D. Hoch. 1997. Signed, numbered clothbound, out of print. Trade softcover, out of stock.

Do Not Exceed the Stated Dose by Peter Lovesey. 1998. Signed, numbered clothbound, out of print. Trade softcover, $16.00.

Renowned Be Thy Grave; Or, The Murderous Miss Mooney by P.M. Carlson. 1998. Signed, numbered clothbound, out of print. Trade softcover, $16.00.

Carpenter and Quincannon, Professional Detective Services by Bill Pronzini. 1998. Signed, numbered clothbound, out of print. Trade softcover, second printing, $16.00.

Not Safe After Dark and Other Stories by Peter Robinson. 1998. Signed, numbered clothbound, out of print. Trade softcover, second printing, $16.00.

The Concise Cuddy, A Collection of John Francis Cuddy Stories by Jeremiah Healy. 1998. Signed, numbered clothbound, out of print. Trade softcover, out of stock.

One Night Stands by Lawrence Block. 1999. Out of print.

All Creatures Dark and Dangerous by Doug Allyn. 1999. Signed, numbered clothbound, out of print. Trade softcover, $16.00.

Famous Blue Raincoat: Mystery Stories by Ed Gorman. 1999. Signed, numbered clothbound, out of print. A few signed unnumbered cloth overrun copies, $30.00. Trade softcover, $17.00.

The Tragedy of Errors and Others by Ellery Queen. 1999. Numbered clothbound, out of print. Trade softcover, second printing, $16.00.

McCone and Friends by Marcia Muller. 2000. Signed, numbered clothbound, out of print. Trade softcover, third printing, $16.00.

Challenge the Widow Maker and Other Stories of People in Peril by Clark Howard. 2000. Signed, numbered clothbound, out of print. Trade softcover, $16.00.

The Velvet Touch: Nick Velvet Stories by Edward D. Hoch. 2000. Signed, numbered clothbound, out of print. Trade softcover, $16.00.

Fortune's World by Michael Collins. 2000. Signed, numbered clothbound, out of print. Trade softcover, $16.00.

Long Live the Dead: Tales from Black Mask by Hugh B. Cave. 2000. Signed, numbered clothbound, out of print. Trade softcover, second printing, $16.00.

Tales Out of School: Mystery Stories by Carolyn Wheat. 2000. Signed, numbered clothbound, out of print. Trade softcover, $16.00.

Stakeout on Page Street and Other DKA Files by Joe Gores. 2000. Signed, numbered clothbound, out of print. Trade softcover, second printing, $16.00.

Strangers in Town: Three Newly Discovered Mysteries by Ross Macdonald, edited by Tom Nolan. 2001. Numbered clothbound, out of print. Trade softcover, second printing, $15.00.

The Celestial Buffet and Other Morsels of Murder by Susan Dunlap. 2001. Signed, numbered clothbound, out of print. Trade softcover, $16.00.

Kisses of Death: A Nathan Heller Casebook by Max Allan Collins. 2001. Signed, numbered clothbound, out of print. Trade softcover, second printing, $17.00.

The Old Spies Club and Other Intrigues of Rand by Edward D. Hoch. 2001. Signed, numbered clothbound, $42.00. Trade softcover, $17.00.

Adam and Eve on a Raft: Mystery Stories by Ron Goulart. 2001. Signed, numbered clothbound, $42.00. Trade softcover, $17.00.

The Sedgemoor Strangler and Other Stories of Crime by Peter Lovesey. 2001. Signed, numbered clothbound, out of print. Trade softcover, $17.00.

The Reluctant Detective and Other Stories by Michael Z. Lewin. 2001. Signed, numbered clothbound, $42.00. Trade softcover, $17.00.

The Lost Cases of Ed London by Lawrence Block. 2001. Published only in signed, numbered clothbound, $42.00.

Nine Sons: Collected Mysteries by Wendy Hornsby. 2002. Signed, numbered clothbound, $42.00. Trade softcover, $16.00.

The Newtonian Egg and Other Cases of Rolf le Roux by Peter Godfrey. 2002. "A Crippen & Landru Lost Classic." Clothbound, $25.00. Trade softcover, $15.00.

The Curious Conspiracy and Other Crimes by Michael Gilbert. 2002. Signed, numbered clothbound, $42.00. Trade softcover, $17.00.

Murder, Mystery & Malone by Craig Rice, edited by Jeffrey A. Marks. 2002. "A Crippen & Landru Lost Classic." Clothbound, $27.00. Trade softcover, $17.00.

FORTHCOMING SHORT-STORY COLLECTIONS

The Sleuth of Baghdad by Charles B. Child ["A Crippen & Landru Lost Classic].

Jo Gar's Casebook by Raoul Whitfield [published with Black Mask Press].

The 13 Culprits by Georges Simenon, translated by Peter Schulman.

Come Into My Parlor: Stories from Detective Fiction Weekly by Hugh B. Cave.

The Dark Snow and Other Stories by Brendan DuBois.

The Iron Angel and Other Tales of Michael Vlado by Edward D. Hoch.

Hildegarde Withers: Uncollected Riddles by Stuart Palmer ["A Crippen & Landru Lost Classic"].

One of a Kind: Collected Mystery Stories by Eric Wright.

Problems Solved by Bill Pronzini and Barry N. Malzberg.

Banner Crimes by Joseph Commings, edited by Robert Adey ["A Crippen & Landru Lost Classic"].

Cuddy Plus One by Jeremiah Healy.

Kill the Umpire: The Calls of Ed Gorgon by Jon L. Breen.

Marksman and Other Stories by William Campbell Gault, edited by Bill Pronzini ["A Crippen & Landru Lost Classic"].

Karmesin: The World's Greatest Crook — Or Most Outrageous Liar by Gerald Kersh, edited by Paul Duncan ["A Crippen & Landru Lost Classic"].

14 Slayers by Paul Cain [published with Black Mask Press].

The Adventure of the Murdered Moths and Other Radio Mysteries by Ellery Queen.

The Mankiller of Poojeegai and Other Mysteries by Walter Satterthwait.

You'll Die Laughing by Norbert Davis, edited by Bill Pronzini [published with Black Mask Press].

The Spotted Cat and Other Mysteries from the Casebook of Inspector Cockrill by Christianna Brand, edited by Tony Medawar ["A Crippen & Landru Lost Classic"].

Hoch's Ladies by Edward D. Hoch.

A Pocketful of Noses: Stories of One Ganelon or Another by James Powell.

Slot-Machine Kelly, Early Private-Eye Stories by Michael Collins.

Murder! 'Orrible Murder! by Amy Myers.

The Couple Next Door: Collected Mystery Stories by Margaret Millar, edited by Tom Nolan ["A Crippen & Landru Lost Classic"].

An untitled second volume of Dr. Sam Hawthorne puzzles by Edward D. Hoch.

Crippen & Landru offers discounts to individuals and institutions who place Standing Order Subscriptions for its forthcoming publications, either all the Regular Series or all the Lost Classics or (preferably) both. Collectors can thereby guarantee receiving limited editions, and readers won't miss any favorite stories. Standing Order Subscribers receive a specially commissioned story in a deluxe edition as a gift at the end of the year. Please write or e-mail for more details.